# BLOOD IS THICKER

*Sarah Cox is a serving police officer based in South London which brings authenticity to the situations described in this, her first novel. She is the youngest of a large family, and is married with three children.*

# BLOOD IS THICKER

## A DS Matt Arnold Mystery

## Sarah Cox

This first world edition published 2008
in Great Britain and in 2009 in the USA by
SEVERN HOUSE PUBLISHERS LTD of
9–15 High Street, Sutton, Surrey, England, SM1 1DF.

British Library Cataloguing in Publication Data

Cox, Sarah
  Blood is thicker
  1. Police - England - London - Fiction 2. Toddlers - Crimes
against - Fiction 3. Problem families - Fiction
  4. Hit-and-run drivers - Fiction 5. Detective and mystery
stories
  I. Title
  823.9'2[F]


ISBN-13: 978-0-7278-6715-5    (cased)

*All Severn House titles are printed on acid-free paper.*

Typeset by Palimpsest Book Production Ltd.,
Grangemouth, Stirlingshire, Scotland.
Printed and bound in Great Britain by
MPG Books Ltd., Bodmin, Cornwall.

To John

# Acknowledgements

To my sister Dee whose own writing provided the inspiration for me to put pen to paper and to my husband, John and three beautiful daughters, whose patience and encouragement allowed me the time and space to develop my ideas.

# Prologue

The moon was full as PC John Arnold walked the short distance from Streatham police station to Granville Road, SW16. He wasn't superstitious, but something about the way the light slanted down across the roofs of the tall Victorian houses made him feel a little nervous. A cloud passed across its face and in the ensuing darkness, the frontage of number seven appeared as sinister as in any nightmare.

Number seven. Lucky for some, he repeated to himself as he walked up the winding footpath towards the front door. His uniform trousers snagged on a bramble overhanging the path and he pulled his leg sharply away. He brushed at the coarse material, feeling the safe strength of the standard issue wooden truncheon in his trouser pocket. Still he felt ill at ease.

As he looked up at the austere brickwork and the large, flaking sash windows, he didn't notice the slight twitch of the curtains, or the shadow that flitted quickly behind them. The house was in darkness.

'Lima Sierra,' he called into the handset of his radio. 'Is anyone backing me up?'

'There is no one,' the reply came back.

He frowned, but knocked sharply on the door. It was only a domestic disturbance, after all. He'd dealt with hundreds.

The door swung open of its own accord and a waft of warm, pungent air drifted into his nostrils. It brought with it a scent of danger. He fought the desire to withdraw, a sense of duty preventing his retreat. He stepped forward into the bowels of the hallway and felt the silence envelop him. From up above he heard a faint scuffling noise.

He felt the adrenalin pounding in his head as he climbed

the stairs one by one, listening, watching, feeling for the presence he knew was there. From somewhere inside his throat, the words 'Police, who's there?' cut through the stillness, but he didn't recognize the voice as his own.

There was no reply but he thought he could make out a muffled noise from an upstairs room. He took his helmet off and placed it on a stair, edging upwards towards the sound. His heart was beating faster and stronger now and he could feel the sweat prickling on his brow. Although he'd dealt with many calls like this before, domestics were always an unknown quantity. Passions ran high, and all parties involved inevitably knew the layout of the venue intimately, not to mention where weapons or escape routes were to be found.

He stopped and listened. Nothing. As he took the last step on to the landing a floorboard creaked beneath him, inflaming his imagination still further. He heard the muffled sound again. It was coming from a front bedroom. Slowly he stepped towards the door, listening for any whispered conversation, any sound or movement that would prepare him for the likely conflict ahead. The sound came again. This time he recognized it as a high-pitched but muted scream, a cry for help hidden beneath a swathe of material or wadding. No other sound could be heard.

He knew he had to act. Kicking the door wide open he leant into the room, flicking the light switch and illuminating the final moments of his nightmare. Everything appeared in slow motion as he took in the scene. A woman lay in the centre of a double bed, her arms and legs spread wide apart, manacled to each bedpost with ligatures. Another ligature was pulled across her mouth, forcing her teeth and lips apart and preventing her from uttering anything but a muffled cry. Her eyes instead screamed for help, wide and full of panic. She was totally naked and he could see several deep stab wounds across her abdomen from which blood still seeped. A large wound in the side of her neck gaped open and a pool of blood was clotting on the mattress alongside the laceration.

Adjacent to the bed, an arm raised high over the woman's naked torso, stood the motionless figure of a stocky, bare-chested man. Blood was splattered across his body too and a large kitchen knife glinted in the moonlight thrown across the room through the translucent net curtains.

In the split second the light illuminated the grisly scene, the man brought the knife down into the woman's chest. PC Arnold watched horrified as the blade bent before entering her soft flesh. He let out a shout on impulse, pulling his truncheon and handcuffs out at the same time, and launched himself at the knifeman. The handcuffs made contact with one of the man's wrists and the impact of PS Arnold's weight knocked him backwards against the wall behind. The man struggled, lashing out and hitting him across the face. He felt a blow go into his body, winding him momentarily. The man laughed and he glimpsed wild eyes and yellow teeth. He pushed the man's arm downwards and a radiator came into view, attached to the wall against which they were pinned. Grasping the spare handcuff he pushed hard towards it, clamping the man to the pipe and immobilizing him.

It was only when he slumped to the side, away from the man, that PC Arnold acknowledged the sharp pain in his chest, how laboured his attempts to inhale had become, how it had become impossible to draw enough breath even to mumble into his radio for help. Feeling a warm stickiness seep around his chest and a muzzy darkness start to blot out the nightmare, he glanced down to see the hilt of the kitchen knife still sticking out from his uniform tunic.

Matthew John Arnold was only just twelve years old when he arrived at the gateway to the small country church of the village in which he lived. The day was cold but the bright winter sun glared down through the branches of the gnarled, ancient oak trees standing guard at the gateway to the graveyard, reiterating with a brutal clarity the injustice he felt. His father, aged only thirty-three, was dead, taken from him by the cruel, serrated coldness of a knife. Now everything, both externally and internally, felt cold and dead to him too.

He was supposed to feel proud, or so he was told. Proud of the heroic act which had not only saved the life of a defenceless woman but at the same time prevented the escape of the perpetrator. Proud that it was his father who had acted so courageously, sacrificing his own life to the public need for a heroic, unarmed, *Dixon of Dock Green* style bobby. The senior officer who had knocked on their door just two weeks earlier had told him so. When he'd finished explaining to them how the woman's life had been saved and that they'd done everything in their power to save his father, he'd put a hand on his shoulder and told him that he shouldn't feel too sad and should hold his head up high. 'You should feel very proud of what your father has done. One day you might want to follow in his footsteps and if you're as brave as him, we'd be only too pleased to have you,' he'd said. But at the moment Matt wasn't proud. He was angry. Angry that he no longer had a dad to play football with. Angry that his mother kept crying and his little sister was waking in the early hours of each morning with nightmares. Angry because at that moment he couldn't feel proud.

A car door slammed behind him and he stared, as the coffin carrying his father's dead body was slowly manoeuvred through the archway into the silence of the churchyard. Everything was quiet now, the general hubbub curtailed at the sight of the stationary hearse. Along each side of the pathway winding into the old stone church a silent, parallel row of policemen and women stood smart and upright. Uniforms were pressed and brushed; shoes were gleaming, white gloves stood out against the black of the belted tunics; helmets, with badges polished shiny and bright, crowned each row.

His father, lifted carefully and respectfully, lay surrounded by a thousand memories, inside a light oak casket, underneath a soft black blanket emblazoned with the insignia of the Metropolitan Police. His duty helmet and truncheon were positioned on top, alongside a large oval bouquet of pale blue and navy blooms and white lilies. The pall-bearers, six uniformed police colleagues, shuffled forward into position and Matt, his mother and sister took their place behind it.

They moved forward and the crunch of the gravel broke the silence, signalling an unspoken end to the stifled emotions. As they moved down through the centre of the line Matt saw with astonishment that some of the policemen and women were crying. They stood stiffly to attention with the tears running down their cheeks, unashamed and unwilling to wipe them away. By the time he entered the stillness of the church, Matt felt himself accepted into the unspoken family of the police force, a subconscious but growing knowledge that he too would join them and serve the public in any way he could.

# Prelude

*3rd December 2007*

The last thing three-year-old Ryan Clarkson heard was the voice beside him.

'This'll teach you, you little bastard,' it said.

The words didn't make sense to him, but he recognized the tone of voice. It was an angry voice. The words were spoken loudly and he couldn't understand why they sounded cross when he was having so much fun.

He'd been so hungry that he'd been eating from the dog's bowl when Mummy had caught him. He'd tried to hide under the table but she'd pulled him out and told him off, said that the food was Scamps and he was not to take it. She said he would have to wait, but he couldn't. He was hungry and his tummy was rumbling. He'd cried, screamed to be allowed to finish Scamps' food, but Mummy had got cross and smacked him. Smacked him hard and his legs hurt and he'd cried some more. And then Daddy had grabbed him by the arm and shouted at him too. Shouted at him to shut his fucking mouth and he was trying to watch the match. He had lifted him up by the arm and dragged him up the stairs and his back had scraped against the bare floorboards. His back was sore now. He'd wriggled, tried to pull free, but his arm had twisted and now his arm hurt too.

Daddy had thrown him into his bedroom and he'd banged his leg on the bed. Then he'd heard the bolt being slid across the bottom of his door and Daddy was thumping about on the landing and going back downstairs.

He'd cried again then and screamed on and on, standing by the door. His arm hurt and his leg hurt and he was hungry and he wanted food. And his tummy was still rumbling. He reached up to the door handle but the door wouldn't open.

He was frightened that he'd be locked up here for a long time, like he always was. He didn't want to be on his own; he wanted to play with his brothers and sisters. And he wanted food, and he wanted to be cuddled. So he'd screamed louder until he felt sick. Then he'd been sick and it smelt horrid and tasted horrible and it was down the front of his outfit and on the floor. It looked like Scamps' food, brown and runny, and he was so hungry he'd been tempted to try and eat it again. He'd looked at the mess and knew that Mummy would get cross if she saw it and Daddy would get angry and he wasn't sure what he should do.

Then he'd heard footsteps outside the door and he'd hidden behind the bed in the corner, under a duvet. He heard the bolt being slid back and he was frightened. He stopped crying. Mummy and Daddy didn't like him making a noise.

Now he was having fun though and everything was all right. That's why he couldn't understand the angry voice. He was laughing and felt giddy. The room was spinning round and round and he flung his arms up over his head, feeling the air rushing through his hair and round his face, drying his tears. He closed his eyes and the sound in his ears got louder. Then he heard the voice over the sound of the rushing air and he couldn't understand why it should sound so angry.

He stopped giggling and opened his eyes, trying to see if the face that the voice came from was also angry, but he couldn't focus on the face at all. All he could see was his poster of Spider-Man on the wall and it was getting closer to him. He could see the red outfit and the black eyes of his favourite cartoon figure, crouching on top of a wall, ready to launch himself out on a thread. For an instant he thought he was Spider-Man, flying through the air on a daredevil mission to save the world.

As his head impacted hard with the poster on the wall, the very last thing he heard before everything went black was the voice again. It was laughing now and through the chuckling he could just make out the words.

'Fly, Spider-Man, fly.'

# One

The frost crunched under his feet as DS Matt Arnold made his way back across the school field to the car park. He liked these sorts of days. Days when the sky was a brilliant blue and his breath came out in large clouds of tepid vapour, which danced around his face before disappearing into the atmosphere.

He smiled wryly at the memory of his young son Ben, pretending he was smoking a cigarette on the way to school, putting a small pencil to his lips and exhaling breathy rings of pretend smoke in noisy puffs. He'd been told they were like two peas in a pod, with Ben's thick dark hair, olive complexion and brown eyes, twinkling behind long lashes, almost identical to his. There was certainly no doubting Ben's paternity, a fact of which Matt was secretly rather proud. He basked in the relative glory of regular comments made about his son's good looks, as well as his mischievous sense of humour and inherited taste for adventure and excitement. Ben though was obviously now trying to emulate his vices too. He frowned at the recollection of Ben's actions and his own guilty response, bending down as he'd scooped the boy up and chastised him in mock anger for giving his game away. He'd recently started smoking again on the quiet, or so he'd thought, but judging by Ben's imitations, his evening sorties into the back garden had clearly been spied. He made a mental note to make sure he didn't stand in full view of Ben's bedroom window next time he chanced outside.

It was only three weeks before Christmas and the school preparations were in full swing. Ben, at five his elder child, was to be a sheep in the nativity production, a fact his son had proudly announced one evening a few weeks previously. He and Jo, his wife, had solemnly congratulated him on his achievement, taking care to avoid him seeing the broad grins that swept fleetingly across their faces as he turned to go. Three-year-old Chloe, his daughter, younger and cheekier, had stood in wonderment at the first sighting of the woolly mask, before her excitement had got the better of her. It had taken the best part of ten minutes before her natural childish exuberance had abated sufficiently to allow her to calmly try it on. She and Jo were still at home now, grateful not to have to brave the elements for the daily school run.

Matt walked briskly, passing the huddles of slow-moving mothers pushing buggies with kids buried under mountainous arrays of hats, scarves and gloves. The talk was all of Christmas. The difficulties in obtaining the latest must-have Christmas present, the traumas of family gatherings with awkward in-laws and too much alcohol and the mounting, uncontrollable excitement of the children. Matt listened to the conversations but usually left participation in them to Jo. He did however like to hear the gossip, hot off the press, as Jo repeated the stories of illicit affairs, bust-ups or ill-advised comments and slights between the school fraternity. It kept his feet on the ground and made him appreciate what he'd got.

He checked his watch. 8.45 a.m. Plenty of time to buy a paper and make his way up to his base at Lambeth HQ. The office had been decorated by some of the typists and he smiled at the thought of the tinsel stretching sparsely across the room, the obligatory mistletoe hanging above the kettle ready to catch unobservant detectives as they stood waiting for their caffeine fix. Several small Christmas trees were dotted around the desks and he himself had found a singing tree, in pride of place on top of his filing cabinet, on his arrival a few days ago.

He glanced up at the conifers that edged the tall wall around the school grounds and noticed the frost on the upper branches was just beginning to disappear under the glare of the early morning sun. It looked beautiful and his mood was high as he reached his car and pressed the key fob. His mobile vibrated in his trouser pocket just as the locks clunked open and he was temporarily confused. The vibration came again, this time accompanied by the polyphonic ringtone Ben had chosen for him.

He flipped the handset open and saw the number was withheld. Guessing it was work he answered easily.

'Hi, Matt speaking.'

'Ah, Matt,' the voice of his boss, Detective Inspector Blandford intoned. 'Are you on your way in?'

'Yes, guv. I'll be in, in about half an hour.'

'In that case then, Matt, don't come to the office. I need you to go straight to 53 Station Road, SW16. The body of a young boy has just been found. Looks like he's been dead for some hours. His parents phoned for an ambulance this morning but there was nothing the paramedics could do. Rigor mortis had already set in. At this stage it looks as if he may have died from a head injury.'

'How old's the boy?' Matt asked.

'About three. 2004 date of birth. Uniform have got all the details at the scene. Can you let me know the score when you get there?'

'Yep, will do. I'll give you a ring ASAP.'

He put the phone back in his pocket and suddenly felt the chill of the early morning frost whip around his neck. He hated dealing with dead kids. Dead adults were bad enough, but children were far, far worse, even more so at this time of year.

Twenty minutes later and Matt was pulling up outside the address. It was in a residential area, narrow streets criss-crossing each other in a tight grid of small terraced houses. Alleyways allowed access to the rear of the properties and a single railway line ran down the back of the opposite terraces, bisecting the area. Most of the houses were well laid out and the gardens were maintained to a nice standard.

Matt took in the look of the street. He guessed most would be either occupied by young families, eager to take the first step on to the housing ladder, or older couples downsizing for more equity towards their retirement. He could almost feel the curtains twitching as he got out of his car.

This house, however, was shabbier than the rest. Paint was peeling off the window sills and porch front and the garden was messy. A crazy-paved footpath led through the mass of tangled weeds to the front door and piles of discarded rubbish and bin bags lay haphazardly along the front of the house. A uniformed policewoman stood guard outside the front door, filling out a crime scene log as people came and went.

She looked up as Matt approached.

'Hi, Sarge,' she said, smiling towards him. 'Wondered when you'd get here. I was told you were on your way. You're the first CID as yet.'

Matt smiled back, although the early joy of half an hour ago was fast being replaced by a grim apprehension of the scene to come. He recognized the WPC as Sandra Harvey from Lambeth HQ, having come into contact with her when she worked in one of the admin offices while on restricted duties, expecting her first child. As if sensing his apprehension, she grimaced.

'It's not too good in there. The little boy's body is still upstairs in his room. The paramedics think he died sometime yesterday evening as the body's cold and rigor mortis has set in. He's lying in his bed, looks like he's been put there. All dressed up in a Spider- Man outfit, his favourite apparently.'

'Do we have a name for him yet?'

She checked her pocket book. 'Yes, his name is Ryan Clarkson, date of birth September twenty-third 2004. He's just three.'

Matt scribbled the details down in a large notepad. 'What about a cause of death? Any theories on that yet?'

'There's not much blood around but he does have a head injury consistent with his head coming into contact with a hard surface or object. Apparently there's a mark on the wall that could be the point of impact. There's a small amount of blood on it too.'

She paused, looking up into his face, and he noticed her eyes cloud over. 'How can anyone do that to a young kiddie like that? Some people don't deserve to have children.'

'I don't know,' he agreed quietly. 'If anyone ever laid a finger on one of my kids, I can't imagine what I'd do. I think I'd do time myself.'

They fell silent, both transported into their own thoughts. After a few seconds Sandra spoke again.

'There are three other kids in there still. They're in the lounge with Dave Wilcox and the duty officer. Social services have been contacted and are making arrangements to house them for the time being, until we speak to them. They thought it would be less traumatic staying there than having to sit around in a police station for ages. It shouldn't be too long until they're gone. We've got all their names and contact numbers for when we need to interview them.'

'How old are they?'

'There are two boys aged eight and twelve and a girl of ten.'

Matt nodded. That could wait. In any case they would need to be interviewed properly, with appropriate adults and solicitors if requested and tape or video recording.

'What about the parents?'

'They've both been arrested on suspicion of murder. One's at Streatham and the other's at Brixton.'

'Have they said anything as yet?'

'Nothing of any note. Both denying any involvement. Both saying the kid was all right when he'd gone up to his room yesterday evening.'

'Did they mention why it took so long before he was found and an ambulance was called?'

'Nothing. They're a right pair though. He seems like a right thug and she seems to be a bit simple. Copies everything he says.'

Matt nodded. He knew the sort: inadequate, feckless parents who put their own needs before those of their kids. He'd seen it countless times before. Sometimes when he'd gone home to his comfortable house and orderly lifestyle he'd lamented to Jo the state of some of the dysfunctional families with whom he'd been forced to deal. These sorts of parents were barely capable of taking care of themselves, never mind the children they brought into the world. The poor kids didn't stand a chance. They were doomed to repeat the cycle, before they even got started.

'I'd better go in and take a look, I suppose,' he said, focusing on the job in hand.

'Mind how you go then, Sarge. There's more dog's muck on the floor in there than in the garden out here.'

Matt grimaced.

Stepping through the outside door into the porch, he could smell exactly what Sandra meant. The front door was wide open and he could see piles of dog excrement in various stages of decomposition lying on the bare floorboards. The stench was unbelievable and the urge to gag hit him immediately. Aside from the dog mess which appeared to be dotted all around the lower floor of the house he was immediately aware of the dirt and clutter reaching into almost every corner of each room. He picked his way along the hall to the kitchen, which was straight ahead.

Dirty plates and dishes were piled in the sink, lying mouldy and rancid in the brown stagnant water. Remnants of food lay rotting on work surfaces, encrusted in months of dried-on dirt. The cooker was thick and black and the floor lino was sticky and ripped. He pulled open the cupboards and was amazed to see numerous tins of dog food, with only rare packets of anything suitable for a family of six. The fridge was similar, containing several open tins of dog food and very little else. The only food suitable for human consumption that Matt could see was the remains of a loaf of bread, some butter in a container without a lid and several cartons of milk. Empty fast-food containers were stacked up all about the place and he surmised this must be what the family survived on.

Not for the first time, he wondered how people lived in these conditions. He pushed the door into the lounge and looked in. Three children sat on a sunken sofa gazing at a large television. A satellite channel blared out cartoons and the two boys and a girl sat mesmerized by the rapidly moving action. They appeared unkempt with matted, unbrushed hair and ill-fitting clothes. They were barefoot, their faces and hands unwashed and grubby. A small black and white Staffordshire terrier was sandwiched between the two boys on the sofa, licking itself. The duty officer, Inspector Munroe, came to the door, breaking the children's line of vision, and they turned to see who the intruder was. Matt looked down into their faces and saw the bewilderment in their eyes.

'Have you been upstairs yet?' Munroe enquired.

Matt shook his head.

'I'll show you then.' He slid past Matt and climbed the stairs, his heavy boots loud on the bare planks. At the top he paused, before pushing open a door into a large bedroom. Matt took a deep breath and stepped forward. The curtains were still closed and the light was off, leaving the room immersed in a dim half-light. He looked across to a bed which ran parallel to the far wall and could just make out a figure lying under the duvet. The bed seemed to dwarf the tiny shape. A mattress lay on the floor just to his right, its bedding thrown down in an untidy heap to one end. He picked his way past it and headed across the room towards the motionless figure. As he reached the bed Inspector Munroe switched the light on and Matt found himself staring down into the sleeping eyes of the toddler. Except that he wasn't sleeping: his skin was pale, all the blood vessels that normally made a young child's cheeks glow shrunken down under the surface, his face white and waxy. His eyes were closed and his arms were lying outside the duvet, his small hands folded one on top of the other. He looked as if he had been carefully laid out, so precise was the way in which he was positioned. Not the haphazard way a young child would normally sleep, arms and legs thrown out at random angles. Not like how he remembered Ben or Chloe would sleep.

He bent down over the little boy and saw the blood congealed on the side of his skull. There wasn't much, but what there was showed dark against the blond of his short wavy hair. It was on the right side of his head, hidden from immediate view of the door. A large swelling rose up underneath the blood, making his head appear distorted and misshapen. He wondered whether the toddler had been aware of what was happening, whether he'd felt pain, whether he'd lain suffering for hours with no way of gaining respite from the agony. Subconsciously, he hoped the blow had been quick and brutal, ending his life in an instant, rendering him unconscious and unfeeling. Not left to die slowly.

'We haven't examined his body for other injuries,' Inspector Munroe was saying. 'It was obvious he was dead as soon as the paramedics saw him, so they left him as he was. We've left him in situ as well, ready for forensics and photographs.'

'Did the parents not touch him or move him when he was found this morning?'

'Apparently not. It was the mother who raised the alarm. She says she knew it was too late as soon as she saw him, but still phoned the ambulance service just in case.'

'But she didn't try to revive him or anything?'

Inspector Munroe shook his head.

'What about the father?'

'He was still in bed when the ambulance arrived. Couldn't even be bothered to get up until they'd nearly finished.'

Matt was incredulous. He couldn't believe that a normal

loving parent could be so callous, that they wouldn't at least try to revive their child, sweep them up in their arms and try to breathe life back into them. Cradle them, hold them, do anything, everything possible. He knew without doubt that he would have.

He pushed the thought from his mind. Even thinking about the possibility sent a shiver down his spine.

He looked back down at the child's body and noticed the Spider-Man costume, covering his arms, down to his wrists. The bright red and black spider's web was in marked contrast to the pallor of the skin on his hands and neck and seemed to heighten the pathos of the circumstances.

'What's with the Spider-Man outfit?' he asked.

'Apparently Spider-Man was his favourite cartoon character. He liked to pretend he really was Spider-Man, jumping off the settee and chairs and suchlike.'

'Any chance he could have received the head injury accidentally?'

'I don't think so. This is where we think his head impacted with the wall. It's too high for it to be accidental and there's nothing much around that he could have jumped from.'

Inspector Munroe pointed to a large Spider-Man poster on the wall nearest to the mattress. Matt looked closely at where he was pointing and saw a thick smudge of blood on the paper. Several strands of blond hair were stuck to the blood and the mark measured about three and a half feet off the ground, about waist high for an adult and slightly higher than the toddler himself. He checked around. Apart from the bed and the mattress, which wouldn't have been near enough, the only other furniture was a wardrobe in the far left corner. Its doors hung open and the shelves inside were buckled and uneven. Its contents had fallen to the floor and lay in piles, unwashed and dirty, spilling half out of it. There was nothing else from which it was possible to leap, that would allow his head to have impacted with the wall at such a height.

To Matt's mind, Ryan's death could only be as a result of him being thrown or hit against the wall by another person, the same person who had then attempted to hide their actions by positioning him in his bed. It would remain to be seen whether a post-mortem would be able to pinpoint an exact time of death or show whether the child had died instantly.

Or for that matter whether he could have been saved, had either parent bothered to check him when they went to bed themselves. One of them would obviously have had a reason not to check, but the other . . .

'Who does he share this room with?' His thoughts returned to the grubby mattress on the floor.

'His older brother, Jake. He's eight. He's one of the lads downstairs. Apparently the older boy and the girl, Mikey and Christina, are the father's from a previous relationship. Jake is the mother's from a previous marriage. Ryan was the only child from the pair of them together.'

Matt nodded and noted down the information in his notepad. It was very common to have a mix of children from various relationships all forced together by ensuing pairings. Sometimes they got on, but often rivalries and jealousy built up, causing an explosive family situation. Add to that the difficulties of step-parents adjusting to children from previous relationships and it was easy to see why these volatile home arrangements sometimes combusted.

'I don't think there's anything more we can do here until the Scene of Crime officer and photographer has arrived. I'll pop downstairs and have a quick word with the other kids.' He stared down for one last time at the toddler's face, so peaceful in death. Maybe it was better for him to have died so young, rather than be brought up in this environment. He turned away smartly and walked out of the room.

Before returning to the lounge he visited the other upstairs rooms, taking stock of the hopeless conditions. Nowhere was there any sense of pride in what they had, or enthusiasm for the future, or love. The adults who lived there existed in their own squalor and the children were being forced into the same way of life. He wondered how it had been allowed to get so bad, how social services hadn't intervened; or whether it was possible that police hadn't been called to any domestic disturbances.

'Have you seen this?' Inspector Munroe queried, pointing to the bottom of Ryan's door.

Matt looked down at where he was indicating and saw a heavy sliding bolt.

'Don't say they locked the poor little chap in there?'

'We don't know as yet. The door was obviously open when

we were called but it's there for a reason and my guess is that it does get used when his parents want a bit of peace and quiet. It slides across quite easily and it's obviously well worn.'

Matt bent down and pushed the bolt. It did indeed move without any hint of rust or obstruction. He had to agree with the inspector. He could imagine it was used quite regularly.

Next to the door he noticed the vomit.

'Looks like he got himself into quite a state too, being locked in.'

The inspector nodded. 'There's some dried vomit down the front of his outfit and on its sleeves which matches this.'

As he descended the stairs Matt felt a great sadness that such neglect and abuse could still happen in Britain.

He entered the lounge and the three children looked towards him. The older boy and girl were sitting close to each other at the far end of the settee. They looked like siblings, thick eyebrows and heavy features highlighting their similarities.

'You must be Mikey and Christina?' Matt asked. He noticed the pair of them were holding hands, which he thought strange for two children of that age. Mikey nodded and, as if in agreement that this would be their only communication, both turned away from him. He took the hint. Obviously the shock of their youngest brother's death had rendered them unwilling to talk. He watched as the girl extricated her hand from her sibling's and placed it protectively around his shoulders.

The younger boy was still gazing up into his face expectantly. He appeared different from the others, blond with a smattering of freckles across his nose and cheeks. His eyes appeared to have a hidden depth, a deep olive green with a dark glint which alternately made him look sad and lost or slightly secretive and intense. He was set apart from the other two, the gap exacerbated by the body of the dog, which lay with its head on Mikey's lap. He appeared to be slightly ostracized from the others and the sight immediately induced a feeling of sympathy from Matt. He bent down so that his head was at the same level.

'And you must be Jake?'

Jake nodded but didn't avert his gaze.

'When will Mummy be coming home?' he said evenly.

'I don't know. Not for a while. We need to talk to her about what happened to Ryan.'

'Why don't you ask Lee? He's the one that locked Ryan in his room last night.'

The older girl swivelled her head quickly to look at him. She appeared angry, an expression immediately conveying her displeasure at his words. Jake saw the warning in her eyes and shut his mouth in an instant, biting on his bottom lip nervously.

Matt knew instinctively that it wouldn't be the right time to ask anything further. Instead he jotted down what Jake had said in his notebook and made a mental note to probe this comment later on.

He stood up and smiled down at the young boy. Already he felt a strange bond growing between himself and this young witness.

'For the time being the three of you are going to a children's home while we speak to your mum and dad. You'll all be together and they'll look after you well. It's just until things get sorted out.'

Jake's face crumpled and he started to cry. Matt bent towards him and patted his shoulder. For some reason it bothered him to see the young boy distressed.

'I'll come and visit you at the home. I promise.'

Jake rubbed his eyes hard with clenched fists, and Matt couldn't help notice the grubby, bitten fingernails and tear stains across his dirty cheeks. The child raised his eyes towards him and he could just make out a challenge in his expression. He ran his fingers through his tangled hair and stared unblinkingly into Matt's own eyes.

'I don't want you to visit me and I don't want to go to a children's home. I just want my mummy back.'

# Two

M att strode quickly into his office and sat down. He couldn't get the memory of Ryan's small, lifeless body, dressed in his favourite Spider-Man outfit, and the words of his older brother Jake, from his mind.

DI Roger Blandford came in, clutching a handful of paperwork.

'You OK?'

'Could be better. There's something about this time of year that always makes kids' deaths worse.'

'I agree.' His boss nodded. 'Christmas is for kids. They're the only ones who seem to enjoy it. The rest of us just find the whole palaver too much.' He paused briefly. 'Unless you happen to be religious, of course,' he added as an afterthought. 'Here, I've got the arresting officer's notes and printouts of previous convictions and the call message.'

He threw the bundle down on Matt's desk and was gone as quickly as he'd arrived.

Matt flicked through the papers carefully, concentrating on the previous convictions and histories of both parents. Not much was shown for the mother. Denise Pamela Clarkson, as she now liked to be known, had only a few previous convictions, mainly for petty theft, shoplifting and driving offences. There was a relatively long list of other names she had used in the past, along with numerous addresses. Stephenson, Moore, Chandler and Bryant were all listed as aliases or names she'd given previously. Matt flipped open his notepad, in which he had scribbled Jake's surname as Bryant. Maybe she'd changed her name to go with every boyfriend she had. He checked her date of birth: 12th September 1981, making her twenty-six years old. She certainly seemed to have gone through some men in those years, particularly as she'd obviously been with Lee Clarkson for the last few. He wondered how Jake had coped with the steady stream of new men in his life and the constant moves from one address to another. It must have been very unsettling for the young boy, impossible to get any kind of education, friendships or stability.

He checked the list of addresses. She had also obviously moved around the country a fair bit too, notching up court appearances in Birmingham, Bristol, Hastings and Exeter. She didn't seem to have many family ties and he wondered whether she had parents who were still alive or any siblings. He typed her name into the intelligence records. Only two reports sprung up, both detailing domestic assaults by her partner, Lee. He read one:

> *On 03/08/2006 police were called to a domestic disturbance at 53 STATION ROAD SW16 where the female occupier Denise CLARKSON dob 12/09/1981 FEMALE IC1 alleged she had been punched several times around the face by her partner and thrown across the room, hitting the back of her head against a wardrobe. Injuries found consistent with Actual Bodily Harm.*
>
> *Partner Lee Ryan CLARKSON dob 09/02/1972 MALE IC1 denied any assault stating she had fallen while drunk. He was aggressive both verbally and physically towards police, punching one police officer on side of head. He was restrained and arrested for ABH on both the female and officer and was very violent.*
>
> *Once removed from the premises the female withdrew the allegation stating she had fallen during an argument and he had not hit her. She stated she just wanted him out of the house and refused to co-operate any further.*
>
> *There are four children in the house – Mikey and Christina CLARKSON, older children of father, Jake BRYANT, older son of mother and Ryan CLARKSON, 2-year-old son of both subjects. Jake, aged 7 years in particular was vocal against father, taking side of mother.*
>
> *The allegation of assault against female was dropped due to lack of evidence but Lee CLARKSON was charged with ABH on police and was bailed to attend Camberwell Green Magistrates Court on 07/08/2006.*

Matt sighed. It was all too familiar. Abusive relationships usually continued for far too long, with the battered victim unable or unwilling to substantiate the allegation, either too fearful of the partner's reaction or too emotionally confused to do more than call police to remove the imminent danger.

The other report was of a similar nature. Lee Clarkson was a violent bully who seemed to assault his partner regularly and with impunity. Matt flipped through his previous convictions and wasn't surprised to see the long list of offences, mainly for violence and drink-related crimes: robbery, GBH, ABH, affray, threatening behaviour, drunk and disorderly, breach of the peace. A catalogue of violence. A catalogue of victims. He felt sure there was now a new young victim to add to the list.

He looked up, suddenly aware that his boss had returned to the office.

'Looks like chummy here likes beating up women,' Matt muttered across to him. 'I wonder if he's added kids to his agenda now.'

'If I was a betting man, I think I'd have him odds-on favourite,' the DI agreed.

Denise Clarkson looked up at the small barred window at the top of her cell, through which a bright shaft of sunlight shone. It seemed like the only brightness in the dark of her day. She concentrated on the beam until her eyes watered with the strain. She didn't care though; it took away the pain from other parts of her body. Her face still hurt from the backhand she'd been given the night before. She remembered Lee's face, even now, contorted with rage. She'd stifled her sobs, gritted her teeth and turned away. He didn't like the sound of crying.

'Don't you dare bring him back down,' he'd snarled at her. 'He'll stay in his room until the morning.'

She couldn't bear to hear the sound of crying either, but for different reasons. It made her feel tense, inadequate and fearful. Now it was gone and she'd never hear her little boy cry again. And that bastard had lain in bed while she screamed for help this morning and hadn't lifted a finger to call an ambulance. He hadn't even got out of bed, while his son's broken body was being examined by the paramedics and pronounced dead. He was too hung-over from the booze, too callous to care what happened to his own flesh and blood. She didn't know what she had ever seen in him.

She saw a movement at the door wicket and heard a key being turned in the lock. Still she sat staring at the shaft of light.

'Denise, you can come out now,' a voice said.

She turned and saw the kindly face of the custody officer, a middle-aged sergeant with an old face and grey wisps running through his beard and hair.

'You're going to be interviewed. Your solicitor is here and we've also got a social worker to be with you, seeing as you said you'd had learning difficulties. She'll just be there to make sure everything is done fairly and you don't feel it's getting too much.'

She followed him along the passageway and into the bright lights of the custody area. There were no other prisoners there and it all felt surreal. A gust of fresh, cold air blew in from an open door into a small caged area and made her shiver. She pulled the blanket she'd been given tightly around her shoulders and shook hands with two women who were walking towards her, arms outstretched. The handshakes were not firm and authoritative, but soft, friendly, mere brushes against hers.

She was ushered into a small interview room and the two women introduced themselves. Dawn Kelly was the social worker, but not like some of the others she'd met. They'd been brash, inquisitive and rude, poking their noses into her business. This one seemed nice – smiled at her, offered her support, said that if there was anything she could help with she'd just to ask. The other woman was more formal, dressed smartly in dark trousers, a white blouse and a grey cardigan. She looked clever and introduced herself as Rachel Mears, a duty solicitor who was going to be acting for her. Her hair was tied up in a ponytail but several strands kept falling forward as she wrote notes in a pad and Denise wanted to push them back behind her ears. She looked to be in her mid thirties and appeared too smart and tidy to have children of her own.

She glanced down at her own clothing. It was shabby and ill fitting, with dried-on stains across the shoulders and sleeves from dealing with the kids. All her clothes were like that. These had been taken from the back of her wardrobe, before they left the house earlier. The police had wanted the clothes she was wearing when they'd gone there.

Rachel was asking her questions about Lee. How long had they been living together? Was it an abusive relationship? Did he beat her up often? Did he beat the kids up? What had happened the night before?

'Will I get my clothes back?' The thought was suddenly important to her.

The solicitor looked up.

'Maybe, but not for some time. The police will be carrying out tests on them.'

'But they won't find anything on them and they're my favourites. I only put them on this morning.'

Dawn Kelly smiled at her. 'Don't worry about your clothes. If necessary we can fix you up with some new ones.'

She relaxed. She'd need some new clothes if she was to move away. When she left Lee. She'd have to start afresh again where he couldn't follow. She couldn't take any more violence from him.

'Just tell the officer what you've told us,' Rachel was saying. She too smiled. She reached over and squeezed Denise's hand, before opening the door and indicating they were ready.

Matt glanced surreptitiously at the young woman sitting behind the desk in the interview room. He'd dealt with many suspects and victims before and this one looked like a definite victim. Her whole appearance and posture screamed defeat. She looked browbeaten and weary, her young face having the lines and texture of an older woman. Creases ran across her forehead and frown marks were etched between her eyebrows. Her eyes were green and she had fair, mousy hair, short but unkempt, clipped untidily away from her face. Matt could see immediately where Jake had inherited his features. Her hands were gripped together and she twisted and squeezed them continuously.

Matt was to be conducting the interview with DC Alison Richards, one of the members of his squad, the Area Murder Investigation Team or AMIT. Alison, although the same height as Denise, was the direct opposite in both shape and character. Her hair was longer, falling loosely about her shoulders, and her face and voice burst through the wild strands that framed her face, loud and exuberant, but with the ability to still when required to exhibit care and empathy. She regularly wore an ill-fitting grey suit that laboured around the waistband to restrain a slightly overfed torso. Matt liked and admired her, not just for her friendly, warm qualities but also for her strong work ethic. She could be relied on not only to do what was required but to do it with a smile on her face and a comment to brighten up everyone else's day too. He glanced across as she introduced herself to the three other women in the room and endeavoured to make everyone feel comfortable and at ease.

It wouldn't be easy, though. Denise Clarkson had educational needs. She'd had learning difficulties as a child and her reading and writing ability was below average. In view of this, the social worker was to act as an 'appropriate adult' for her, there to oversee the interview and ensure she was treated fairly and her needs met. He didn't think she'd be a hard nut to crack but he would have to do it carefully.

He introduced himself and switched the tape on. As he started to caution her and explain her rights she started to cry.

'Are you all right to continue?' he asked.

She sniffed noisily and started to sob out loud.

'Of course I'm not all right. I found my little boy dead in his bed this morning and I've been carted off here and banged up all day. I should be with Jake and the older kids.' She stared at him accusingly. 'I'm the one who called the ambulance, you know.'

'Tell us about it. We need to hear your side of the story before we can decide anything.'

'But what's happened with Jake?'

'Don't worry. He's being looked after. He's with Mikey and Christina. They're all together. Nothing will be arranged permanently for them yet until we know what's happened and can make some decisions.'

'I don't really know what happened. All I know was Lee was in a bad mood last night. He was trying to watch the match but Ryan kept disturbing him, crying and that. I tried to quieten him down but he wouldn't stop bleedin' crying. In the end Lee grabbed him by the arm and took him upstairs. I could hear him shouting at him, telling him to shut his mouth or there'd be trouble. Then Lee came crashing back downstairs and said he'd locked him in and no one was to let him out. He was drinking beer, getting angrier and angrier. When Ryan didn't stop screaming, Lee started swearing, like. He went storming off upstairs again and I heard him go into Ryan's room. I could hear him stomping around on the floorboards, in and out. Then it all went quiet and I heard him shut the door and lock it.

'I went upstairs to the toilet and passed him coming down. He told me not to go into the room, that Ryan was sleeping now and I'd be in trouble if I went in and woke him up. He was right in my face. He pushed me up against the wall with his hand round my throat. I was frightened about what he'd do to me if I went in. He looked really mad. He's beaten me up lots of times before.' She looked up at him. 'I've had you lot round and he's been nicked a couple of times.'

She started pulling her sleeves up, showing Matt an array of bruises that reached from her wrists up to her shoulders. He looked at the varying sizes, shapes and colours, noting the angry blotches merging through to greeny, yellow faded smudges.

'Look what he's done to me. He's an animal.'

'Has he ever hit the kids before?'

'He's hit Jake and the older ones, pushed them around, like. I've seen him kick them an' all. I haven't seen him hit Ryan before, proper like, but he's always rough with him. Grabs him up and pushes him about. He was really mad though. I wouldn't put him past it to crack his head against a wall.'

She started to cry again, great racking sobs forcing themselves up her throat and exploding into the silence.

'He's a bastard. A lying bastard,' she whispered through the sobs. 'And to think that my poor little lad was lying dead or dying while he told us he was asleep.'

The thought left them all speechless, each quietly visualizing the scene. The silence was broken as Dawn Kelly reached for a tissue and passed it to Denise. She took it and wiped her face ferociously. She couldn't wipe away the spark of anger and determination that had suddenly showed itself, though.

'Do you know what he did after the football game had finished? He wanted sex, like, so he grabbed me up and pushed me upstairs. Made me spread my legs, while my boy lay in the next room. Bleedin' bastard, I want nothing more to do with him. Now that Ryan's gone he's got nothing to come after me for. I hope he rots in hell, for all I care.'

She sniffed loudly, blowing her nose on the tissue. Matt looked at her.

'Did you not get a chance to check on Ryan at all?'

'I looked into the room just afterwards when Jake was settling down and I thought Ryan was asleep. It was all dark and he was in his bed. I didn't go over to him because Lee called me back.

'It wasn't till this morning that I got the chance to check on him proper, like. He hadn't moved since I last saw him. I touched his face and it was all cold, then I saw the blood on his head. I knew he was dead, I just knew it. He'd gone.'

She went silent for a few seconds as if remembering. The tears fell down her cheeks unabated and she let them fall.

'But I still called the ambulance though, just in case. I was screaming for Lee to phone, but the bastard wouldn't get out of bed.' She looked up at them, pleadingly, as if this statement would make it all right. 'I did try, I really did, but it was too late.'

Matt looked at the woman in front of him. Twenty-six years old with one living son, one dead and an abusive partner. Her life was obviously so full of fear and trepidation that she'd chosen to neglect checking on her son rather than risk another beating. Now she seemed to think she'd be exonerated from any blame because she was the one to phone an ambulance. Her expression was pitiful. She was like a child pleading for praise, for one correct answer in a failed exam, for one success in a lifetime of failure. He felt sorry for her. Sorry for the life she was forced to lead. Sorry that she could even start to believe that a belated phone call was enough.

Leaving the desolation and misery of her family home just a few hours earlier he'd been sure that he would know nothing but anger and contempt for the parents responsible for forcing such conditions on their child. Now he was surprised to be looking at this woman with a completely different attitude, pity even.

'Interview concluded,' he said. 'You need to see a doctor to have your injuries logged and I'll speak to you again later.'

# Three

'What do you make of her then?' Alison Richards asked, as Matt drove towards Brixton police station. Tom Berwick, another member of the squad, had joined them and was to sit in with Matt on the next interview, while Alison went through the previous one collating any points that Denise had raised. Tom was one of Matt's best mates; the two had joined the police and trained together at Hendon training school. He and his wife, Sue, were the couple with whom Matt and Jo mainly socialized. Tom was a giant of a man, six foot five, heavily built and with a personality as large as his muscular physique. His was the voice that was always heard over the crowd, the laugh that was always the loudest, the stature that commanded respect. His shaven head and imposing size made him Mr Nasty to Matt's Mr Nice Guy, and Matt knew he would come in very handy for the father's interview.

'She seems a bit simple to me,' Matt replied. 'I was talking to Dawn Kelly briefly before I left and she said the same. Apparently she'd made a big issue about getting her clothes back. She seemed to be more concerned about that, than really taking in what's happened to Ryan – and more importantly, who's done it.'

'Well she's definitely blaming Lee,' Alison added, leaning forward from the rear. 'She's put him up in the bedroom at the right time and says little Ryan went quiet after he left the room. Pretty damning I would say. And anyway, she doesn't look as if she'd be capable of it, to me.'

'I tend to agree with you,' he nodded. 'She's your typical battered wife, although she's not even married to him. Frightened to do a thing without Lee's say-so. Judging by the look of those bruises on her arms, I'd guess he has a pretty short fuse as well.'

'The next interview should be interesting then,' commented Tom, smiling.

'Yeah, let's just see if he can keep his temper under control with us.'

Matt smiled wryly. It certainly wouldn't harm the prosecution case for a suspect to snap during an interview. Some even did it in court occasionally. He'd seen the jurors looking petrified in more than one case, even with the defendant safely secured in the dock at the other side of the courtroom.

As he drove into Brixton, Matt scanned the bustling crowds of people. It was always busy there, whatever time of day or night. By day, inhabitants and visitors alike browsed the shops and cafés, while at night they frequented the bars, restaurants and nightclubs or just hung around on corners, talking in small groups, the Caribbean culture transferred on to the London streets. Drug dealers too would be out on the front line at all times, touting for business, while in the evenings prostitutes would emerge, plying their trade, lingering in any dark alleyway, away from prying eyes. The streets came alive at night.

He turned off the main road and after rounding a few side roads, crossed the colourful street market. Stalls groaned under the weight of the wares for sale and a throng of rainbow bright shoppers of all nationalities milled around, touching, feeling, purchasing the goods. The crowd parted to let his car through and he was soon at the back of Brixton police station, waiting as the heavy outer gates swung open. The yard was large, having until recently housed some of the mounted branch of the Metropolitan Police. Matt had always thought the smell of freshly piled manure strangely irreconcilable with the concrete and tarmac of the city all around. The sights of horses too had always seemed out of place, but not unwelcome in the midst of the high-rise buildings.

They walked to the metal cage through which prisoners entered the custody area. Unusually, it was empty. Through into the custody reception, Matt found himself nodding a greeting to the custody sergeants and peering up on to the white board on which the detainees' names were written. He saw Lee Clarkson's name written against Cell 5, the words MURDER in capitals next to it. He had already been fingerprinted, photographed and seen a police doctor and he was ready for interview, pending the arrival of a duty solicitor.

While he waited, Matt took the chance to walk down to Cell 5 and peer in at the man against whom his wits would be pitted shortly. Lee Clarkson was lying on a mattress, gazing upwards. He didn't turn his head at the movement at the door but smiled lazily. He wasn't tall but he was stocky, his bulk filling the white jumpsuit prisoners were sometimes given. His hair was black and unruly and he had a dark growth of stubble across his chin. His knees were drawn up and his arms were tucked round the back of his head. A thick growth of hair was visible on his arms and shins and some had escaped from the front of his suit, curling out over the zip.

As Matt watched, Clarkson swung his legs round and stood up, walking straight towards the door. He put his face directly in front of the large toughened-glass spyhole and spoke.

'When the fuck are you going to let me out of here?' His voice was low and threatening, impotent now behind the thick cell door but edged with barely contained menace.

Matt didn't like him. Instantly.

'You'll get out if and when we say you can. Your solicitor will be here soon and then you'll be interviewed. Until then you might as well lie back down and wait.'

Clarkson turned away, but swung back quickly, lashing out at the door. Matt jumped, taken mildly by surprise. He walked away and as he did so, he heard Clarkson kick the door again, and again, and again. As he left the custody area he could still hear the continuous dull thud of the cell door being booted, as Ryan's father took out his rage in controlled and monotonous anger.

Lee Ryan CLARKSON, date of birth 09/02/1972, MALE: WHITE, born Hastings, sat in the interview room of Brixton police station with his solicitor. His boy was dead and they were blaming him. He always got the blame. All his life he'd got the blame. From the moment he'd landed the first punch on his older bullying sibling, he'd been in trouble. With his mother, his school teachers, his neighbours. It was always his fault. Always his fault that his victims didn't fight back, didn't return the blows, but chose to grass on him instead.

Now, as he sat waiting for the coppers to come and start asking questions, he felt the usual frustrating sense of perse-cution settle firmly on his broad shoulders. It wasn't his fault he was violent. It was in his genes. His father had been violent too and he had watched his own mother become his punch bag, until a gang of three other violent men had snuffed out his lights in a dark and dingy alleyway on the estate in which they lived. Lee remembered it vividly. Word had reached his mother that there'd been a fight and her man was badly injured. She'd run through the night to reach him, with eight-year-old Lee right behind her. She'd watched as her husband had breathed his last, fantasized that he'd died defending her honour, and ever more sainted him as some kind of hero. The violence and terror of home life was forgotten and Trevor Lee Clarkson lived on as some kind of role model. In Lee's young mind he had equated violence with honour and couldn't understand why he should get in trouble when he used it to settle disputes and differences.

As he'd matured the violence had increasingly become a problem, one that he could neither overcome nor understand. If his mother nagged, he'd respond by pushing her to the side; if school chums said anything against him or taunted his lack of education, he'd replied with his fists; if his employer was too demanding, he'd told him where to go, smashing the place up and making threats as he slammed out of each new workplace.

The violence had grown in line with his physique and so too did the blame he got for using it. Women, however, seemed to fall at his feet, enticed by his strength and masculinity. He could have virtually any woman he wanted and was always aware of eyes staring at his body, mesmerized by his taut muscles and easy smile. And he'd had them too. Plenty of them of all shapes, sizes, ages. He didn't care. He wooed them, loved them, fucked them and left them when they started to become too demanding, as they always did. They loved his strength but didn't like to be put in their place when he used it. Some of them had lied to get their revenge, lied to get him dragged away from his own home by the cops, lied to have him banged away in prison. As the sentences had grown in length, so too had his sense of injustice and persecution.

He'd done time in various prisons and although he believed he didn't deserve the sentence, he seemed to feel strangely at home behind the heavy, unyielding bars. He knew where he stood with the other cons. They were like him and they respected him. He didn't take any shit from them and after the first few scuffles wasn't given any. The places were well ordered and he liked the routine, liked the fact he didn't have to make any decisions and liked the time available to work out. He was strong, hard, muscular and able to fight his own corner. He could push himself to his limits and take out any frustrations on the equipment. On each occasion when he'd been discharged he'd felt a sense of loss, a hint of panic, of fear, an emotion he was not used to feeling and one that set him on edge.

He'd returned to some of the women who would have him. Like Angie. Mikey and Christina were proof of that. He'd tried to control his fists, tried to remain monogamous, but inevitably his lust and temper had got the better of him. Angie had taken her own life, unable to cope with any more beatings. It wasn't his fault though. She'd wound him up, provoked his fists, and he'd silently been blamed for her death by her family and friends. He'd felt it in the way they'd stared at him, unspoken looks of fear and loathing piercing through the despair of the funeral service.

Now Denise was causing him grief too. She couldn't control the kids and didn't seem to be trying. His own two children, Mikey and Christina, were left to their own devices. She barely spoke to them, hardly even carrying out her duty to feed and clothe them. Jake seemed to receive the most attention and it was the boy with whom she spent the most time. It was as if he himself wasn't there sometimes. She let Jake get away with more and took his side in arguments, even over Lee's own. Things had got so bad that they were barely talking, at least not civilly. It seemed it was down to him to deal with all the kids, except Jake who he was barely allowed to admonish. He didn't like the situation and now it was out of control. Ryan was dead and he wished he had been able to control his violence the night before. He would get the blame, as always. This time, though, he was determined he wouldn't let it happen. This time, the bitch would pay for her lies and deceit. This time she could take the blame. He'd had enough.

A shiver of anticipation ran through him. He wanted to get on with it and didn't know why they had to wait.

He stood up and took a step towards the interview room

door. He was nervous, frustrated and angry and he couldn't stay still any longer. He felt a hand touch his elbow and drew his arm back quickly. It was instinctive and as he swung round, he saw his solicitor pull away from him sharply and put his arm up to his face for protection.

'Calm down, Lee,' a small voice pleaded from behind the arm.

'What the fuck are we waiting for then?'

Matt Arnold and Tom Berwick opened the door into the interview room and immediately took in the scene before them. Without a moment's hesitation Tom grabbed Lee Clarkson's arm and forced it behind his back, pushing him up, face first, against the wall. Matt too moved forward, taking hold of Lee's other arm, and felt the muscles tense under his fingers.

'What's going on?' he said, peering round towards the solicitor who was obviously trying to regain his composure.

'Nothing. Don't worry. My client's just getting a little frustrated with the wait. Bearing in mind he's lost his son today he just wants to get on with the interview.'

'Are you going to behave yourself then?' Tom turned to Lee. 'Because otherwise you can go back down to your cell until you calm down. Do you understand?' He gave Lee's arm a tweak upwards and Matt heard his suspect gasp.

He nodded, wincing in obvious discomfort, and his muscles relaxed slightly.

'Sit yourself down then,' Tom said. 'And we'll start.'

Lee sat down on the seat, slowly folding his arms and leaning backwards, legs spread open in front of him. Matt watched the man as Tom prepared the tapes. He appeared arrogant and confident. Too confident. Maybe he thought they would be intimidated by his presence like others around him, including his own solicitor. He settled back in his own chair. He was going to enjoy this.

He read out the words of the caution and went through the preliminaries.

'Tell me in your own words, Lee, what happened last night.'

Lee stayed in exactly the same position but shifted his gaze to Matt, staring straight into his eyes. He sighed out loud.

'I was watching the football. Ryan was misbehaving and crying. Denise couldn't sort him out. She's fucking useless.

So I took him upstairs to his room and shut the door. That's all. He was all right when I left him.'

'So you're saying that the last time you saw him he was alive?'

'Yeah, that's right.'

'What sort of condition did you leave him in?'

'What do you mean by that?'

'Well, Denise says she saw you drag Ryan up the stairs and go into the room with him. She heard you shouting at him and then you locked him in the room.'

'Yeah, that's right. And he was still screaming then.'

'Do you always lock him in his bedroom?'

'No, not always. Only when he's playing up. So does she.'

'Did you smack him then, or hit him?'

'No, I just put him in his bed and told him to stop crying.'

'By that you mean you told him to shut his mouth or there'd be trouble?'

'He was disturbing the match.'

'He's three years old.'

'He's got to learn some time. He needs to learn respect. He needs to know when he's got to do as he's told.'

'So you think it's all right to drag a three-year-old up the stairs by the arm and threaten him and lock him in a bedroom?'

'Yeah, if it teaches him.'

'And did it teach him?'

'No, he still wouldn't stop bleedin' squealing.'

'So what did you do then?'

'Nothing.'

'What do you mean, nothing?'

'I mean, I did fucking nothing. I told the others to leave him up there. That he'd quieten down if he was left alone.'

'Did you go back up there again?'

'No.'

'Denise said that Ryan wouldn't stop crying so you went back up to the room.'

'I went up to the toilet. I was drinking beer so I needed to have a piss.'

'She says she heard you go into the room and shout at him. Then she heard the sound of banging and crashing and then it all went quiet.'

'I didn't go back into the room.'

'Were you drunk?'

'No, not drunk.'

'But you'd had a few?'

'Yeah.'

'How many?'

'I don't know. I didn't fucking count.'

'I think you'd been drinking and Ryan was making a noise and he was annoying you so you went back into the room to shut him up.'

'That's bullshit.'

'Denise also says that you wouldn't let anyone go back into the room afterwards. Was that because you'd really shut him up? Shut him up for good and you didn't want anyone to see what you'd done?'

'No. I just thought he'd fall asleep if he was left.'

'Why would Denise say that?'

'I don't know. She's lying.'

'Why would she lie about something like that?'

'Because she's a fucking lying bitch, that's why. She's always getting me into trouble. Calling you lot.'

'So you've never hit her before, when she's called us.'

'I didn't say that. She winds me up deliberate, like. Always nagging me to do stuff. Always leaving me to sort out the kids.'

'So you really sorted out Ryan this time?'

'I didn't touch him. Maybe you should ask her what she did. Maybe she wants me out. Maybe she wants to get rid of me for good, so she thought she'd drop me in it.'

'By killing her own son?'

'I wouldn't put it past her. She's always on my case these days. Nothing I do is right.'

'So what you're saying is that she's killed her son to somehow get back at you. Even though you're violent towards her and the kids, even though you dragged your own three-year-old son up the stairs, shouted at him, threatened him and locked him in his room. Even though you were drunk and angry. But it's not your fault?'

Lee was on his feet. Taking hold of the table in front of him, he tried to lift it, but it wouldn't budge. With veins bulging on his temples he banged his fists hard against it.

'No, it's not my fucking fault,' he shouted. 'I'm fed up with always taking the blame. She's a fucking lying whore. I'll get her, the bitch. I'll teach her to fucking lie.'

The door was flung open and Lee was manhandled, kicking and struggling, back down to his cell for the night. His eyes were wild with rage and he screamed obscenities through gritted teeth. Matt listened to his shouts. Through the commotion, the words came across clear and loud.

'Ask her what she did, the bitch. Ask her why she was up there at the same time. Ask her what happened to our baby daughter.'


# Four


T he entrance to the mortuary reception was decorated by a solitary Christmas tree. Small white lights glowed on and off and a smattering of silver tinsel and ornaments hung disconsolately from the lower branches. There was no star on the top; no overtly religious signs or symbols were allowed in public buildings.

Matt glanced at the tree as the three of them entered and felt immediately depressed. Several of the bulbs had gone out and their absence reminded him of why he was there. Death was absence, loss, abandonment. A small life snuffed out, where the energy and joy of childhood should have shone. A small life ended before it had begun, in squalor and pain.

Tom stopped behind him, his attention also drawn to the tree.

'Looks a bit sad, doesn't it. Still, goes well with the building, I suppose.'

The pathologist, Dr Peter Karlsson, came through from the back. They shook hands warmly, having worked together on numerous jobs.

'Happy Christmas, ladies and gents,' he said smiling. 'Everything's set up and ready to go.'

Matt couldn't quite bring himself to respond to the seasonal greeting. It seemed out of place. Still, he supposed that working daily in this particular environment, it would be necessary to maintain a veneer of normality. He followed the pathologist through to the laboratory.

The sight of Ryan Clarkson's tiny body was a shock.

Naked, white and lying straight, with his eyes closed, it looked almost doll-like, until Matt stepped closer. That was when he noticed the scars and bruises, the scratches and burn marks. That was when he noticed the ribs, standing out from his chest, the skinny arms and legs, the emaciated body. That was when he noticed the dried blood and bruising to the side of his head.

'Christ,' he said quietly. 'What a mess. What have they done to him?'

The four of them stood silently for a few moments looking down at the child. Matt guessed that each of them would be thinking of their own children, or relatives, like he was. He couldn't imagine in his worst nightmare having to see Ben or Chloe lying on a cold mortuary slab. The thought made his heart race and sent an icy chill through him. Chloe was the same age as this little boy, but his body was smaller than hers; underfed, undernourished, un-nurtured, unloved. Its stillness appalled him. Children were never still, always running when they should walk, screaming when they should be quiet, fidgeting, squirming, laughing, breathing.

The silence was broken by Alison, whose face had lost its usual cheeriness.

'How could someone do this to a toddler?'

The question hung in the air, unanswerable. And yet it was their job to find its answer.

The catalogue of injuries made grim reading. Most of Ryan's ribs had been broken at one time or another. Left to mend on their own, some had slipped slightly out of position and the pain the youngster must have learned to live with was heartbreaking to imagine. He also had historic breaks to the radius bone of his lower right arm and to several fingers on his left hand.

The list of scars seemed endless, ranging from small round burn marks, probably caused by cigarettes being pushed into his skin, to large, jagged scars two to three inches in length, whose cause could only be imagined. Matt watched the list grow in morbid fascination. He didn't want to watch but the horror kept his eyes riveted to the entries, counting them as they were added. His own son, Ben, had a fair few scars from his own endeavours – toddlers' legs and arms were particularly vulnerable to the scrapes and bruises of their growing enthusiasm to explore – but to see the number on display on this young boy's abdomen, chest and back was extremely abnormal.

Dr Karlsson was thorough and precise, working his way from top to toe, front and back. It took several hours before the list was complete. In the end, ninety-three injuries were listed.

He weighed Ryan's body, measured the body fat and worked out his body mass index: 13.5. Underweight and under-nourished for a boy of that age.

The more recent injuries he listed separately. Injuries caused in the hours leading up to Ryan's death. He was able, by their appearance, to gauge at what time they were likely to have been sustained and whether they had contributed to the death.

Ryan's right shoulder was swollen and bruised, and he had recent heavy bruising to his left upper leg and grazes down the length of his spine. He examined the colour of the bruises, the amount of swelling and fluid around the joint and the depth and consistency of the scabbing around the grazes.

Finally he noted down the swelling and laceration to the right side of Ryan's head. He swabbed the blood, cleaning it away from the wound so that he was able to measure its length. He measured too the swelling around the wound. Only when the boy's body had been opened and his skull and brain examined was the cause of death clear. He had a fractured skull, causing the brain to swell; the resulting build-up of pressure had led to his death.

'Would he have been killed instantly?' Matt found himself asking. The question was important, one that most parents whose youngsters had died needed to know. Had they suffered?

'It's hard to tell exactly,' Dr Karlsson replied. 'He would almost certainly have been unconscious from the initial blow to his skull. It's possible that he could have lived for an hour or so more, while his brain continued to swell. Perhaps if he'd been taken to a hospital quickly, they'd have been able to operate and relieve the pressure. I'll have to run a few more tests first and then I'll be able to say more accurately whether death was instantaneous or not.'

Matt felt relieved in one respect. At least Ryan wouldn't have known too much about it, shielded from pain by unconsciousness, but to think that he might have been saved made his blood boil. He thought of Lee's replies: *'He's got to learn some time. He needs to learn respect. Needs to know when he's got to do as he's told.'* He thought of Denise's pitiful pleas that at least she'd phoned the ambulance the next morning. It was too late then to save their son. And it needn't have been too late. If she'd plucked up the courage to check earlier, if she'd put her son's needs before her own fears . . .

He watched as the pathologist's scalpel sliced through the pale young flesh in front of him, probing, cutting, examining, and he felt his anger grow. Body parts were lifted out to be minutely examined and he tried to put the sight to the back of his mind and concentrate on the investigation to come.

'Take a look at this,' Peter Karlsson was saying.

Matt peered at the bloody space indicated by the pathologist.

'See that, that's part of the digestive tract. That's the stomach and oesophagus.' He pointed down and Matt tried to make out precisely what he was supposed to be looking at. 'It looks as if he vomited shortly before his death. There are traces of the stomach contents in the oesophagus and the back of his mouth. I'll obviously have to do further tests but the contents don't look like normal remnants of food. Do they have a dog in the house?'

'Yes, they do, why?'

'Because the only food remnants I can see in his stomach appear to have the consistency and appearance of dog food.'

By the time Matt returned to Lambeth HQ he was raging. He climbed the stairs two at a time rather than stand and wait passively for the lift. He needed to do something positive, something that would let the parents know they couldn't treat their kids like they had and get away with it.

DI Roger Blandford was waiting to speak to him.

'We need to decide what we're going to do with the parents,' he said. 'The first thirty-six hours are nearly up and we'll have to get further authorization if we want to keep them in any longer.'

'I know what I'd like to do with them, especially the father. I'd like to put him in a ring with Mike Tyson. Let him see what it feels like to be a punch bag. And that would be far, far too easy. He deserves to stay inside for the rest of his life. At least the cons would square him up. They bleeding hate child-killers. It might give him a taste of his own medicine.'

'Come into my office and we'll talk.' The DI guided him down the passageway to his own small room. He opened the window wide and beckoned Matt over. The sounds of the city exploded into the room – cars hooting, traffic, people shouting – and Matt realized how much the double glazing shielded them from life outside. It seemed to keep them cocooned from reality, in a world of computers and paperwork and wordiness. Yet decisions made in this separate world would affect those on the other side of the glass. Taking a packet of cigarettes out of his pocket the inspector offered Matt one.

'Looks like you need one,' he said simply.

Matt smiled back at him. Although the new no smoking law had recently come into force throughout the building, everyone knew that Roger Blandford's office remained a safe haven for those who needed the odd nicotine refreshment. His boss was too long in the tooth to bother about laws which he mischievously decreed were both irrelevant and in breach of his human rights, and the senior management team turned a blind eye too, rather than incur the wrath of their stubborn and somewhat eccentric inspector. Matt took one and sucked at the lighter flame, enjoying the guilty presence of the smoke as it hit his lungs and brain.

'Thanks. I do need it.'

He blew the smoke out of the window, watching as it drifted away from the glass, small wisps of grey against the glow of the late afternoon sunset. He watched it drift downwards towards the queue of rush-hour traffic. It wouldn't be long before it was almost at a standstill, slowly and painfully allowing the besuited commuters to return, ruffled and impatient, to their homes and families. He thought of the family ripped apart by a parent's violence, the discordant, dislocated family he was now dealing with.

The post-mortem had taken most of the day but now it had

been officially established that the death was suspicious, non-accidental, a deliberate act against a defenceless toddler, they had to come to some decisions.

Roger Blandford came straight to the point.

'I've been liaising with the CPS and the custody officers. At the moment, we know it's a murder but we don't have enough to charge either parent. We need to get the other children in the family interviewed, but that obviously needs to be done carefully and without rushing them. Forensics won't be back yet although we can get them processed through the lab a bit quicker if I put a bit of pressure on.'

'I don't know if forensics are going to be able to help us much this time anyway. We know Ryan was murdered but it's one word against the other. We need one of the kids to finger either parent actually doing it.'

Roger Blandford nodded.

'Hopefully one of them will, but until then we're going to have to let them out on bail.'

'You're joking!'

'I wish I was, but even if we ask for an extension it won't give us enough time to thoroughly interview the children. Besides, we can put restrictions on them while they're on bail, make sure they can't contact the kids and try to influence any of them. They don't know where they are anyway. Neither of them have any previous convictions for failing to answer bail, and we've got no other reason sufficient to keep them in. They're not likely to commit a further offence of this nature and they're safer out than in. Kick them out for two weeks with conditions that they live and sleep in addresses that we're happy with, don't contact each other or attempt to contact any of the other children and report daily at their respective police stations.' He checked his diary. 'Eighteenth of December should be OK for them to return. I can't see what other option we have at the moment.'

Matt was quiet. He knew his boss was right but the thought that the pair of them would be out on the streets while their little boy was lying dead on a mortuary slab just did not seem right. They stood silently, both absorbed in their own thoughts. Matt watched as a young woman struggled on the street below to keep control of a baby buggy and two small children on either side. He gazed down from on high as she smacked one of the errant children smartly across the back of their legs.

'What happens if we can't prove which one did it?' he said quietly.

He knew the answer but was hoping for a different one. Roger Blandford sighed.

'Then they both get away with murder.'

# Five

Jake Bryant gazed around his small room. He missed his mother, missed the way she held him, stroked his face, smiled at him. He didn't miss Lee though. Lee hit him sometimes. Sometimes he hit his mum. In fact Lee hit her a lot and he didn't like it. He didn't like to see his mother crying in fear, the way she cowered away from his angry fists. He wanted to hit him back. One day he would, when he was bigger. One day he would make Lee leave them alone. One day he would like to kill him, but until then he was on his own.

He looked around. At least he had a room to himself. He had always had to share one before. The room had a bed with a little bedside table by the side of it. There was a wardrobe in one corner and a small chest of drawers with a bit that stuck out from one end and acted as a desk. He only had a small bag of clothes and these had fitted easily into the drawers. The wardrobe was empty.

He walked over to his bed and lay down. The bed was soft and the duvet smelt nice. Clean. Not like their house. He loved his mum but she didn't keep the house very clean, and Scamps did messes all over the place and no one cleaned them up. He never brought his friends back to his house, what friends he had. He'd done so once and the boy had turned his nose up, refused to stay and told all the other boys at school that Jake lived in a shit-hole and his mother was a tramp. They'd all laughed at him then and called him names and his mum names. He hadn't gone back to school much after that.

Anyway, they never stayed in one place long enough to make really good friends, and his mum and Lee never really bothered about making him go to school. Sometimes he did. Sometimes he didn't. Occasionally some people from the school or the education office would come and visit them. Then he would have to go to school for a while, but he didn't really fit in and school was boring.

He was only really happy each day when he came home. Glad that his mum would be waiting for him. And it didn't take long before he stopped going again. Sometimes he felt that his mum was the only one who cared about him in the whole world. Lee didn't. Lee hated him. He'd told him enough times. And Mikey and Christina didn't like him either. They were jealous because his mum would give him more food than them. Not that she gave them much food. Normally she didn't bother to cook, or do much shopping. Normally they just got burgers or chicken or chips.

He felt his stomach. He was full up after eating a big meal. He'd eaten so much he felt sick. It was more than he normally had in a week. He couldn't stop. When they'd said he could have more, he had. Some of the other kids had laughed at him for eating so much. Called him a pig, but he didn't care. He quite liked it at the home. He liked the food. He liked having his own room. He liked it because it was clean and warm. But he didn't like the other kids and he missed his mum.

But Lee was going to get everything he deserved now. He was going to pay for hitting his mum, hurting her and for hitting him and Ryan. For hurting all of them. And soon he would be back with his mum just like they always were. When that nice policeman Matt Arnold spoke to him he would tell him all about what Lee had done.

Tom Berwick was regaling the squad with his failed attempts at Christmas shopping when Matt walked in. He slid backwards on his chair and watched as his boss ran his fingers through his mass of dark hair, trying and failing to tame the spikes sticking out at all angles.

'Give up, Sarge. You'll never get it to stay down without a good handful of gel. Maybe you should ask for some for Christmas.'

Matt turned towards him and laughed.

'You're just jealous,' he replied. 'It'll be a sad day for my barber when my hair gets as thin as yours. I think I keep him in business these days.' He combed his fingers through his hair again, pouting good-humouredly.

A couple of the other detective constables sauntered over. Matt Arnold was a good laugh but he was also hard-working and enthusiastic and commanded respect. Tom particularly enjoyed working with him. Matt knew his stuff and was only too willing to get stuck in. In addition to that, he was obviously proud of his history and the way his father had died in the course of duty. Tom knew the story well. It was no secret, but it was something that Matt rarely spoke about openly, preferring his men to judge him on his own endeavours. The photograph on his desk nevertheless spoke volumes.

Tom knew that his friend was ambitious to further his career but that this dream wouldn't be fulfilled at anyone else's expense. Matt backed his staff up and wasn't afraid to lock horns with any senior officer who undermined any of his team. In return he expected, and received, his squad's loyalty and hard work. He asked only that they give their best, and they all did.

'What's got to be done with the case today then?' one of them called over.

Matt walked up to the main noticeboard and started pinning up photographs. The group crowded closer to see better the close-ups and stills of Ryan Clarkson's scarred and broken body. At the centre he pinned one of the youngster dressed in his Spider-Man outfit, taken a few months earlier. A broad grin lit up the little lad's face, although it couldn't hide the obvious pallor.

'Little Spider-Man, here, had the smile wiped off his face by one of his parents. He was made to eat dog food, dragged up the stairs and locked in his room. When he dared to cry, his head was smashed against a wall, fracturing his skull and causing his brain to swell and kill him. He was laid in his bed and no one bothered to check him until the next morning when an ambulance was called, but by then it was too late. He had ninety-three injuries, either past or recent, and it's our job to find out whether it was his mother or father who caused them. I interviewed both of them the day before yesterday and they both blamed each other. I know you've been out trying to get witnesses and researching the case but last night we had to bail them. They went to separate addresses and they'll be returning on Monday the eighteenth of December. We have two weeks to find out which one of them killed little Ryan or else neither will be able to be charged.'

Tom looked at Matt as he spoke. The man was passionate about the job, passionate to do the best for the victims and passionate in his hatred of injustice. He had sat in bars with him and listened as Matt berated the courts for the sentences handed down to convicted criminals. He didn't believe victims received justice these days and he passionately believed they deserved better.

'I need a couple of you to go to the venue and speak to the neighbours,' Matt was saying. 'Find out what they know about the family, what they've seen, anything that will give us a bit of history on them. Who's interviewing the other children?'

Three of the group indicated that they were.

'Steve and Karen, can you take Mikey and Christina? Look at their records, phone up social services, find out as much about them as you can before you go in. They're both Lee Clarkson's kids from a previous relationship. I've a feeling they'll not say too much for fear of dropping their own father in it. They looked as if they didn't want Denise Clarkson's kid Jake to open his mouth the other day.

'Barry, likewise with Jake. Find out as much as you can before you go in. This one's a bit different though. I think he'll talk more. He's obviously seen his mum beaten up by Lee, quite regularly. Probably been on the receiving end himself a few times. He's not likely to shield his stepdad so much.

'Make sure you take your time though. Don't rush it. If you need to re-interview them another day, don't worry. I think the kids will be the key to who murdered Ryan and we've got two weeks to gently prise out the truth.

'The rest of you, sift through the list of exhibits and forensics and see what needs to be chased up. I want to know everything I can about Lee and Denise Clarkson. Listen to the interview tapes so you can get an idea of what the two of them are like. I personally think Lee's a violent bully and

Denise seems to be a typical victim, but see what you think. There's something about the pair of them that makes me uneasy.'

The squad broke away. Those with set jobs got straight to work. A small group huddled together discussing who was to do what.

'What are we doing then, Sarge?'

Tom walked over to where Matt stood and followed his eyes to the picture of Ryan in his Spider-Man outfit.

'Like I said, I think it will be the kids, and particularly Jake, who'll be the key to this. When Barry's ready I want us to go with him to speak to Jake. We need to befriend him and make him feel at ease with us all. I want him to know that he can really trust us. That way maybe we can hopefully get behind his fear of Lee and get him to tell us the truth.'

Tom nodded. If anyone could get to the truth, it would be Matt.

By lunchtime the officers tasked with interviewing Mikey and Christina had left. Matt was sitting in a car with Barry Tate and Tom on their way to the children's home.

'Have you got much on Jake?' Matt asked.

'No, not much,' Barry said. 'It's strange really. You'd expect a family like that to be well known to social services but they know very little. It seems that the family turned up at Lambeth Town Hall en masse about a year ago, claiming they were homeless. They refused to say what area they had come from so social services have no records from beforehand. They were shown to the housing office and fixed up with temporary accommodation in various bedsits around the area as an emergency measure. Jake never really settled in any school. About four months ago, they were offered the house they're in now and they've been there ever since. Jake is supposed to attend Middlemarch Junior School but he rarely goes. He's been visited several times and spoken to on the doorstep. He goes for a few days and then drops out again.

'Apart from that social services have very little. The older two, Mikey and Christina, seem the same with regards to school. Mikey's in high school now but rarely attends and Christina is supposed to go to the same school as Jake.'

'I would have thought the education authorities would be

working with social services on this one then.' Matt was puzzled.

'Well, they have obviously referred the case on. Social services have tried to visit the family several times but the parents won't let them in. They'll speak briefly on the doorstep or go to an office but they've never allowed a social worker to set foot inside. Little Ryan has been seen by social workers, but always fully clothed and always at the office. The parents have never allowed anyone to examine him properly and to be honest, since they've been in Lambeth there's not been any real reason to suspect the kids were actually being abused. Until now.'

Matt snorted out loud.

'Apart from the fact that they never turn up at school and the parents refuse to allow any of the officials over the threshold. Or that they've never allowed the little one to be examined under his clothing. Didn't they suspect anything was going on?'

'Seems not. They had the family pegged as being awkward and Lee Clarkson was known to be aggressive towards some of the workers, but no calls had ever been made by concerned family or neighbours about the family and they've never attended hospital with any untoward injuries.'

'That's because the parents can't be bothered to take them there until it's too late.'

Matt thought back to the mother's pitiful excuses.

Barry continued.

'Social services are obviously carrying out a rearguard defence now though. They're being a bit cagey about answering any of my questions. Worried about another load of bad press for not doing enough, I suppose.'

'So they should. It makes you wonder how these sorts of things can keep on happening in a so-called civilized society. After the Victoria Climbie inquiry things were supposed to have been tightened.'

The three men sat quietly for a few moments. Matt still felt angry at the memory of Ryan's body and this information didn't help.

At last Tom spoke. 'I suppose social services are snowed under just like us. There's too much work and too few of them to do it.'

Matt nodded. His own father had been murdered because he was on his own. If someone else had been available to assist that fateful night, he might still have had a father. He closed his eyes angrily, willing the thought to go.

'Too few of them and too few of us and too much bloody red tape and arse covering.' He spat out the words. 'When are the people who need it going to be allowed more time and facilities to deal with these sorts of people without having to constantly account for their every move?'

He knew the answer. It was *never*. He peered out of the window angrily, suddenly aware that Barry was swinging the car into the driveway of a large house.

Looking up he saw several faces squashed against the window, peering out at the new arrivals. He knew the house well. The police were in and out regularly. The only question on each visit was whether the occupant involved was being treated as suspect or victim. He thought they were actually both. Victims destined to become suspects in future years. It wasn't really their fault. They were already on the scrap heap of society, cast aside on to an overburdened care system. The house was bland, with no particular features to give it a focal point of interest. The windows were shut, with washed-out curtains giving it a tired appearance. Several panes of glass had been broken and small wooden boards covered the gaping holes. The front door too had suffered repeated attempts to kick it open or shut, he didn't know which, displaying cracks and splits in the paintwork. Everything about the place was depressing.

As they approached the front door, it swung open and they were greeted by a young black man. He exuded enthusiasm and seemed at odds with the building in which he worked.

'Hi, I'm Tyrone Weeks. I'm the new care manager here. Come in, come in. Jake's been waiting for you.'

He ushered them inside and Matt was surprised to see the dull cream walls had been covered with brightly coloured posters encouraging the residents to make the most of themselves, take charge of their lives and do the best that they could. He couldn't help a wry smile. He wondered how long it would be before Tyrone too capitulated to the constant pressure of failure.

'Nice to see you're making an effort,' he ventured.

'Well, trying to, but it's hard with the kids that we got. They've seen so much and been exposed to too much already to really care what happens to them. Anyway, Jake seems to have settled in well. Here he is.'

He pushed the door to the office open and Matt saw Jake's face turned towards him. He didn't look afraid of them, in fact he didn't appear to be fazed at all. He seemed to have filled out already, despite having been there for so little time, but Matt didn't know whether he was imagining the change. His face also seemed to be rosier, less pale than before, and his blond hair was clean and brushed neatly. He looked like a different boy to the one Matt had seen just a couple of days earlier, squatting in the filth of his home.

'Hi Jake,' Matt said. 'Do you remember me?'

'Yeah, you're the one who said he'd come and visit me, aren't you?'

'That's right. My name is Matt Arnold and this is Tom and Barry. Barry will be asking you some questions about what happened to your little brother.'

'Can't you?'

'I'm afraid I've got other things to do, but I did want to come and see you, like I promised I would. How are you?'

'I'm fine, but I miss my mum. When can I see her?'

'I don't know yet, but we might be able to arrange a visit soon.'

'Do you want to see my room? I've got a room of my own and there's lots of food to eat and they've even said we're all going to get presents this Christmas.'

'That sounds good. It sounds like you've settled in well. Can I see your room on my next visit?'

Jake looked disappointed. He turned away, staring resolutely at the wall. Matt didn't want him to clam up. He walked over and put a hand on the boy's shoulder.

'Come on, cheer up,' he chivvied. 'I said I'd come and see you and I have. Next time I'll make more time and I promise I'll come and see your room. We have to go now though, so get your gear and you can have a ride in our police car with us.'

Jake brightened up. Grabbing a small rucksack, he jumped to his feet. As he followed them out of the room Matt felt a small hand take hold of his own. He looked down and saw Jake was gripping his hand firmly and staring up at him.

He stopped and stared back down into the same olive-green intensity that he'd noticed before. Jake's expression was calm, his eyes unblinking, and Matt couldn't quite make out why it troubled him so much. He watched the young boy's mouth as it started to move, mouthing the words that followed evenly and seriously.

'Do you always keep your promises, Matt?'

# Six

Matt still felt uneasy with Jake's words as he re-entered his office. The words disturbed him. The boy disturbed him, and he wasn't sure why. He seemed so pitiful in his desire to be visited, to have someone listen to him, stick to their word. Matt decided he would keep his promise and return to see him. It was the least he could do.

He sat down at his desk and pulled out the image of Ryan in his Spider-Man outfit that now adorned the office notice-board, the photo of the toddler alive and with his whole life in front of him. Sliding it into a vacant frame he placed it on the desk next to the photo of his own father standing proudly in uniform, tall and upright. He sat silently gazing at the two images, both victims of violence, both cut down before their time. On this occasion, however, Ryan had no real family for whom to get justice. They were all guilty of participation in his early demise, either by actual violence or through neglect. He would be working to achieve justice for the child himself.

He looked at the pile of paperwork on his desk. There was something niggling him from what Barry had intimated on the car journey. Leafing through the various files he found a report on the family's previous history, gleaned by Barry from the information passed on from Lambeth Social Services. It was as small and meagre as he'd said. No previous history at all until the family had arrived in Lambeth. There had to be a lot more. A family like this should have been well known wherever they lived. He just had to find out which part of the country they had moved from and which social services department had dealt with them before their move.

He got up and walked back into the main office.

'Tom. It's imperative we find their previous history. Have they or the kids come across with any details of where they've moved from?'

'Not that I know of so far.'

'In that case I've just thought of a way of finding out. Can you get a few of you together and look at Lee and Denise's previous convictions. Phone up the courts they attended. They must have lived nearby. Try to get any previous addresses and names they used and then phone up the local police stations and social services and give them all the details you manage to find. There must be a huge amount of information out there about them that we haven't got as yet.'

'Will do. I'll let you know as soon as we find anything.'

'Thanks Tom.'

He returned to his office and picked up the phone. He needed to make sure all the kids were seen by a police doctor in order to log any injuries they might have received from either parent.

Mikey and Christina were still in the process of being spoken to, but talking to a spare officer outside the offices in which they were being interviewed, it appeared they were still loath to say much about their situation. It was clear they didn't want to get their father into any more trouble than he was in already.

Jake was being interviewed at a separate station. Matt phoned the office and Barry was available to speak, having just stopped for a break.

'How's it going?' he asked.

'Pretty much as we thought,' Barry responded. 'He doesn't like Lee. Says that he's hit him and kicked him on numerous occasions and that he's always picking on him, rather than Mikey and Christina. He also says Lee was violent towards Ryan too. He's seen him lock Ryan in his bedroom many times and has recently begun to give him a bit of a shove or throw him down across the bed before he leaves. And that's what he lets the others see. What goes on behind that closed bedroom door is anyone's guess. Lee doesn't like any of them crying, it makes him snap and get angry. It wouldn't take too much more for him to throw Ryan up against the wall, as opposed to the bed, I don't suppose?'

'Can he say if he saw Lee being violent towards Ryan the night he was killed?'

'He says he saw Lee shouting at him and dragging him up the stairs. He can say Lee went into Ryan's bedroom and shut the door. He also apparently went back in a short time later when Ryan wouldn't stop crying and he heard more banging and then it went quiet. He says his mum went up the stairs at about the same time and he heard Lee shouting at her. He was sitting on the stairs and he saw Lee grabbing Denise and threatening her. He claims Lee hit her but he gets very angry and upset when he talks about that sort of thing. He's very defensive of his mum. Won't say anything bad about her and gets upset if she's criticized in any way. There's obviously a very strong bond between them.'

'If she was to have done anything to Ryan, do you think he'd tell us?'

'I don't know. I don't think he would at the moment, but maybe if he got to know us more he might feel a bit more confident. I have a feeling he knows more than he's letting on but is too frightened or worried to say.'

'Do you think he'd tell us if he saw Lee actually throwing Ryan up against the wall?'

'Again I don't know. I get the impression he's frightened of what Lee might do to his mother if he says anything. Maybe in time though.'

'OK, thanks Barry. Make sure he sees a doctor before you finish.'

'Will do, Sarge.'

Matt put the phone down thoughtfully. He still felt Jake held the key to the puzzle. It was a matter of gaining his confidence and persuading him that his mum wouldn't be put in danger if he told the truth. He needed to see that Lee couldn't get to her or him and they would all be safe.

He checked his watch. Time was getting on. The days seemed to fly past so fast and everything took so long when they were collating evidence. Forensics took time, interviews took ages, even phone calls were time-consuming being moved from one department to another. Before he knew it Lee and

Denise Clarkson would be reporting back on bail for a decision and he had to be ready.

His thoughts were disturbed by a loud knock on the door. Before he had time to answer, Tom was striding in.

'Sorry to barge in, Matt, but we've just found something that will be of great interest to you, I'm sure.'

He pulled a chair up next to the desk and leant forward towards Matt.

'We've done what you asked and it appears that both parents have moved around a fair bit. Denise in particular seems to move on whenever she has a problem with relationships or convictions or trouble with social services. The most recent information we can find, prior to them moving up to London, is from an address in Hastings. It's obviously where she met Lee Clarkson. He was born in Hastings and he'd probably returned there for a while. She was still using the name Bryant initially. It appears that they set up home together there about four years ago, with Mikey, Christina and Jake. Ryan was born soon afterwards and Denise changed her name to Clarkson. While there they notched up a fairly long record with social services – just the usual stuff; domestic assaults, truanting from school and injuries to the children, consistent with minor assaults. The kids were on the At Risk register, but there wasn't enough to take them into care. Same as here though. The family were known to be uncooperative with any social workers attached to them and Lee to be aggressive.

'Anyway, it appears that in the year before they left Denise got pregnant again and had a baby girl by the name of Bryony. The baby was born fit and healthy but about eight weeks later was the subject of a cot death.'

Matt gasped.

'I thought you'd find that bit interesting.' Tom frowned. 'I did too. But apparently there were no suspicious circumstances. A post-mortem was inconclusive as to an exact cause of death and so it was put down to sudden infant death syndrome. Both parents denied any wrongdoing. Denise said she found the child dead in her cot when she woke up and called an ambulance straight away.'

'Rings a bell, doesn't it?' Matt commented.

Tom nodded.

'As soon as the baby girl was buried, they upped and left.

An inquest is apparently not required in cases of SIDS as the death was non-suspicious. Didn't give any notice to the council of their whereabouts or the fact that they'd moved. Just walked away as if nothing had happened. I don't suppose they've even bothered to return and visit the grave. The flat stood empty for a few months before the council realized and it's now been re-let. Hastings Borough Council have had no further involvement with the family and weren't able to forward their files on as they didn't know where they were living now.'

'Can you get hold of the file, or a copy of it?'

'I'm not sure whether the local council will allow us to see their files but I'll give it a go. I have already spoken with East Sussex police though and they're quite happy to make the cot death file available to us. It should arrive in the next few days. They'll also send us any other reports and information they have about the family. At least that will give us some idea of their history before they moved up here.'

'Thanks Tom. Keep digging and see if you can go back any further. I'm sure we'll find that both Lee and Denise have a pretty chequered past.'

Tom nodded and walked back out, leaving the scraps of paper with the details on his desk. Matt picked them up and looked at the name. Bryony Mary Clarkson, born 18th September 2006, died 11th November 2006, another tiny life cut short. There had to be a link. Two deaths in the same family within two years. It was too awful a coincidence. Maybe the baby's death was more suspicious than had been previously thought.

The file, when it arrived, made harrowing reading. As always, Matt found the photos the worst. It was the reason he insisted on his squad seeing the pictures of the victims for whom they were working to get justice. It was the reason his father's face stared out from the frame on his desk, next to Matt's latest murder victim.

The little girl had a thin, downy covering of light hair across her head and a small, perfectly round face. Long blonde lashes framed her closed eyes and her nose turned upwards slightly. She appeared as if sleeping; except that her cheeks were pale, instead of exhibiting the normal rosy, baby blush, and her lips were tinged blue. She was dressed in a pale pink babygro with a picture of a kitten across the chest.

In the following photos she was shown naked in the mortuary, her tiny limbs and fingers still, against the cold of the slab. Matt couldn't help wishing she had been laid on a warm blanket, shielding the softness of her skin from the stark, cold metal.

Looking at the images of the tiny baby sent a shiver down his spine. He remembered when his own children had been tiny, defenceless scraps of humanity, totally dependent on their parents, totally vulnerable.

He turned his attention to the next photos, pictures that showed where she had died. They were not dissimilar to Ryan's room. A white cot stood against one wall opposite a single bed. She obviously shared the room with one of the other children. He wondered why such a tiny baby was not positioned closer to their parents, rather than in a different room. Posters of Buzz Lightyear and other *Toy Story* characters surrounded the single bed, giving the backdrop the appearance of a young boy's room. Toys and clothing littered the bare floorboards, making the room appear shambolic and messy. Close-ups of the cot revealed that the frame was scuffed and dirty and the bedding was also smeared with stains and traces of excrement.

He read through the pile of statements that accompanied the photos.

Lee Clarkson's was the first. He described being away from home when the discovery was made. He stated that he first realized what had happened when he returned from the pub and an ambulance and police car were outside their house. He admitted becoming abusive with police who had refused to allow him through the front door. He denied ever mistreating the baby and said that he left the day-to-day care of the child almost totally down to Denise, but interestingly stated he didn't believe she was a very good mother. He refused to expand any further on this comment.

Matt remembered the words he had shouted as he was being taken down to his cell so recently. *Ask her what happened to our baby daughter.* Maybe for some reason he held her responsible for the baby's death. He made a mental note to question Lee about the comment when he returned on bail.

Next he read Denise's statement. She had been interviewed
as a relevant witness, as had Lee, because at that stage a post-
mortem had not taken place and the cause of death had not
been suspected or found to be suspicious.

He scanned the document until he came to Denise's description of Bryony's illness. The little girl had been taken to the
doctor with a temperature, runny nose and cough, and a virus
had been diagnosed. Finally he reached her account of the
day in question:

*On Monday 11th September 2006 I woke in the morning
and took Mikey and Christina to school. Ryan and Bryony
were sleeping so they stayed at home with Lee while I
was gone and Bryony was still sleeping when I returned.*

*Jake was also not feeling well and had a bad cold so
he was allowed to be off school and he was also at home.
During the morning I didn't really do much. Jake was
watching telly with Ryan and Lee stayed in bed. Bryony
was coughing quite a bit and not very happy and I had
to hold her to try to stop her crying. At about midday,
Lee got up. He was in a bad temper and said he was
going off to the pub because all the crying was disturbing
him.*

*I fed Bryony at about 1.25 p.m. and put her down in
her cot for her afternoon nap, like she normally has. I
laid her on her back like I've been told and covered her
with her duvet. She was snuffling and coughing a bit but
didn't seem to have a temperature. She started to cry
but I left her and after about twenty minutes she fell
asleep.*

*I was also really tired because I hadn't slept much
and Lee doesn't help me with the kids so I thought I'd
try and have a sleep. Jake came upstairs with me to my
bedroom and lay down next to me. He fell asleep first
and then I did. I woke up about an hour and a quarter
later at nearly three o'clock. I had to collect Mikey and
Christina at 3.25 p.m. from school. When I went in to
see to Bryony, she was still lying on her back and looked
like she was still sleeping. I didn't really want to wake
her but as Lee wasn't back from the pub I thought I'd
have to take her to the school with me. I called out her*

*name but she didn't stir so I lifted her up, putting my hands under her armpits. She was all floppy and she couldn't hold her head up. I panicked a bit and shook her to try and wake her but she still wouldn't open her eyes and her lips were all blue. I didn't shake her hard. I was calling her name time after time but she wasn't responding.*

*I think I must have screamed because Ryan started crying and Jake came running in. I shouted at him to get my mobile and I phoned 999 for an ambulance. While they were on their way, the operator told me what to do to try to see if she was breathing and to do mouth to mouth resuscitation on her. I did what they told me but when I put my face right next to Bryony's mouth I couldn't feel any breath and I couldn't feel a pulse either. Although she wasn't cold, she felt strange. She was very white. I knew she was dead then. I did try to do what the operator was telling me but my hands were shaking too much and I was in a panic.*

*The ambulance arrived quite quickly and the paramedics tried to work on her but they couldn't get her breathing. They carried her straight into an ambulance and Jake and I went with her to Hastings General Hospital. Ryan stayed with a neighbour until Lee came back, because he was too small to come with us. The doctors and nurses tried really hard to revive her. I was watching them, but they couldn't get her breathing again.*

*After a while a doctor came and spoke to Jake and me. He said that Bryony had been dead on arrival and they hadn't been able to save her. I started to cry then. Bryony meant the world to me. I loved her to bits and I can't believe my beautiful little girl has gone.*

Matt put the statement down. The sequence of events seemed to flow but his gut instinct was that something was not right.

He turned to the pathologist's report.

The baby's description appeared unremarkable. There were no overt injuries and no internal injuries logged. Bryony was slightly underweight for her age but nothing to give any real cause for concern. The post-mortem had revealed evidence of a mild respiratory infection, consistent with a cold or virus, as her mother had intimated, and a small amount of blood and mucus was found in the lungs and nasal passage. The baby was also slightly dehydrated; a condition that may have been exacerbated by the respiratory infection and may have contributed towards her death, but not one that would give rise to a suspicion of neglect or abuse.

Leafing through the technical data, most of which made no sense to him, he turned to the conclusion.

Sudden Infant Death Syndrome was listed as the cause of death, there being no other injury or illness found that could be held responsible for it.

He frowned. On the face of it, it seemed like a straightforward cot death, but two deaths in the same family was a bit too much of a coincidence, especially with the second definitely confirmed as suspicious. He wondered why Denise hadn't mentioned it in her interview, or Lee, except for the shouted comment. There was something not right with the family. Hints were dropped, allegations made and information withheld. Even the children were reluctant to speak about what had gone on. Not the normal actions of an innocent family. Each implied the others' guilt, each covered their own back and each knew more than they were willing to say.

He stood up and stretched. Another day was coming to an end and time was ticking by. He owed it to little Ryan to bring his murderer to justice. It was his job to stand up for the victims who couldn't stand up for themselves. On this occasion though, he was fast coming to realize that the truth would be extremely hard to find among the mass of lies, omissions and deceit.

# Seven

Jake was sitting opposite Tyrone at the desk in the main reception office. The chair was too upright and he wriggled about on its hard, plastic surface trying to make himself comfortable. His belly was full after a large breakfast and he was wearing a new hooded sweatshirt given to him the evening before, but he was unhappy. He was waiting in the office to be collected by Barry the police officer. He didn't really like him. He had a beard and a moustache and didn't smile very much. He tried to be friendly but Jake didn't think he really cared. He was just like all the others who talked the talk. Nothing ever happened though. He was still stuck with Lee and Mikey and Christina. All he wanted was to be with his mum. She was the only one who loved him.

Mikey had been horrible to him all week, threatening to beat him up if he said anything bad about his dad. He was in the room next door and kept coming in without being invited. Jake didn't like him either. Mikey was spiteful, called him names, grabbed him, pinched him, hit him. When they'd been at home he'd been left alone. Mikey knew that Denise would take his side and that he and Christina would be given less food or treats if he gave him hassle. Now though everything was different. He didn't have his mum to protect him and the people at the care home thought that Mikey was being friendly when he kept going into his room. He was all alone.

He really wanted to tell the police it was Lee, but he was frightened. Frightened that if Lee was put in prison Mikey would guess that he'd bubbled him up and would hurt him. Mikey was bigger than him.

He thought back an hour. After Tyrone had told them that he was to be interviewed again, Mikey had pushed Jake up against the wall in his room.

'If you grass on my dad, you're dead,' he'd whispered into his ear, pulling a small flick knife from his pocket and pressing the catch. The blade had sprung out and Mikey had placed its cold, metallic point against the warm skin of his neck.

'Do you understand me?' his stepbrother had asked, but he didn't want to speak to him.

'I said do you understand me?' he'd repeated, pressing the blade against his neck so that it hurt.

He'd nodded slightly. 'OK, Mikey. I won't say nothing. Where did you get that from?'

Mikey sneered down at him. 'Never you mind. Just remember. If I find out you've been saying anything against my dad, you're goin' to get it. OK?'

He'd nodded again.

Now, as he waited for Barry to arrive, he knew that he couldn't say what he wanted to say. He recognized that, should Lee be put inside for Ryan's murder, Mikey would take over where Lee had started and the bullying would get worse. He knew that he and his mum would be stuck with Mikey and Christina for good and would never be left in peace.

He loved his mum and wanted to see her again.

Maybe he could ask Barry if he could see her again, but he didn't trust Barry. He wanted to speak to Matt Arnold. He was the boss. He could make things happen and sort things out.

There was a knock on the door and Barry poked his head round.

'All right, Jake? Shall we go?'

He bristled. It wasn't a question, it was an instruction, and one that he didn't want to follow.

He nodded. Slowly he dragged his body up from the uncomfortable chair, wishing now that he could remain seated. He could see Tyrone standing too, smiling back at the police officer, but he didn't want to smile. He lifted the hood of his sweatshirt up over his head, pulling it forward so that his face could barely be seen, and sighed.

He would get this over and done with but he wouldn't say what they wanted to hear. He wouldn't say what he wanted to say.

Barry Tate was disappointed.

He'd thought he was getting somewhere with Jake but the boy seemed to have clammed up this morning. He'd been different from the moment he'd walked out behind him from the care home office, quieter and surlier. Mikey had been sitting on the steps outside smiling at them as they left the building. He seemed to be a friendly sort of lad and Barry thought it lucky that social services had been able to place the three children together.

The car journey had elapsed into silence. He'd tried to make small talk and explain what was happening but Jake didn't respond to any of his prompting. He sat silently, brooding, and nothing Barry said could penetrate his thoughts.

Nothing changed in the interview either. Jake slumped

morosely on a sofa, refusing to expand any further on his previous statements. He'd seen Lee drag Ryan up the stairs and put him in their room, he'd seen him re-enter the room a short time later and Ryan had gone quiet. He'd seen Lee hitting his mother. He did not see Lee hit Ryan, swing him around or throw him against the wall that night. He hadn't seen exactly how Ryan was killed, nor did he want to say anything further.

Barry tried to coax some more information out of him but Jake was adamant he had nothing more to say. It was disappointing. He'd been hoping to be able to go back to DS Arnold with something a bit more useful.

He drove back in silence.

Towards the end of the journey they stopped at traffic lights adjacent to the local park. A boating lake lay silent, its grey waters reflecting the murky sky above. A small array of wooden boats bobbed serenely to one side, tied up for the winter out of harm's way, their brightly painted numbers the only colours to pierce the gloom. Tall trees surrounded the edge of the lake, stretching outwards across the ripples. A mass of leaves floated beneath their naked boughs, frozen solid in brown ice.

From between two of the largest trees a young boy appeared, wrapped warmly in a bright blue jacket and white woollen hat. He ran towards the lake and stopped at its edge, bending down to pick up an assortment of sticks. An older man followed and the two stood side by side as the boy leant backwards and threw a stick out across the lake. A collection of ripples shot out from the impact, slowing gradually as they made their way towards the opposite bank. The older man clapped his hands together as the boy threw another and Barry could see their heads thrown back in laughter. He looked in his mirror and saw Jake staring out from behind him at the same scene.

'Will Matt come and visit me again?' he suddenly asked.

Barry was taken aback. It was the most animated he had seen Jake all day.

'I don't know, but if he said he would, I'm sure he will at some point. Why?'

'Because I want to show him this park.'

# Eight

The train was not quite stationary at the platform of Hastings Railway Station when Matt stood shakily, trying to retrieve his briefcase from the luggage rack. He, Tom and Alison were visiting the area and the police station in order to get a better idea of the family background and to speak with the officer in charge of the cot death investigation.

As he stepped down on to the platform he could smell the freshness of the sea air. A cold wind was blowing in from the Channel, freezing unprotected flesh and bringing with it a dampness that pierced his clothing, seeping straight through every thin layer.

He pulled his collar further up around his neck and felt a violent shiver run down his spine. He checked his watch. They still had two hours before their scheduled meeting with DI George Martin, time to see the area where the family had lived.

Jumping into a waiting minicab, Tom called out the address and the driver was soon steering through the back streets of Hastings, giving them a guided tour on their way. The town was divided into the Old Town and New Town, and there was a marked difference between the two. Lee and Denise's address was in the modern part, set further back from the sea and recognizable by its concrete shopping malls and blocks of council flats in rundown estates. The driver stopped by the entrance to an estate and pointed to a block, set a short distance away.

The building used to be white, but was now a dowdy cream with graffiti smeared around the lower regions. As they walked towards it, Matt noticed a small group of street drinkers huddled in a bin area, out of reach of the biting wind. Cans grasped firmly in gloved hands, they seemed determined to continue their alcohol-fuelled exploits however wintry the conditions.

The flat itself was on the third floor, up a stairwell littered with discarded needles and foil. They walked along a balcony overlooking the town, which appeared to nestle snugly between hills and spilled down to the stony beach. The wind whistled through the metal grilles on the balcony, sending concentrated blasts through each gap that they passed. The flat itself, with its new occupants, was of no particular interest to them, but they were hoping for a brief conversation with any neighbours who might remember the previous tenants.

Matt knocked at one of the neighbours' doors. It looked as if someone was in but there was no immediate answer. He knocked loudly several more times and eventually an elderly woman peered though the window at them. He held up his warrant card and after a few minutes, she shuffled round and opened the door, ushering them in to the warmth of her home. He explained briefly why they were there and watched as a frown flickered across her brows.

'Best you sit down while I make you all a cup of tea,' she said firmly. 'And I'll tell you all about them.'

Alison went to help the old lady while he and Tom were shown through to a small lounge without a chance to decline the offer and perched themselves on a small two-seater settee, their bulky frames tilting uncomfortably towards each other. As soon as they were seated, a long-haired tabby cat jumped gracefully down from its perch on the back of an opposite armchair and wound itself around their legs, pressing its body hard against the firmness of their shins and purring gently. Matt reached down and stroked its well-groomed softness.

'I see Tabitha has introduced herself,' the old woman said fondly, as she shuffled back into the room. Alison followed directly behind bearing a tray, set with four cups and saucers, a large teapot and a small plate of digestives. 'She's very friendly and keeps me company now I'm on my own.'

'How long have you had her?' he asked, not wanting to appear rude.

'I've only had her for about eight months. I got her from the cat sanctuary when I realized that the lot you mentioned weren't coming back.'

Matt's interest was fired immediately. Quickly he introduced Tom and himself properly and learned the lady's name was Edna Barnett.

'Edna, can you tell me what you know about the previous tenants, Lee and Denise Clarkson and the family? Why did you wait until they'd gone before you got Tabitha?'

The old lady's face clouded and he thought for one minute that she was going to cry. Alison moved forward and touched her arm, and she smiled back gratefully.

'Because they killed my last cat, Bessy,' she said at last, composing herself. 'I don't know which one exactly did it but one of them did. She was such a friendly cat and when I let her out she would go to some of the flats along the balcony. All the residents knew her and would give her scraps and a lot of fuss and attention. We're not really supposed to have pets but the council turn a blind eye and like I said, she's company. She always seemed a bit wary of them next door though and would skirt around their flat to get to some of the others. I noticed it but I didn't really know why.

'Anyway, one evening she didn't come back. I looked everywhere for her but I couldn't find her, then one of my neighbours came around and said they'd found her body and she was dead. She'd been tied in a black bin bag and thrown off the balcony. Some of the other residents said they'd seen the kids from next door throw her. And they'd been spotted with a black bin bag, swinging it around and hitting it against walls. It was awful. When they'd finished beating her, they tried to set fire to her. That was how she was found. Beaten and half burnt. It nearly broke my heart and I swore I'd never get another cat while they were still there. I thanked God when I found they'd gone.'

'And you say you don't know which of the kids it was?'

'No, I don't. I'm sorry. The three older ones were seen together. I think they were called Mikey, Christina and Jake. They were all as bad as each other. Out of control they were. And the noise!'

'What sort of noise?'

'All sorts. The man would be constantly shouting and swearing. Using terrible language. The woman would shout too, but mostly she would scream. I've seen her with bruises all over her face, black and blue sometimes. I didn't actually see him being violent towards her but you could hear it. I never knew quite what to do, whether to call the police or not. I didn't want to interfere.'

'What about the children? Did you ever see or hear them screaming?'

'Yes, quite a lot. A couple of times I did call the police, but it was after one of those times my cat was killed. I did call the police again after that when the screams were particularly bad but I didn't leave my name. I was frightened what else they might do if they found out it was me that had called.'

'Did you ever get invited into the flat?'

'Only once. They usually kept themselves to themselves. He was definitely the boss. Didn't like her going out much or socializing with other people. It was at the beginning when I did go inside, soon after they'd moved in, and even then it was really dirty, I don't mind telling you. I don't think she ever cleaned the place. Stuff and mess everywhere. He came home and saw me there and had a real go at her for inviting me in, right in front of me as well. Raised his arm to her but changed his mind at the last minute, probably because I was there. He's a nasty piece of work and I wouldn't put anything past him. After that she never really spoke much. Seemed a bit embarrassed. I felt sorry for her actually. She seemed quite a nice lady but couldn't really cope.

'I did see her a bit when she had the babies. A little boy first, I think they called him Ryan. And then, very soon afterwards, a beautiful baby girl.'

She looked up at them and shook her head.

'It was a real tragedy when that little girl died.'

'Do you know what happened?'

'Only what I've been told really, although I did see a bit of what happened. I remember the baby crying quite a lot during the night and seeing Denise taking the older two kids to school in the morning. They walked past my window, you see. When the mother came back she looked exhausted. She had to do everything for them kids. I don't think he did a thing. Just before lunchtime I heard him shouting again then the door slammed and I saw him going off. The baby was still crying but after a while it all went quiet. I couldn't even hear the TV and that was usually on. I guessed they were all sleeping and I remember feeling glad because of how she'd looked when I saw her earlier.

'The next thing I knew was when I heard the ambulance turning up and then all hell broke loose. The baby was being worked on and the mother was crying. I came out on to the balcony to see if I could help and she asked if I could look after Ryan until Lee came back. It was the least I could do. One of the older kids was there, I think it was Jake, and he seemed quite calm for such a little boy and was helping his mum with everything. I don't know what she would have done without him.'

'So you heard nothing until the ambulance turned up?' Matt queried.

Edna paused, thinking for a moment.

'No, it was all quiet, silent even. The first I knew anything was wrong, was when the paramedics were running along our balcony. I heard afterwards it was a cot death. So tragic though. She seemed such a fragile little scrap. I heard her coughing sometimes at night. Mind you, the condition of the flat when I saw it probably didn't help. Not exactly a healthy environment for a young baby.'

'How long did you look after Ryan for?'

'Oh, not very long at all. He was such a skinny little thing. I gave him a few biscuits as he looked as if he hadn't eaten for a week. He would have had them all if his father hadn't returned. Got right nasty with the police who had arrived and ended up dragging Ryan away from here. Poor boy was crying. I think he wanted to stay and have some more biscuits but that thug wouldn't let him. Didn't even say thanks, not that I particularly cared. I wanted to help anyway, but you'd think he would be glad his little boy was being cared for and say something.'

'Did you notice any injuries on Ryan while you had him?'

'No, I didn't really have time. Do you know how the little lad's doing?'

Matt was dreading the question but knew it would eventually be raised.

'I can't say this any easy way, but he died the other day. I can't really go into details but suffice to say, there are suspicious circumstances and what you've told us has been very useful.'

Edna Barnett pulled a cotton handkerchief from the sleeve of her cardigan and dabbed at the tears that had immediately sprung to her eyes.

'How awful,' she said, stifling a sob into her hankie. 'The

poor little scrap. If you ask me though, you don't have to look too far from home for your suspect. I'd lay a bet, judging by the way I saw him treat his son, that that thug Lee Clarkson is responsible for the little lad's death.'

An hour later and the same minicab driver had been summoned to return. A cheerful, pot-bellied man with a penchant for chain-smoking and beer drove them back towards the Old Town. He had lived in Hastings all his life and proudly extolled its virtues, while trying to ignore the obvious deterioration in some parts. It was certainly a town with character. Its history stood all around it in the gaping ramparts and jagged stone walls of the castle built by William the Conqueror. The remnants looked resolutely seawards and the fishing town that had sprung up as a result nestled at its feet. An old pier jutted precariously out into the white-tipped waves. All around, gulls squawked and shrieked into the wind.

As they passed an old church Matt felt a sudden compulsion to take a few minutes in its graveyard. After calling to the driver to stop and telling the others to wait, he scrambled out and wandered round to the rear of the imposing square tower of the Norman church. The small graveyard lay silent, ringed by an old, layered stone wall. Animals had made nests among the many gaps and hollows and rabbit burrows were scattered at its footings. Some of the tombstones were ancient, their writing and dates made illegible by age and weather. Others, although now in disrepair, were large and grandiose, with structures and crypts built to exaggerate the worth of the person entombed inside.

He wandered towards the rear, and soon found himself staring down at a row of more recent graves. Several still had mounds of raised earth above them, with flowers spread out across the bare soil. A child's grave lay nearby, with a collection of soft toys, teddy bears and framed photos of a small boy, barely five years of age. The grave was well tended, and care had been taken over its layout and appearance. He found the sight of it both touching and shocking, the bright colours of its modern decoration seemingly at odds with the age and gravity of its surroundings. He turned away, realizing that the time of his appointment at the police station was fast approaching. As he picked his way back towards the main footpath, he noticed a small wooden cross, standing askew in a lumpy, grassed area. An empty vase lay next to it on the grass and he realized with a shock that he recognized the name etched into the small plaque at the base of the cross. There were no words of love introducing the deceased, no verses, no Bible passages, nothing. Just the name of a tiny baby girl and the dates between which she had existed in a filthy flat, with feckless parents, who finished mourning her loss in a matter of weeks before moving on.

DI George Martin, although trying to appear welcoming, was obviously a little put out that Matt and his entourage were casting aspersions on his previous cot death investigation. He was obviously proud of the way he worked; the deep creases running along his brow and forehead showed the hours of concentration and worry resulting from his caseload.

The file lay on the table before them, the photo of baby Bryony on display, the piles of statements stacked to one side.

'Our actions had to be guided by the pathology report,' George was saying. 'The post-mortem was inconclusive. There was no evidence of foul play or any previous injuries. The only slightly disturbing element, as far as I can recall, was that blood was found in the lungs.'

He ran his fingers through his fast-diminishing hair, pushing the longer strands back over his ears, and leafed through the file to the pathology report.

'Ah, here it is. Examination of lung tissue found evidence of bleeding into approximately four per cent of the total lung surface. We queried that with the pathologist but he said that bleeding into the lungs was not in itself a cause for concern, unless there was other evidence to back up any suspicions.'

Matt knew he had to be careful, so as not to appear to discredit his colleague.

'I've shown the report to our own expert,' he said quietly. 'And he explained that they now use a digital method of measuring the amount of blood in the lungs. This means that more deaths previously labelled as SIDS deaths have been reclassified as "unascertained". Apparently in seventy-three per cent of infants deemed to have suffered accidental smothering, and in forty-five per cent suspected of suffering intentional smothering, this technique has found bleeding in as little as five per cent of the total lung surface. Is it possible that there could have been slightly more blood present than your pathologist measured, which may have led to a classification other than SIDS?'

'Are you saying you believe the baby was smothered?'

'I'm just asking if it could be a possibility.'

George Martin was clearly rattled now. 'Well, you need to read the rest of the report properly then.'

He scanned through the report, précising the facts. 'There was also evidence of slight dehydration, which evidently in itself would not be fatal but might sometimes cause bleeding into the lungs. Apparently recent research has shown, however, that if a minor respiratory infection or virus is also found to be present, this may sometimes exaggerate a pre-existing state of dehydration. In this case a respiratory infection was found and the pathologist believed that the dehydration, exacerbated by it, may have contributed directly towards the baby's death.

'In addition,' Martin continued, clearly unwilling to accept any criticism and referring to the report lying on the table in front of him, 'the mattress the baby was sleeping on was an old one, used for some of the previous children, and tests carried out on it showed that there was a high number of fungal and toxic gases present within it. It was believed that these substances were probably breathed in by the baby and, added to the slight dehydration and respiratory infection, were believed to have contributed to the cause of death. So, you see, there was a combination of issues and not one specific factor that led to the decision to classify the death as SIDS.'

DI Martin shut the file decisively. Matt knew that any further argument about the post-mortem report would fall on deaf ears. As with so many investigations, different experts gave different opinions. He just wished that instead of the case being classified as a straightforward SIDS death, it could have been classified 'unascertained' and at least opened up to an inquest. He tried a different tack.

'What about the condition of the premises? Was any consideration given to a charge of neglect?'

'Yes, we did consider it. But with no evidence of any previous injuries and with the mother confirmed as having recently taken the baby to the doctor's, the CPS said there wasn't a case to be answered.'

'And the previous history of domestic violence and abuse in the household?'

'That was also looked at. Certainly the mother, Denise Clarkson, appeared to have received injuries from her partner, as had some of the other children possibly too, but none that Lee was ever prosecuted for. Added to that, he was clearly shown to have left the house at the time of the baby's death. We have statements from Denise Clarkson and Jake Bryant and also from a neighbour that confirm that.'

'We went and spoke to the next-door neighbour, Edna Barnett, before we got here. She was very interesting. She told us about the family and the violence and her suspicions that her cat had been deliberately killed by some of the kids.'

George Martin was frowning now.

'Is there anything else you've done to try to undermine my investigation?' he snapped angrily.

Matt plunged on. 'She said that on the day Bryony died, everything was quiet until she heard the paramedics on the balcony. But in Denise's statement, she said she was screaming and crying as soon as she found the baby dead, before the ambulance arrived. Don't you think that's a bit strange?'

The DI folded his arms defensively, his frown deepening. 'Edna Barnett is nearly eighty years old and clearly going a bit deaf. What she said at the time didn't make any real sense and was refuted by both Denise Clarkson and her son Jake, both of whom were very distressed on the arrival of the ambulance. Much as I too didn't like the family, there was nothing more to substantiate any suspicions. The pathologist said it was a cot death, the witnesses' statements point to it being a cot death, and I for one also believe it was a tragic but unavoidable cot death.'

He rose to his feet and held out a hand towards Matt. 'Now, if there's nothing further I can assist with, I'm a busy man and I have plenty more things to do.'

Matt recognized their dismissal and felt his frustration growing. Every suspicion he'd tried to throw at the DI seemed to have an answer, every action an explanation, every discrepancy a reason. It seemed that nothing could be changed. And yet everything about the little girl's death screamed 'suspicious' to him.

As he turned and walked from the office, the condescending

words and expression of his Sussex colleague still fresh in his mind, his memory returned to the words of Edna Barnett and the vision of a small, wonky cross that would forever symbolize the last journey of a tiny baby girl and her forgotten existence.

# Nine

M att waved as Ben skipped happily into school. The air was full of noise and laughter, the children animated in their last few days before the Christmas break. His own home was a hive of activity with presents hidden away from prying eyes, food stockpiled in any available space and preparations for the coming festivities. Most of the children's gifts had already been bought, thanks to Jo's organizational skills and a task he was always glad to devolve to her.

'Don't be late tonight,' Ben shouted before disappearing into the gloom of the school building.

'I won't. I promise,' Matt shouted back into the empty space.

He felt his mouth turn up into a wide grin at the thought of that evening's nativity play. Ben was the most highly rehearsed sheep in the history of Christmas productions, and the thought of his treasured bundle of energy skipping on to centre stage was almost enough to make him forget the trials of his day ahead.

It was 18th December, the day that Denise and Lee Clarkson would be returning on bail. Prior to that he had a meeting with the Crown Prosecution Service representatives to decide which charges the evidence supported.

He turned from the playground and made his way along the path to the car park. The day was overcast and cold, a light mist suffusing the air with droplets of water that settled on clothing, hats and hair, leaving them wet and icy. According to the weather forecast there was even the chance of a white Christmas, and Matt relished the chance to take the kids out into a white, gleaming wilderness. The city looked so clean and bright when covered with a fresh blanket of snow.

A car horn returned him abruptly to the present and he stepped to the side sharply to avoid a slow-moving people carrier. By the time he'd climbed into his own car and made his way to Lambeth HQ his mind was firmly set on the day ahead.

DI Blandford was waiting for him in his own office, a fact made clear by the small line of smoke issuing from the open window as he glanced heavenward. Hurriedly he collected together his files and made his way to his boss's den. The majority of the evidence had already been taken to the CPS office for their perusal and his boss had been furnished with copies of each statement and interview.

'Morning, Roger,' he said, pulling up a chair next to the desk. 'Have you had a chance to look through the file?'

'Yes. I've gone through the lot and spoken to the CPS already. They're still coming later to give a final decision but I've got a fair idea of what they're likely to say.'

'And that is?' Matt sat back anxiously. He so much wanted a charge of murder levelled at Lee, who he felt sure had been the one guilty of smashing his son's head against the wall.

Roger Blandford looked up.

'I'm sorry, Matt, but they don't think there's enough to charge him with murder. I know he's admitted to going upstairs to Ryan's room twice and on the second time it's alleged Ryan went quiet. That's good circumstantial evidence. But the fact is neither Denise, who also appeared to be upstairs at about the right time, nor Jake who witnesses his mother getting a beating just afterwards, can say they saw what happened in that room.'

'But it must be him. He's in the right place at the right time, and the kid's not heard from again after his visit.'

'I agree, and so do the CPS, but the evidence just doesn't support the theory. Lee denies hitting Ryan and points the finger at Denise, saying she must have done it while he was in the toilet. And we have nothing to say she didn't.'

'Except Jake, who was sitting at the bottom of the stairs while it was all going on.'

'I know, but he's an eight-year-old boy and Denise's son. He's hardly independent. The defence is just going to allege that he would say anything to defend his mother, especially in the light of Lee's behaviour towards him. And they'd probably be right.'

'But why would a mother do something like that to her own son? It doesn't make sense to me.'

'Who knows why anyone would do that to a little child, but people do. Time and time again. Maybe she reacted out of fear of what Lee might do, maybe she'd had enough of the screaming herself and lashed out, maybe she thought he might start on Jake if Ryan didn't stop crying. I don't know. All I know is that there's not enough for a murder charge.'

'So he gets away with nothing?'

Roger Blandford opened a notebook.

'No, he won't get away with nothing, nor will she. There's a new law that's been passed fairly recently which covers just this scenario. I didn't even know about it myself until the CPS pointed it out. I think it was brought in for exactly this reason. Where neither parent can be proved to have actually done the killing they can be charged with S5, Domestic Violence, Crime and Victims Act 2004. I don't know of any other case yet where it's been used but the CPS is happy to run with it for our job.'

Matt read the notes out loud slowly.

'Causing or allowing the death of a child or vulnerable adult. A person is guilty of an offence if a child or vulnerable adult dies as a result of the unlawful act of a person, who was a member of the same household and had frequent contact with him. If there was a significant risk of serious physical harm being caused to the victim by the unlawful act of such a person, they commit an offence if either they are the person that committed the act, or they are a person that ought to have been aware of the risk or they foresaw it happening and failed to take such steps as could reasonably have been expected to take to protect the victim from the risk.'

Roger Blandford jumped in. 'I know it's a bit of a mouthful but basically, both Lee and Denise are part of the household. We believe Lee committed the act that killed Ryan and so is guilty. We also believe Denise was aware of what was happening and did nothing to protect Ryan, so she is also guilty. It's not down to the prosecution to prove which way round it was, so if, as Lee maintains, Denise must have killed

Ryan while he was in the toilet, then it still applies. They can both be charged with causing or allowing the death of a child and fight it out in court.'

He smiled. 'And of course there's also a range of lesser charges of assault and neglect, et cetera, that the CPS are also advocating. Some of these aren't quite ready as yet, but as soon as the pair of them are charged with the substantive offences, they can be brought back to the police station to be dealt with for the others.'

Matt smiled back, relieved. 'Great. At least we've got something more substantial. What's the sentence likely to be?'

'I don't really know, as there have been no others to compare it against, but the statute states that . . .' He ran his finger down to the bottom of the page. 'Ah, here it is. A person guilty of an offence under this section is liable on conviction on indictment to imprisonment for a term not exceeding fourteen years or to a fine, or to both.'

'A fine. For something like this?' Matt frowned. 'Let's just hope they both get banged up for a good long time. It's nothing more than they deserve.'

His boss nodded. 'Of course, if we can come up with anything further that points to one or the other's guilt, they'll certainly be willing to look at it again. A murder charge isn't out of the question.'

'What about the information about the previous cot death? Is there anything we can do with that?'

'It's a non-starter I'm afraid. The case is closed and there's insufficient evidence to get it reopened. In any case it would mean digging up the grave to carry out a further post-mortem and that's just not going to happen. An exhumation is only ever carried out in exceptional circumstances, where definite new evidence has come to light. It would be impossible to check whether there was a slightly larger amount of blood in the lungs sufficient for us to prove Bryony might have been suffocated, no matter what we think. It's too long ago.'

Matt frowned philosophically. He had guessed when George Martin had closed the file so emphatically that nothing further would come of his suspicions. In addition, he had since been made aware that Roger had received a phone call from the disgruntled detective inspector, complaining about his visit

and continued questions. It was obvious he would do everything in his power not to have his decision reversed.

'Best I see what I can do then.' Matt was on his feet. 'I
was going to do one last interview with Lee and Denise but
I don't suppose they'll come up with anything different to
what they've already said. I still think Jake holds the key. I'm
sure he knows more than he's letting on.'

It was 11.30 a.m. when Denise Clarkson was chauffeured
through into the custody office, accompanied by her appropriate adult and solicitor as required. She'd been told not to
say anything more. There was no more to say, anyway. All
she wanted now was to be able to leave and collect Jake from
the home and disappear. She needed to start afresh. Lee would
take the rap for Ryan as he deserved to and she would be
free. After all, he was the bastard. He was the one who made
their lives hell. Now maybe his life too would become hell.

The interview room was set up and she was ushered inside
by the same two police officers as before. She was smiling
now though. It wouldn't be long. She did what she was told,
saying 'No comment' to each question, and then they were
back out. No untoward incidents. Codes of conduct complied
with.

'Take a seat in this cell until we've spoken to Lee. We'll
return soon.'

Then she'd be leaving, ready to start over. She ran her hands
through her hair, smoothing the underlying tangles, and
straightened her new clothes. Lying down, she relaxed back
on to the blue mattress and closed her eyes. It wouldn't be
long.

It was 2.05 p.m. and Lee Clarkson was ready this time. He
was clean, washed and deodorized and prepared for anything
the cops might throw at him. For two weeks he'd been deciding
on his course of action. He needed to place the blame squarely
at Denise's feet. There was no way he was going to take the
punishment for his son's death. He'd done enough time inside
and he was enjoying himself in the outside world at the
moment. Until this. It was all her fucking fault anyway. If
she'd only controlled the boy better this would never have
happened.

He allowed himself to be directed through the waiting rabble
in the foyer of Brixton police station and found himself back in
the custody area. It was heaving with a mass of people of all
shapes and colours and as he threaded his way past them to
the reception desk, he scanned the names on the white board,
wondering idly whether he recognized any of them. Most of
his prison mates had been in and out of the nick pretty regularly,
as had he.

When it came to the interview he said what he wanted to.
It wasn't him. They had no proof. Denise was the one they
should be looking at. She could have done it when he was in
the toilet. She was a lying, scheming bitch who wanted him
out of her life.

He didn't answer any of the questions they put to him. He
said only what he wanted to and nothing else. DC Berwick
and DS fucking Arnold could go to hell if they tried to pin
Ryan's death on him.

Three and a half hours later the two police officers were on
their way to hell and Lee Clarkson was listening to the charge
read over to him. Causing or allowing the death of a child or
vulnerable adult, contrary to S5 Domestic Violence, Crime
and Victims Act 2004. He didn't understand. Causing the death
of a child sounded like a clever way of saying he'd killed
Ryan. So he was being done for his son's death after all. They
were just using different words. The duty solicitor tried to
explain that it was to cover the times when it couldn't be
proved who exactly had done the killing and who had allowed
it to happen, but in his mind he was still getting the blame
while that bitch got away with it. At least, the solicitor had
said, the offence did not bring with it a mandatory life sentence,
as with a conviction for murder, but the maximum term of
imprisonment was still up to fourteen years. Fourteen fucking
years.

Whichever way he looked at it, he'd be taking the rap. He
ran his hands though his hair, feeling his anger fast reaching
boiling point. The evil, lying fucking bitch. She'd dropped
him in it and she would pay.

'There may be other charges relating to previous injuries
found on the children,' he heard a voice saying.

'Haven't you lot got enough?' he screamed in anger. He

felt hands taking hold of him. 'Don't fucking touch me.' He wheeled round suddenly and felt himself being propelled towards his cell.

As he heard the heavy, grey cell door slam shut behind him, he turned and saw the face of DS Arnold staring through the Perspex window at him. He was smiling, his face drawn up into a smug, self-satisfied grin. Lee Clarkson immediately wanted to get rid of it. He launched himself at the door, hammering at the Perspex and spitting at the face that was even now backing away.

'You won't get away with this, you bastard. She's a lying bitch. You can't fucking believe her. I'll make you pay when I get a chance.'

Denise Clarkson was sleeping soundly when the custody officer roused her. It was gone 6 p.m. and dark outside the small toughened-glass window at the top of the wall in her cell. She rubbed her eyes and stood up.

'Are you ready to go?' he was saying. 'You can leave your jacket there if you want.'

She nodded, but it didn't make sense. Why should she leave her jacket if she was going? She pulled it on, ready for the coldness of the outside, and followed as the young sergeant led the way down the passageway to the main reception area and sat down behind the custody computer.

'Right, let's get going. Come up here and listen carefully.'

She waited for the words telling her that no further action was to be taken, but they didn't come. Instead she heard the charge being read through and then she was being further cautioned.

'Anything you do say will be taken down and given in evidence.'

'But it wasn't me. It was Lee,' she spluttered, looking round wildly towards her solicitor. The elegant woman shook her head in her direction and put her fingers to her lips. Denise shut her mouth abruptly, her mind spinning. Her solicitor was speaking again, objecting to a request by DS Arnold to keep her in custody. She sounded very eloquent and well spoken but the custody officer was shaking his head.

'I believe you need to be kept in custody due to the serious nature of the offence you're charged with,' he said, turning

towards her. 'And for your own protection. Should details of
the offence become public knowledge I believe you might be
at risk of physical danger. Do you understand?'

She didn't though, and her solicitor was just accepting the
decision. She felt tears springing up and let them fall un-
hindered down her cheeks. She couldn't comprehend what
was happening. She should be walking out of the police station
now, ready to track down Jake and move on.

The solicitor turned towards her and was speaking quietly.

'Don't worry. I'll make a bail application as soon as I can.
Lee is being kept in too so at least you're not getting all the
blame. Hopefully he'll admit to his involvement when he hears
what's happened to you, and you'll be out. Your part of the
charge will no doubt relate to *allowing* the death of a child,
rather than causing it. If Lee does admit his culpability and
they charge him with murder then your charge will be dropped.'

She couldn't think straight. This wasn't supposed to have
happened.

'What will happen to Jake?'

She started to sob noisily, trying to imagine how he would
cope without her. Her solicitor passed her a tissue and she
wiped her face, feeling the material go limp with the wetness
from her cheeks.

A policeman in uniform entered the custody office, striding
straight over to where the boards for each detainee were kept.
He looked young and fresh-faced and eager. He peered at her
details and turned to stare at her, his eyes following the length
of her body from her feet to her face. She saw his expression, the disgust unmasked, his mouth twisted up in a sneer.

He turned away, his eyes remaining momentarily fixed on
her tear-stained face.

'It's a bit late for her to be crying now,' he whispered loudly
to the custody officer. 'Pity she didn't think of what might
happen before she sat back and did nothing while her child's
head was smashed against the wall.'

Matt felt little pleasure as he thought about the day's events.
He'd succeeded in getting a charge, but not the one he really
wanted. He drove round the block, trying and failing to find
a space. All the nearest spots had been taken and he was
forced to park further away from the school. He was late for

the nativity play and the evening Ben had been so eagerly awaiting. He felt his mobile phone vibrate in his pocket and saw Jo's name highlighted on the screen.

'Are you nearly here?' Jo asked urgently. Her voice was edged with panic and annoyance. 'It's about to start and Ben's already upset. He thinks you're not coming.'

'I'll be there in two minutes,' he puffed down the phone, walking quickly towards the school. He hung up, his mind was still at work, firmly set on the strangeness of the day. At least both Lee and Denise would be accountable to a jury for their actions and even if neither could be proved to be the murderer, they should at least both receive a hefty sentence. Or he'd like to think they would. And there was still the opportunity of a subsequent charge of murder, if only he could come up with the crucial evidence. He broke into a jog as the lights of the school hall came into view, shining like a beacon through the dark, foggy atmosphere.

The hall was full to bursting as he squeezed though the main doors at the back and tried to worm his way forward through the hordes of video-bearing fathers. Mary and Joseph had just entered on the prompting of a small group of narrators and were making their way across the stage, dragging behind them an obstinate donkey with an equally obstinate-looking child inside. A slightly discordant piano struck a chord and a straggly choir stood up to the side of the stage and burst into a lively rendition of 'O little town of Bethlehem'.

Matt seized the opportunity to squeeze his way down the outside of the audience to where he saw Jo sitting, with Chloe peering up excitedly from her lap. As he drew level Jo glanced across towards him and smiled thankfully. He stood to the side watching as Joseph knocked at the door of various inns and was turned away, before eventually being ushered through into the confines of a straw-covered stable with his pregnant wife and surly donkey. As the choir started their own version of 'Away in a Manger' he managed to apologize his way along the line until he reached the empty seat next to Jo.

'Ben's on next,' Chloe piped up, her eyes glowing with anticipation. She knew the scene almost as well as Ben did and her excitement was almost palpable.

The scene cut away to a dark mountainside. A young girl holding a large yellow star crossed slowly into the centre of the stage. She was followed by a group of five tea-towel clad shepherds leading their flock of sheep. Matt watched eagerly as a trickle of woolly children skipped across the stage behind the shepherds. He stared at each of the participants trying to work out which one was Ben, finally realizing with disappointment that he wasn't there.

'Where's Ben?' Chloe's voice called out plaintively. 'I can't see him.'

A small disturbance in the wings heralded his arrival as another rather shy sheep was coaxed, a little roughly, out on to the stage. The audience stirred in a murmur of suppressed laughter, followed by a small voice calling out. 'There he is.' Matt realized with a shock that the stage-struck child at the side of the curtains was Ben. Jo's words of rebuke came into his head and forced him up on to his feet to show his young son that his father was indeed watching. The sheep looked in his direction, waved shyly and made its way on to the hillside, before being rounded up and led away to see the baby Jesus.

The rest of the nativity play went by in a blur of pride. At the end, the shy sheep got a special round of applause and removed his furry mask to reveal a happy young boy who ran towards his parents at the conclusion.

The hall exploded into happiness as children were reunited with smiling parents and grandparents and the Christmas spirit was passed around in the shape of mulled wine and mince pies. Matt chatted with the other parents who were trying their best to provide for their children, but his thoughts were of Ryan killed by his parents in a senseless display of violence. He thought too of Bryony, the tiny baby girl, whose life he believed had been taken from her. He felt he had let them both down.

He scooped Ben up in his arms and walked towards the exit, feeling the cold air surge in, swapping place with the warmer, musty interior. He hugged his young son against his body and kissed him gently on the cheek. Ben nestled his head on his father's shoulder, the trauma of performing suddenly taking its toll. Walking out into the dark, Matt looked up into the grey night sky, the clouds obscuring even the light from the moon and stars, and thought of Jake, both parents in custody, his older stepbrother and sister excluding him, his younger siblings dead, all alone in the world. For his sake he would keep trying, keep the pressure on, until the truth was exposed and Ryan's killer was brought to justice.

# Ten

The atmosphere at the children's home was tense as Christmas approached. Among the decorations and frivolity, a nervousness was taking root and Jake felt it all around in whispered conversations and unexpected outbursts. Some of the children were allowed to be with family for the holiday but were fearful of how they would be received and treated. Some had family visiting, but were worried whether they would actually show up. Some had nothing and no one to look forward to. On the whole, these children seemed better off to Jake. They had nothing to fear because there was nothing.

He fell into this category and he'd accepted it. His mum and dad were both in prison, his younger siblings were dead and Mikey and Christina were there with him, whether he liked it or not. There was no one else. He had nothing to prove, no one to talk up, no one that was going to let him down and make him look foolish in front of his peers.

He had watched as numerous bags of groceries were carried though to the kitchens. Some of the other kids had told him that there were loads of extras at Christmas, treats, sweets, even presents. He'd never really had much before. True, they had been bought presents. He'd been given new computer games and toys in the past, but the house had never been decorated, they'd never had a Christmas tree or lights and there'd never been boxes of chocolates and a fancy Christmas dinner like other kids seemed to have. Their Christmas festivities had consisted of Lee downing extra booze, getting steadily drunk in front of the TV, and the inevitable consequences of screaming, arguing, fighting.

At least he had had his mum though. And he wanted her

now, really badly, even though she didn't give him the material things that other children had, didn't care about feeding
them properly. He lay down on his bed and felt tears stinging
the back of his eyes. He wouldn't cry, he wouldn't. It would
all be all right in the end, she'd said it would. He remembered her, with her arms around him, the feel of her soft hands
on his skin, her voice whispering gently in his ear, and knew
she loved him, from wherever she was. And he loved her too.
And it was only a matter of time before they'd be together
again.

There was a knock at the door and Tyrone peered in.

'Are you all right? You've got a surprise visitor downstairs
when you're ready.'

Jake sat up, rubbing his eyes fiercely to prevent any tears
seeping out. He yawned lazily, pretending he didn't care, but
inside he was curious.

'Who is it?'

'Come down and you'll see.'

Tyrone was already halfway along the corridor and Jake
had to run to catch up. By the time he reached the office, his
curiosity had got the better of him and he was half jogging
in order to arrive more speedily.

He peered around the door and saw the smiling face of
Matt Arnold. He wanted to like him, after all he'd kept his
promise to visit him, but now he wasn't so sure. This was the
policeman who'd been responsible for having his mother
locked up.

'What do you want?' he said carefully.

He glanced across as the policeman stood up, and tried to
fix him with an angry stare. Matt Arnold walked towards him
and put his hand on his shoulder.

'I'm sorry it hasn't turned out how you wanted.'

'Why have you locked my mum away? I told you Ryan
went quiet when Lee went in there. What more do you want?'

'Unfortunately, your mum was also up there at about the
same time. You said yourself that you saw Lee attacking your
mum. Both of them are blaming each other. So they'll both
have to go to court and make their claims, and let a judge
and jury decide.'

'But it shouldn't be my mum. She loves me. It should be
Lee. He's the bastard.'

The door swung open again and Mikey and Christina shuffled in. Jake stopped talking as soon as they entered and shut his mouth hastily.

Matt greeted them both and changed the subject abruptly.

'I've come to see you, like I promised. Everyone at work wanted to buy you all something for Christmas so we had a whip-round and . . .' He paused, reaching into a holdall on the floor and pulling out three brightly wrapped parcels. 'Anyway, I hope you like them.'

Mikey and Christina stepped forward and took their presents, thanking Matt politely and retreating from the room, back to the safety of their bedrooms.

Jake reached out and took the gift. He didn't know what to think. He'd rarely received presents before and never from a man that he'd only recently met. He was a man, however, that he instinctively liked, and he wanted to trust him again.

He opened the wrapping and took out the gifts, looking at each one in turn. The first was a box of magic tricks complete with cards, mystery boxes and magic wands. The second was a small blue diary with a page for each day of the year and the third and best was a ten-by-eight wooden photo frame in his favourite football team's colours. He knew exactly what photo he would select to be displayed.

'Sorry, they're not much, but I hope you like them,' Matt was saying.

'Will you come and see my room now?'

He turned and walked from the room. If Matt followed he would gain his trust again. If he failed, Jake knew he was only going through the motions, trying to be friendly out of an ulterior motive, not really bothered enough to give him the time. He'd said he would on the last visit. He turned and saw the policeman was following. He climbed the stairs quickly, pacing out in front until he reached his room.

Matt was right behind and Jake closed the door tightly after he'd entered.

He studied the policeman's face as he took in the room, following his eyes as they skirted each wall, taking in the sparseness and lack of personal items. He didn't care though, it was all his own. Lifting his pillow, he pulled out a picture of his mother, holding a tiny baby. The baby was wrapped in a white shawl and held tight against her body.

'That's me as a baby, with my mum,' he explained to Matt. 'There were just us then. It was before Lee and Mikey and Christina came along.'

He slid the photo into the frame and stood it by his bed, pausing before he put it down, as the memories came flooding back.

'When will I get to see my mum again?' he said quietly. 'Will it be quicker if I say what really happened?'

'I don't know. It depends what the truth is.'

He nodded, but noticed the flicker of interest that glinted in the policeman's eyes.

'I'll only talk to you, but I want to speak to my mum first,' he said firmly.

Matt was thoughtful as he drove away. It had been a pleasure to visit the home and pass over the gifts to brighten the children's Christmas. It had been something he'd wanted to do, but it was the team's decision to make a collection. Seeing them, he was glad that they seemed settled and were looking forward to the festivities. In some respects, he guessed they would have a better Christmas than usual, although they were missing their parents. Jake still troubled him though. He was so serious and earnest in his questions and so firm in his requests.

It was obvious that the boy wanted to say more, but Matt didn't particularly like the terms. Maybe with Lee safely locked away Jake would be more likely to speak the truth. A meeting between Jake and Denise now appeared to be vital, in order to progress the case, but it would have to be supervised. There was no way that Denise Clarkson could be allowed an unsupervised visit while her court case was still pending. The risk would be too great.

He felt his mobile phone vibrating in his pocket and reached down to extricate it. Jo's number flashed up on the screen. He pulled over, pressing the button at the same time.

'Matt, it's me. You've got to come quickly. Ben's been knocked over.'

The voice that came through the earpiece was not Jo's voice. Or at least not the voice he knew. The fear and panic was obvious and an immediate panic gripped him too. His mind was screaming almost as loud in his head as the unrecognizable voice.

'Jo, what's happened? Where are you? Is Ben all right?' He needed to know, but at the same time he instinctively also knew that she couldn't say.

'Just come.' The voice was sobbing now. 'We're in Brookley Street. They've called an ambulance. Just come.'

The phone went dead.

As his mind processed the information, his hands started to shake. He needed to get there and get there as fast as possible, but his body wouldn't respond. This time it was different. This time it was his own child, his own flesh and blood, his life. He pressed the button to open the window and felt the cold air rush in, stirring him into action. His head started to clear and he reached down feeling for the magnetic blue light, situated by his feet. His hands wouldn't stop shaking but at least his brain was back under control. He stuck the light to the roof of the car and flicked the switch to start the sirens. The noise was loud with the window open but he could still hear Jo's voice.

He pressed down hard on the accelerator and the car moved off, its tyres screeching and its engine roaring. *Just come.* Cars veered out of the way, pulling over to the side, but they weren't clearing his path quickly enough. *Come quickly.* They were moving in slow motion. *Ben's been knocked over.* Last-minute Christmas shoppers filled the streets, each vehicle or pedestrian weighed down with heavy bags and cumbersome boxes, making their movement slow and pedantic. *Just come.* He waited at traffic lights, stuck behind queues of vehicles that tried but failed to give him space. *We're in Brookley Street.* The journey seemed to be taking for ever. He was nearly there now, but he couldn't get through. *They've called an ambulance.* The traffic was stationary. A pedestrian walked past.

'You won't be able to get through there, mate,' he was shouting towards him. 'There's been a nasty accident, the road's blocked.'

Then he was running. Past cars, lorries, buses, their passengers craning to see what was causing the hold-up. He saw the ambulance, Ben's ambulance. It was still there.

He was sprinting now, his head pounding as he closed the distance. Blue lights flashed across the darkening sky. Police traffic cars were situated across the road, preventing vehicular access, their bright fluorescent strips standing out boldly.

A lone policeman dressed in a bright yellow jacket was blocking his way. He held his arm out.

'You can't go through here, sir.'

'It's my son.'

The arm dropped and he kept running, on towards the stationary ambulance. The rear doors were pulled to but not locked. He grabbed the handle, wincing as the bright lights of the ambulance hit his pupils. Faces turned towards him in surprise. He saw Jo. Her face was white with shock, her eyes full of terror. She stood and he stepped up towards her. Then she was in his arms and he could feel the sobs wracking her body, could see the tears coursing down her cheeks.

'Thank God you're here.'

'What's happened?'

'It was so quick. Ben and I were going to the corner shop. Ben was running ahead, stopping to look at every house with Christmas lights. I saw a small animal dart across in front of him. It was an albino squirrel. It ran straight out between some parked cars across the road. Ben ran after it. I screamed for him to stop but he didn't hear me. A car was coming – it was going really fast, you could hear it. It was on the wrong side of the road. It hit him and sent him flying up into the air. I should have been holding his hand and this wouldn't have happened. It's all my fault.'

'How is he?'

Jo started to sob again.

'I don't know. They're still working on him. They want to stabilize him a bit before we leave.'

Matt looked down at the small figure, lying on a red blanket behind Jo. The face that he saw took his breath away. Ben lay motionless, his eyes closed, his figure static, his head to one side. At the back of his head an ugly open wound seeped blood. The surrounding tissues were starting to swell and his hair was matted in the congealed, red substance, but his face remained intact. His clothes had been cut away and his body was white and still. A tube came from his open mouth and various lines and needles were inserted into veins. He was unconscious.

He felt as if all the breath had been squeezed out of him as he took in the sight. Jo moved to the side and he stepped towards his son, his eyes fixed to his static features. Nothing moved except the paramedic's hand, rhythmically squeezing a bag of oxygen, again and again and again. Pushing the life into his small body.

He bent down, taking Ben's limp hand in his own, stroking the soft flesh, wincing at the hard metal needle stuck into his small wrist. He couldn't speak for the lump rising in his throat.

The ambulance was ready to move out. Ben was as stable as could be and the driver was climbing out, ready to take his seat in the front.

'Are you coming with us?' he asked matter-of-factly.

He swung around to Jo, unwilling to let go of Ben's hand.

'Jo, my police car is outside. Are you OK to go in the ambulance? I'll follow on in the car and meet you at the hospital.'

Jo nodded back and wiped her face, preparing to take over the position next to their son.

Matt bent down and kissed Ben gently on the forehead. The skin felt clammy and peculiar to the touch but still warm. He was glad.

'Hang on in there, Ben. Mummy's going with you now but I'll be back by your side again soon. Don't give up. I love you.'

The lump in his throat rose up as he whispered the last words. Choking back the sobs he rose and climbed down the steps into the cold, watching as the paramedic closed the door. The siren started up and the ambulance pulled swiftly but smoothly away, the blue lights flashing across his pupils until they faded from view.

He stayed, rooted to the same position, until a traffic cop joined him.

'Are you OK?'

The answer was obvious but Matt turned towards him and nodded, the policeman in him regaining control of his emotions.

'Yeah. I'm OK. How's the other driver?'

Until now, all his thoughts had been with his own family. Now, as Jo's words began to sink in, he realized that his son had run out into the path of another car, the driver of which must also be suffering from the trauma of watching a child tossed into the air and on to its bonnet.

'We don't know. The other driver failed to stop.'

The words hit him almost as hard as the initial phone call.

'What do you mean, he failed to stop? You mean he just left my son in the roadway to die?'

The traffic cop shook his head. He was a veteran officer, with twenty-seven years experience, the last twelve in traffic patrol. Forty-six years of age, he had three kids of his own, but his expression still conveyed the horror of dealing with such an accident.

'Apparently he pulled up, got out and looked back and then drove straight off again. You're in the job, aren't you? Your wife mentioned you were.'

He nodded.

'I'm Gary Fellowes, from Merton traffic garage.' He held out a hand towards him and Matt shook it firmly. He was struck by the difference between the size and strength of this hand and his son's tiny one.

'Matt Arnold,' he replied shakily, feeling the lump in his throat return.

'Matt, I promise you. I will do everything in my power to catch this bastard and make sure he pays for doing this.'

He nodded, not trusting himself to utter a word without breaking down. Swallowing hard, he forced a smile.

'Thanks Gary. I'd appreciate that very much. I'll be in touch. Now I'd better get to the hospital.'

He turned and started walking back towards his car. The late afternoon gloom had given way to the darkness of the winter's evening. Blue lights still flashed across the scene, bathing everything around in peculiar shades of topaz and glinting eerily off windscreens and house fronts. The road was unnaturally quiet and still, with incident tape sealing off the normal sounds and smells of nearby traffic.

He walked slowly, allowing himself to come to terms with the shock of the accident and its aftermath. He wanted to be at Ben's side at the hospital but at the same time, he was dreading it.

He heard a shout and turned to see Gary Fellowes waving towards him.

'Mind where you're treading,' he shouted over.

He looked down and saw a small blue and white trainer lying on its side in the gutter. A yellow fluorescent wax crayon mark encircled it, charting its position for the coming photographs. He recognized the shoe immediately.

There was almost nothing else to show where the accident had occurred. No vehicle, no debris, just a small pile of used, bloody dressings, a set of long, black rubber skid marks and a lone trainer symbolizing the start of a young boy's fight for life.

# Eleven

It was dark as the blue Peugeot entered the car park to the flats at Clonsdyke House, Martell Street, SE1. All around were tall tower blocks and concrete footpaths. A walkway ran alongside the car park and a row of outbuildings housed numerous bins and rubbish chutes.

The car pulled up and the driver fell from the door, stumbling as he walked round to survey the damage. The front, nearside light cluster was smashed and there was a large dent on the left side of the bonnet. The windscreen was cracked, the glass intact but splintering from the impact mark of a head, close to the centre. Strands of hair were just visible in the light, stuck against the point of impact, their ends blowing gently away from the small amount of congealed red blood that held them firm.

As he looked closer at the damage, Andrei Kachan panicked. He was aware he had no insurance to drive his girlfriend's car. He was aware that he had been drinking and would be over the limit. He was also very much aware that he had hit a kid and not even bothered to go back to see how he was. The kid had been thrown up over the bonnet and crashed into the windscreen, directly in his line of vision. He'd left him for dead in the road and driven off, while the screams of the child's mother still pounded fresh through his head.

His two workmates and drinking friends were climbing out of the other seats now, joining him where he stood.

'What are we going to do?' one of them, by the name of Filipp, was saying. His voice was slurred and he sounded excitable.

'Calm down, I'm thinking,' Andrei responded. Hurriedly he dialled his house, issuing instructions clearly and precisely to his girlfriend. His mind was whirring with ideas which were beginning to form into a plan. He ran his hand through his dark hair as he spoke, allowing his fingers to run through the gelled spikiness at the top of his head. The smell of the engine and burning rubber wafted across to his nostrils, reminding him of the speed and aggression of his previous journey.

As an idea took shape, he walked back round to the driver's door, bending down and looking in. His balance was shaky and he grasped the door frame to keep himself steady. Reaching in, he tugged at the steering column, pulling the hard plastic cover from around the ignition switch until it came off in his hand. He fell backward as it came away, his spine scraping against the hard concrete.

Filipp laughed as he struggled to get up. It immediately made Andrei angry.

'Don't just stand there,' he shouted. 'Fucking help.'

His mate laughed again.

He struggled to his feet, tossing the ignition cowling up on to the flat roof of the outhouses, out of sight.

'What're you trying to do, then?'

'What does it look like? We have to burn the motor.'

His voice came out loud and harsh and he saw Filipp's expression change as the shock of the idea registered. Slowly, his face changed back to one of amusement and he fumbled in his pockets, glancing around as the sound of footsteps came closer.

'Have you got a light, old man?' Filipp shouted out loudly at a figure hobbling slowly across a nearby walkway.

Andrei swung round to look in the direction Filipp was facing and saw the man too. He was a thin, elderly black man, of Caribbean appearance. His hair was beginning to go grey at the sides and he had a sparse moustache and pitted face. He looked nervous at the attention. He was only a short distance away but was elevated above them by the walkway. He stopped, staring down at them for a split second. Andrei immediately realized he'd guessed what they were doing.

'I'm sorry, I haven't,' he called down to them, his hands outstretched and open. As quickly as he had seemed to appear, he was gone, limping sharply away and disappearing from view into the confines of the estate.

'What did you have to do that for, you idiot?' Andrei snapped back at Filipp. He reached into his jacket pocket and took out a lighter, flicking the catch so the spark lit up the gas. His face looked almost manic in the light of the small flame.

'Get your stuff. This baby's gonna burn.'

He opened the boot and took out his coat and several discarded magazines and random papers. Igniting the papers he threw them down on to the front seats of the car, watching as they grew steadily into a larger flame. He rolled one of the magazines up, took the petrol filler cap off and pushed it down into the pipe, lighting the end of the roll still in view. The paper flared, dropping black cinders on to the ground beneath but spitting as the fire took hold, carrying its deadly heat down towards the petrol accelerant.

Retreating to the safety of the garages, Andrei watched in awe as the first blast ripped through the petrol tank and the blaze exploded upwards into the darkness. He started to run, whooping as his friends caught up with him, and the three continued, through the estate and out on to the approach road. The flames were shooting high into the sky, burning in blue and orange flares, as he turned for a jubilant final view.

He had one last thing to do before he could relax. Sirens were sounding from afar as they plunged into the gloom of another estate and headed towards the main road nearby. Pulling out his mobile phone he dialled the number of a local taxi firm.

The accident and emergency room was busy when Matt arrived. Assorted casualties sat slumped on chairs impatiently awaiting their turn. Some were obviously under the influence of too much Christmas spirit, while others, cut and bruised, already bore the marks of alcohol-induced scraps and fights. A few paced the floor, barely concealed tempers meagrely held at bay.

He walked slowly over to reception and waited while an Eastern European man painstakingly spelt out a casualty's name. Jo was nowhere to be seen. He guessed she would be tucked away with Ben in whichever cubicle he was being treated. He wanted to be there for his young son but the fear of seeing him so ill was almost overwhelming.

The middle-aged, bespectacled receptionist was looking up at him, her lips a thin line of impatience.

'I'm sorry,' he apologized. 'I'm looking for Ben Arnold. He was brought in by ambulance a few minutes ago.'

She typed the name in on her keypad and looked back at him, the impatience replaced by a softer, more sympathetic smile.

'Come with me, I'll take you.'

She rose and he stepped across until he was keeping pace with her. His legs moved automatically, propelling him past minor traumas towards the swing doors into the resuscitation unit. Normally when he attended hospital he had a job to do, a victim to be dealt with, a suspect to guard, but this time it was so different. He felt helpless in the face of what had happened. There were only two casualties in resuss, one an old man wired up to an ECG machine, his heart finally giving up to the ravages of old age.

Ben was the other.

As he approached, he saw the boy's small white body still motionless, attached to numerous monitors, lines and machines. The squeeze of the air bag had been replaced by a monotonous low-pitched bleep. His eyes were closed and a large tube forced his lips apart. Jo was by his side, her eyes still rimmed red, her skin almost as white as Ben's.

She looked up and he saw the relief flicker across her face.

'Thank God you're here,' she said. 'He hasn't woken up but they've managed to stabilize him at the moment.'

He went straight to the far side of the bed and took Ben's other hand, feeling its warmth against the cool of his own. He was desperately thankful that it still had life pulsating through it.

'Will he be all right?'

He directed his question to a young Asian male doctor who stood at the foot of the bed, writing on Ben's chart. Matt felt himself wishing the doctor to be older – greying, more obviously experienced. Still he had an air of confidence about him. Matt was, at least for the time being, willing to put his trust in him.

'It's too early to say at the moment,' the doctor replied, glancing up. 'Your son's suffered a severe trauma to the back of the head. He's stable at present but we won't know yet whether his brain has been affected. The skull is almost certainly fractured and there's a fair amount of internal swelling. Until that goes down, it's impossible to assess any damage. We're keeping him sedated and he'll be going to X-ray shortly. When that's done we should know exactly what's occurred and whether any other bones may be broken. His pelvis is out of alignment so there's a good chance that could be broken too.'

'Will he live though?' Matt couldn't stop himself repeating the thought. He didn't hear the other words, the talk of swelling, damage to the brain, broken bones. They were irrelevant beside the need for his son to live.

'It's too early to say. But he's stable, which is the main thing at the moment. The machine's breathing for him to give his body all the help we can, to allow it to start the recovery process. Every hour is a bonus, but he's young. At his age you'd be surprised by the body's ability to pull through.'

Matt nodded, grasping every scrap of optimism that he could find. Ben was stable. He was young and if he was anything like his father, he wouldn't give up. He would pull through. He would fight this. They would fight this together.

He tried not to think about the alternative.

He looked at his boy and wanted to scream out loud. If only Ben hadn't run out. If only he hadn't been distracted. If only Jo had kept hold of him. If only that bastard hadn't been speeding down the wrong side of the road at precisely that moment. If only.

The taxi driver nodded back towards Andrei to signal his understanding.

'I can wait but it'll cost you. And I need payment up front,' he called.

Andrei pulled out his wallet, passing several notes across.

'I'll be back before you know it,' he shouted, walking away from the car. He paused at the corner of the road, checking for any sign of police activity before he plunged onwards to his house. There was nothing. Everything appeared normal.

The house was a small, terraced property, but was huge in

comparison to the tenement flat he'd left in Russia. There, squashed into his parents' abode, he'd dreamt of living in a style he could only imagine. When the European Community had opened up, he'd been one of the early migrants to stand in line for the chance to better himself. His family too had benefited from the regular cheques and were slowly clawing themselves out from the poverty that surrounded them. He'd been in England for nearly five years and his ability to speak the language fluently had enabled him to earn a respectable living in the building industry, as well as charming himself into the life of a pretty, English, divorced, property-owning woman. It was her house that he now regarded as his home and it was her car that he had just been driving.

His home came into view, lit up intermittently by the lights of a flashing Santa Claus that pulsated out from his neighbour's house.

He strode up his driveway, opened the door and walked in, closing it quietly behind him. His girlfriend, Sharon Cunningham, was on her feet as he opened the lounge door.

'What the hell's going on?' she said. Her eyes echoed the bewilderment in her voice. She came towards him, standing in his path as he made for the cabinet. He took her by the shoulders and stared into her face.

'Nothing for you to worry about. I just had a small accident. That's all.'

'So why do I have to tell the police the car's been stolen, if it's nothing to worry about?'

'Because I've been drinking, because I'm not insured to drive your car and because I've only got a Russian driving licence, that's why. I can't afford to get banned. I need to be able to drive for work.'

She was quiet.

'How serious was the accident? Was someone hurt?'

He ignored the question.

'If the police come round, just tell them what I said. Tell them that the car should be on the driveway where you last parked it and that you're the only one who drives it. Be surprised when you see it's gone. Tell them it must have been stolen and show them the keys.'

He rummaged in his pocket and gave her the car keys. They were the only set and it had been imperative that they be returned, in case she was asked for them. It would be too suspicious if the keys were missing at the same time as the car.

She took them and hung them up on their usual hook, frowning.

'Where's the car now?'

He paused, not knowing whether to admit to what he had just done. She saw the hesitation.

'What have you done with it?' she repeated, staring straight up into his eyes.

'Don't worry. I've sorted it.' His voice was edged with impatience and came out a little too roughly. 'Just do what I've told you and everything will be fine. The police may not even come. I don't know if anyone saw the number plate. But if they do, just stick to the story. I'm staying out overnight but I'll be back tomorrow.'

He squeezed past her, rummaging in the cabinet for more cash. When he turned round he could see the worry etched across her delicate features. He needed her on his side. He smiled towards her, gently taking her in his arms, and kissed her lightly on the cheek.

'I'll see you tomorrow, my darling. It'll be OK. Don't be scared.'

Then he was gone.

As the hours ticked by, so Matt's anger grew. Each time he gazed at his sleeping child, more fuel was added to the fire that was burning within him. X-rays had been taken, Ben was still stable and after several hours he had been moved to the intensive therapy unit. He was still unconscious and likely to be so for some time. And until he woke, if he woke, there was nothing to do but wait and hope.

Jo was stronger now. She'd phoned her parents, who had immediately offered to look after Chloe for as long as they were needed. As the minutes grew into hours, she seemed to be gaining inner strength and determination to do everything in her power to help her young son survive. Her guilt at allowing it to happen was still raw, however, and each time she raised it, Matt felt it feeding his anger. He knew in his head that it was not her fault. Ben was of school age; he was old enough to be trusted not to run out. He knew also that he too would have allowed Ben his freedom to walk or run down the street without constantly holding his hand. But he needed someone to blame.

He got up and walked away from Ben's bed, out into the cool of the corridor. It was quiet here, away from the constant sounds of the machines. His head was pounding. He had to do something.

Jo followed him out, slipping her arms around his waist as she came up behind him. He didn't turn towards her, preferring to remain staring out of the fourth floor window. The night sky was black, the stars and moon covered by a thick stratum of low-lying cloud. Traffic slipped by noiselessly, its red and white lights leaving fiery comet trails behind. Christmas lights shone out from rows of terraces and blocks of flats, each gaudy bulb emphasizing the pointlessness of the coming festivities. The only thing they would be celebrating this year would be each hour that Ben survived his battle for life.

A blue light flashed across his line of vision, followed by another. He strained to see where they were coming from. The two lights converged at the same place and he saw another moving towards them. They were centred on a large junction and from his vantage point he could see a fire engine and police car at the scene of an accident. It looked serious. He speculated whether the car's occupants, now being freed by the fire brigade, would end up lying next to his own son in intensive care. He wondered whether all the parties involved had stayed or whether one side had fled in drunken panic. The fire inside him blazed.

He spun round, away from the sight, feeling Jo's arms loosen.

'I've got to go,' he said, staring into her face fleetingly.

'You can't go. Go where?'

'I've got to do something.'

'But there's nothing you can do. I need you here. Ben needs you here.'

He shrugged. 'I'll be back. I've got to do something to help. I can't just stand here doing nothing.'

And then he was striding away, his pace lengthening with each step until he was running. He turned briefly as he approached the swing doors and saw Jo standing where he'd left her, arms by her sides, staring after him. He thought he saw tears glistening on her cheeks. He ran on, down several flights of stairs, until he was out in the cold air. His breath was all around him as he sprinted to the car park and fumbled at the lock. He had to find Gary Fellowes and help to trace the animal that could do this to his son.

# Twelve

G ary Fellowes was just wrapping up at the scene. The photographs had been taken, the Accident Investigation Unit was finished and about to leave and he was bagging up the last few exhibits. He picked up the trainer and placed it in a paper exhibits bag. It looked so small and fitted along the width of the bag, so unlike the normal adult ones. As he was staring down at it, the accident investigator sauntered over.

'How is the little lad?'

'Not good. He's being kept alive on a ventilator at the moment. We're doing two-hourly checks on him but it could go either way. It's just a matter of time. Any estimates as yet as to the driver's speed?'

'Difficult to say until I do all the calculations, but at a rough guess I'd say somewhere between fifty and fifty-five mph. In these road and weather conditions it was an accident waiting to happen. The driver must have been mad or drunk or both. He's on the wrong side of the road and passing a bollard on the offside. By all accounts the boy took the full brunt of the force and was knocked straight up on to the bonnet and hit the windscreen. It's lucky he wasn't killed outright.'

'True. But, if he does die we've definitely got enough for death by dangerous driving?' Gary asked.

'Or death by dangerous driving due to drink or drugs. It's Christmas. The driver's almost certainly pissed.'

'But we need to find him for that.'

They both fell silent.

Gary was the first to break into their thoughts. 'It's a damn shame the boy has to die before the driver can be charged with the more serious offence. That bastard deserves everything he gets. You know the kid's dad is in the job?'

The other man nodded. 'I was at the same station as him years ago. He was a good bloke. Must be awful to find your own child's been involved in an accident. It'd be my worst nightmare.'

'And at Christmas too.' Gary paused. 'I'd better get finished here. The car's registered to a female, Sharon Cunningham, 33 Beauchamp Road, SW4. That's not too far away. I'm going to go straight there and see her as soon as I leave. It hasn't been reported as stolen as yet and it's not unregistered so at least I have somewhere to start.'

'I'm off too, back to base. I'll have the report to you as soon as I can.'

The two men shook hands. Gary watched as the accident investigator climbed back in his car and disappeared. He only had a few last bits to finish and then he and his partner could open the road up again and start on the preliminary enquiries.

He was in the process of piling up the traffic cones when he recognized Matt Arnold walking down the road towards him.

'How's it going? Have you nearly finished here?'

Gary was surprised to see the man again, never mind so soon.

'Yep, we're just opening up the road and then we'll be paying a visit to the registered keeper's address to see what they've got to say about it.'

'Would you mind if I came along? There's nothing I can do at the hospital at the moment. Ben's stable but unconscious and my wife's with him. I just feel I've got to do something to help.'

Gary frowned. He was normally partnered with his colleague, Dave. They knew each other and worked well together. It was always difficult when there was an extra person, never mind the father of the victim.

'I don't think it would be a good idea really. You're too involved.'

'I promise I wouldn't say or do a thing. I can't sit and do

nothing. I won't say a word, but I would like to at least see some of the other people involved.'

Gary sighed deeply. Having Matt there might cause problems but at the same time he could well understand his need to feel he was doing something. In any case Matt Arnold was a sergeant and as such could overrule him.

'You say and do nothing but observe, Sarge, you understand?'

Matt nodded. 'Don't worry. There's no way on earth I would jeopardize any prosecution. I want this bloke arrested and put before a court.'

By 1.30 a.m. they were on their way. The evening had given way to a damp and windy night. Rain was threatening, giving the atmosphere outside the vehicle a heaviness that mirrored the mood in the car. Naked trees stretched overhead, their branches finally stripped of their last foliage.

The radio crackled into life.

'Oscar Victor Two Six receiving?'

Gary responded.

'Oscar Victor Two Six, for your information, the vehicle concerned in your possible fatal accident has been found abandoned and burnt out in SE1. I'll send the message through to you.'

Matt watched as the mobile data transmitter signalled a message was pending. At the touch of a button the text came up on the screen. He strained forward to read the words, frustration building as he read the vehicle had been completely destroyed by fire. It was to be lifted and taken to a garage pending a thorough forensic examination but he knew it would be virtually impossible to find any usable evidence from it. From experience he guessed that it would be just a matter of time before it was reported stolen. It was all too predictable.

'Shit,' Gary muttered, as if reading his mind. 'I was hoping that wouldn't happen. Still, it'll be interesting to hear what the registered owner has to say about it. The car's an old P reg Peugeot, which is a very unusual car to be stolen. It's not exactly a joyrider's normal choice of transport.'

They came to a stop. Matt looked up at a small row of terraced houses. They seemed quite respectable and were situated in a quiet suburban street. The lights were out at number thirty-three and it was in darkness. He hoped the occupants were in.

They parked directly outside the house and walked towards the front door, their footsteps crunching on the gravel. The parking area on the driveway was empty and he stopped to see if there was any sign of a vehicle having been stolen from the space. There was nothing. No tools, no broken glass, no remnants that might give rise to suspicion.

From the corner of his eye he saw the curtains at the front upstairs window move, before quickly falling back into place.

'I think we've got a reception committee,' he said quietly to Gary, casting his eyes up towards the window.

No lights came on and there was no further movement until they'd knocked several times loudly on the door. On the third knock, he heard movement from within and a light came on in the hallway. The door opened and a woman appeared, tying the cord of a dressing gown around her middle. She was tall and slim, with long, blonde hair tied loosely behind her in a messy ponytail. She was in her nightclothes but he noticed that she still had make-up on and her eyes didn't look to have just woken up. She smoothed back her hair and smiled.

'I'm sorry. I hope I haven't kept you waiting. I was asleep.'

'Are you the only one in?' Gary asked.

'Yes my fiancé's at a Christmas do.' Her expression changed abruptly. 'Why? Has something happened to him? Is he all right?'

'Nothing's happened to him. Don't worry, but we do need to come in and speak to you.'

The smile returned to her face.

'Oh, thank goodness for that. When I saw you on the doorstep I thought something had happened to him. Come in, come in.'

She opened the door and beckoned them through. The house was tidy and smelled of vanilla fragrance. They walked into a small lounge with a three-piece suite against one wall, a wall unit against another and a large plasma screen television, complete with sound system and DVD player, directly in front of them. She was clearly quite comfortably off. He glanced round and noticed a small Christmas tree tucked into the corner, tastefully decorated in silver and red, partially covering a small bookcase. Matt saw a number of framed photographs spaced out along the top. He edged towards them and pushed the branches back carefully to peer through at them. Several contained pictures of young children and family portraits. The largest one, however, positioned in the centre of the shelf, showed a dark-haired, smiling man with an arm slung proprietorially around the same woman who was now stepping in his direction. He stared at the face smiling out at him, taking in the handsome features, the tousled hair, the white teeth and the easy smile. He wanted to memorize every part of the face.

'How can I help you?' The woman moved across, stepping into his line of vision and blocking his view of the smiling man.

'Are you Sharon Cunningham?' Gary asked evenly.

'Yes, I am.'

'And you own a blue Peugeot 106XN, registration number P117 FHY?'

'Yes.'

'Where is it now?'

'It should be on the driveway. That's where I left it.'

She walked to the window and pulled back the curtain, gasping out loud as she looked down. A hand flew to her mouth to emphasize her shock.

'Oh, it's gone. It was there last time I looked out. It must have been stolen.'

Matt wanted to laugh. She was playing a game and playing it badly. She was lying through her teeth. Judging by the twitch of the curtain and the mock surprise, she'd been expecting a visit and had had plenty of time to work out the story.

'Who last drove it?' Gary persisted with his line of questioning.

'I did. I parked it there this morning when I got back from shopping. Someone must have taken it.'

'And you didn't hear or see anything or check out the window at all, until now?'

'No, I had no idea.'

'How would they have got it started? Have you had the keys stolen?'

'I don't know how they would have done it. I've still got the keys. They're hanging on the peg.' She walked straight to the line of keys in the hallway and took off a set, holding them up triumphantly. 'Look, here they are. They're the only set I've got.'

Gary examined them slowly before handing them back.

'And you're sure your fiancé hasn't been out in the car earlier?'

'I'm positive. Why do you ask? What's happened to my car?'

'It's been found burnt out in an estate uptown.'

'Burnt out!' This time the look of shock appeared to be genuine.

'Have you any idea why someone would want to steal your car and burn it out?'

She was silent but shook her head in disbelief as Gary ploughed on.

'Are you sure no one you know was driving it? Could your fiancé have borrowed it, or lent it to someone else?'

'No, he wouldn't. He hasn't got a full British driving licence and he's not insured. There's no way he would take it out. It's been stolen, like I said.'

'What's your fiancé's name?'

'Andrei, Andrei Kachan.'

'And how would you describe him?'

She paused as if unsure whether to continue. Finally she spoke.

'He's thirty-one years old, medium to stocky build, average height with dark, spiky black hair. But it wouldn't be him, like I said.'

'A male fitting that description was seen driving your car earlier when it was involved in an accident.'

'Are you insinuating I'm lying to you?' Sharon Cunningham's face was now fixed in an angry expression. Fellowes ignored it.

'The vehicle hit a young boy, on the wrong side of the road, knocking him up on to the bonnet so that his head cracked against the windscreen and then throwing him back down on to the road. The driver got out to have a good look and then got straight back into the car and drove off. He didn't even try to help or find out how the boy was. That five-year-old boy is still fighting for his life.'

Matt felt the colour drain from his face. He hadn't been ready to hear the stark reality of the crash spelt out so bluntly and the shock of listening to the words forced the lump back into his throat. He glanced at Sharon Cunningham and saw the shock mirrored in her face. Her hand came up to her mouth and this time the exclamation she uttered appeared to be genuine.

'Oh my God. Will he die?'

'We don't know as yet. He is very seriously hurt with major head injuries. If he does live, the chances are he might be brain-damaged for life.'

Sharon Cunningham started to cry. Any pretence of acting was stripped away by Gary's words. Matt too felt paralysed with shock at the prognosis. He had not really thought past the question of what would happen to Ben if he did survive. He leaned back against the wall and swallowed hard, turning away from the crying woman and focusing on the face of the smiling man. The smile mocked him.

He could hear the conversation between the woman and Gary continuing. The voices sounded to him as if they were coming from far away. He heard her say that her fiancé had in fact been out in the car and had returned the keys and admitted to her that he'd had a slight accident. She said he'd instructed her to say the car was stolen. She gave her fiancé's details and an address she believed he might be staying at for the night.

Five minutes later he felt himself being propelled from the house by Gary and his partner. The cold hit him as he stumbled back out towards the police car, but the vision of the smiling man and the name Andrei Kachan were firmly planted in his memory.

The police car wove its way along the back streets near London Bridge railway station. Tooley Street was a long desolate road lined with shops and railway arches. The London Dungeon with its vast array of gruesome medieval tortures nestled under one of the arches, sinister at night with a single flame casting shadows down on to the silent cobbles. The River Thames flowed noiselessly, parallel to the street, its dark ripples concealing deadly currents that waited to suck any surface material down to its murky depths, only to regurgitate them on to the glutinous mudbanks at low tide.

They continued slowly, Gary and his partner searching for

the names of the blocks and tenements that lined one side of the road. Matt was deep in thought, looking out towards the river on the opposite side, his eyes following the silhouettes of the City but barely taking in the sights. They passed the shape of HMS *Belfast* looming large with its funnels and vantage points rising high from its decks. They passed the Gherkin, its iconic shape twisting up between the office blocks on the opposite side of the river. They passed the Tower of London, its ramparts and battlements lit up against the skyline. Tower Bridge came into view, standing majestically upright, its towers and spans lit up in gold against the blackness of the night sky. He was surrounded by so many centuries of history but could only think of the last few hours. Everything else was irrelevant.

'This looks like it.' Gary's voice pierced his thoughts and he spun round to follow the direction in which his driver's face was turned. A tall, dark building sat back from the roadside, with just a small bulb illuminating a plaque on the wall. 'Riverside Mansion', it stated grandly, and he couldn't help smiling grimly as he noticed the graffiti that surrounded the words. They stopped next to the entrance and he climbed out, peering at the bars that covered its boarded-up windows. There were chinks of light from some of the intact ones and a distant beat could be heard from one of the higher floors. They ascended a small flight of stairs, clutching on to a wobbly iron railing. The front door was closed and a column of bell pushes lined up vertically against the door frame.

Gary shrugged. 'Looks like we're going to have to wake a few people up to find the room we're after.'

He pushed the top few bells and waited. No one came, so he leant against the door and applied pressure by the catch. It sprung open easily and he almost fell into the gloomy hallway. Mail lay on the floor and was piled up in small bundles on shelves. Matt picked up a few of the letters and read the names. They were almost all different, a testament to the itinerant nature of the building's occupants, but he could find none for the person for whom they were searching.

Ahead of them was a flight of bare wooden stairs with a smooth banister. They climbed the stairs, scrutinizing each door for a plaque bearing the identity of the room's inhabitants. A few bore names but the majority were bare wood, imprinted only with the scratches, splinters and footprints of previous occupants and their unwelcome visitors. As they climbed higher, the thumping of the music became louder. Fewer rooms appeared to be in darkness but fewer too were named. They decided to speak to the occupant of the room housing the sound system. Several times they knocked loudly before a Nigerian man answered, dressed only in a pair of boxer shorts, gazing lazily at them through bloodshot eyes. A strong smell of cannabis wafted out as the door was opened.

'Yeah,' he said in greeting.

'We're looking for a man called Andrei Kachan. He's supposed to be staying with his friend Filipp Ivanovich, who has a room here. Do you know either man or which room Filipp lives in?'

The man shrugged and indicated the noise. 'Who did you say?' he shouted.

'Filipp Ivanovich or Andrei Kachan?' Gary shouted back.

The man indicated a door on the other side of the landing towards the rear of the building. 'Filipp lives there. I saw him come in a few hours ago with another man who I didn't know. Maybe it is this man that you wish to see.'

'Have you seen them leave?'

'No, but I do not see or hear everything.'

He smiled and shut the door abruptly and Matt heard the volume of the music increase. He walked across to the door and listened. A TV was on inside the room and he could feel warm air coming from the keyhole as he bent to look in. He felt a sudden adrenalin rush. The man responsible for hospitalizing his son was on the other side of the door. He banged loudly with his fists and waited, each second seeming to take an age. Gary touched his arm gently, guiding him backwards behind him.

'Leave it to me,' he said firmly.

He knocked again, harder, louder. Still there was no answer. The TV chattered on but they could hear no other sounds from within.

Matt felt his anger lurch. The man was in the room and wasn't going to get away with not answering. He took a step back and, pushing Gary to one side, launched himself at the door. It gave way easily and he tumbled forward into the room. The first thing he noticed as he regained his balance was the

curtain blowing out through an open window. His eyes scanned
the room. It was empty. He ran to the window and looked
out. Underneath the sill ran a metal walkway, leading to the
fire escape. Spiral iron stairs twisted downwards to the ground
below and out into the back yard and a maze of alleyways
that zigzagged between the tenements. He swung round, taking
in the empty sleeping bag laid out across the floor, the cigarette ends still smoking in the ashtray and the half-empty cans
of lager on the coffee table. The bastard had gone, no doubt
alerted by his name being shouted on the landing outside.

He grabbed hold of the table, upending it and sending its
contents spraying across the floor. He kicked at one of the
cans, sending it slamming against the far wall. He could feel
his head pounding with frustration and at that moment knew
he might lash out at anyone or anything. Turning abruptly he
stalked out of the room and down to the street below. The
bastard had gone and with him any chance of measuring the
alcohol content in his blood. It would be too late for that when
they caught up with him. He strode onwards past the police
car, across the green, to the river and stood leaning out over
the stone wall. For a second, he questioned whether he should
throw himself into the freezing waters and allow his body to
be taken on a painless journey into unconsciousness and death.
A journey like Ben's that would take away the anguish he
was feeling and allow him to sleep peacefully, oblivious to
the hurt and sadness that threatened to engulf him.

The reply came in whispered rushes of wind, gusting around
his face and ears and causing him to pull his jacket up around
his neck. 'Don't give up,' it murmured to him. 'Don't give
up.' And he remembered the words with which he himself had
implored his small son.

He turned and walked back towards the car. 'I won't give
up,' he said firmly back. 'I promise I won't ever give up.'

# Thirteen

The streets were buzzing with Christmas Eve shoppers as Gary Fellowes made his way back into his office. All around, groups of office workers bedecked in red Christmas hats were weaving drunkenly in conga lines from bar to bar. The traffic was heavy as it moved haltingly forward along the busy High Street towards Merton garage. A float was causing the hold-up, travelling slowly at the front of the queue, Christmas music blaring and a collection of elves and fairies surrounding a rather too skinny Father Christmas resplendent with ill-fitting beard and sour face. Buckets were held aloft and money was being thrown in their general direction by excited children and harassed mothers.

He checked his watch. It was almost midday and his eyes felt gritty and strained from the lack of sleep. The previous night had finished on a bitter-sweet note. After the accident they were now at least able to identify the driver, but he wished they'd been able to apprehend him as they'd hoped. Matt had been dropped off back at the hospital, quiet but determined. He admired the man's resilience although it had been awkward with him present.

By the time he reached his office he was feeling irritated by the time it had taken. The phone was ringing and although a couple of the others were in the room they were more concerned with their own conversation than answering it. He picked up the receiver in annoyance. The voice he heard on the other end of the line sounded familiar. It asked for him by name. He replied.

'I made a mistake last night,' the female said. 'I spoke to my partner this morning when he came in and he said he hadn't been out in my car. He said he'd been picked up by a friend in his car. They'd had a slight accident but it wasn't in my car. I must have misunderstood him.'

'Is this Sharon Cunningham?' Her voice seemed different from the voice he remembered. More controlled, more official.

'Yes it is. I want to report my car as stolen, like I initially said when I spoke to you. It was taken from my driveway and I only discovered it gone when you came round last night. Whoever stole it must have been involved in that accident. It wasn't Andrei.'

Gary was amazed. After seeing her tears and emotion the night before he couldn't believe what he was now hearing.

'Are you sure you want to make this allegation of theft? It's a very serious thing to allege if it isn't true. If the car's found not to have been stolen you could be arrested for conspiracy to pervert the course of justice.'

'It was stolen and that's all I've got to say about it. I parked it there when I got back from shopping in the morning. Now are you going to report it or not?'

'I will make a report if you wish.' Gary was astounded but he too could be formal. 'But we will still need to speak to your partner.'

'He has a solicitor and he will attend the police station this afternoon if you need to talk to him.'

'Tell him to be at Wimbledon police station at three p.m. and I will speak to him then. I will also need to speak personally with you to report your allegation and take a full statement, so I want you at the same station at seven p.m.'

He put down the phone and cursed. He hadn't expected this to happen. He cursed again. They hadn't taken a statement from Sharon Cunningham the night before as they'd been eager to apprehend the man who fitted the description of the driver. She hadn't been a suspect. Now, though, it appeared she might be attempting to cover up for Andrei and it was her word against theirs that she had made the admissions at all. He took out a statement form and started to write his recollection of the details of the conversation, stamping the date and time at the end when it was finished on the automatic time recorder. He stared at the time. Twelve hours after the conversation had taken place, twelve hours in which he had returned home and slept, twelve hours in which any defence barrister worth his money would no doubt claim his memory was mistaken and the facts were not fresh in his mind. Shit.

He needed to speak to his boss and get some advice about the case. He didn't want to fuck it up for Matt or his family. He'd promised to do his best and that was exactly what he would do. The only problem would be whether his best would be good enough.

By 2.55 p.m. he was ready and waiting at Wimbledon police station. He'd sought advice from his boss and he'd sought advice from the CID. He liked the advice. Play them at their own game. If she wished to report the car as stolen, any person fitting the description of the driver at the time of the accident should also be treated as a suspect for the theft of her car. In addition, the conversation the night before gave him cause to suspect that her partner Andrei had been the driver.

He waited near the front office, watching through the one-way glass to see the entrance of the man whose photograph he had been shown the night before. At precisely 3 p.m. the door opened and his suspect entered, closely followed by a besuited solicitor. He was dressed smartly in casual trousers and jumper and his dark hair was freshly gelled and spiky. He stood upright with his head held high and his broad shoulders thrust back, accentuating a defined chest and narrow waist. He appeared confident and arrogant and Gary took an instant dislike to him. He would enjoy wiping the egotistical expression from his face.

Andrei Kachan held out his hand as Gary opened the door. It was ignored. He smiled towards the uniformed man but the policeman's expression was stern.

'Are you Andrei Kachan?'

'Yes, I am,' he responded, again trying a smile.

The policeman's face remained unchanged.

'Andrei Kachan, I am arresting you on suspicion of dangerous driving, failing to stop after an accident, theft of a motor vehicle and conspiracy to pervert the course of justice. The arrest is necessary for a prompt and effective investigation of the offence. You do not have to say anything, but it may harm your defence if you do not mention when questioned something you later rely on in court. Anything you do say will be given in evidence.'

He smiled again. 'No comment.'

He wasn't worried. They would have to prove it. He wasn't

about to admit to anything and now he'd had words with Sharon she wouldn't say anything more either. She'd made a mistake when she'd sent the cops round last night and she was sorry for it, but at least it had enabled him to be ready. They'd obviously got his registration number from the accident scene, but that was all. Plus, of course, a burnt-out car and an emotional admission from a mistaken woman. Even if they did get his fingerprints from the car it wouldn't be a problem, it belonged to his fiancée and he was always out in it. And now it had been destroyed, he wouldn't have to face any tricky questions about why no one else's fingerprints were to be found. No, he was just too smart for the cops. The car had been reported as being stolen and they would have to prove otherwise.

He followed the policeman through into the custody office and listened intently to the facts of the case. They were clutching at straws. It was a formality and he would be released when they'd done their worst, just as his solicitor had intimated he would.

He listened to the custody sergeant.

'You have the right to have someone informed of your arrest. You have the right to speak to a solicitor. You have the right to see a copy of the codes of practice. You can do any of these things now or if you do not wish to do so now you can do them at any time you are here.'

A police doctor was called to examine him to check for any injuries and ensure he was fit to be interviewed and detained.

He smiled at the doctor when no injuries were logged.

He smiled when he was informed he wasn't to have blood taken from him to check for any residual alcohol, as it was now deemed to be too late.

He smiled at the policeman and his partner when his rights and caution were read out at the start of the interview. This was what he liked about this country. He had so many rights.

By the time his interview was concluded he'd exercised his right to consult with his solicitor and he'd exercised his right to silence.

As he walked from the interview room, a smug smile plastered across his face, he was looking forward to the right of freedom and the right to a family life during the forthcoming

Christmas festivities. He would soon undoubtedly be receiving all the rights he was due.

Sharon Cunningham was not arrogant when she attended. She was petrified. She had never been in trouble with the police before and hated to be in this situation, but Andrei had drilled into her the script, and she needed him and loved him. She loved him more than anything else and was frightened as much for the consequences for him, as for anything that might happen to her. She was fearful that he would get sent to prison, but even worse that he might be deported back to Russia afterwards. If he was sent back to his own country, she would lose him for ever. She couldn't risk that happening.

Andrei was the love of her life. He was handsome and strong, charming and attentive and they had met when life seemed to be passing her by. A disastrous marriage when she was too young had put her off remarrying, but when she was thirty, this swarthy, dark-haired Russian had walked into the gym where she worked and swept her off her feet. He was the type of man she had always dreamed of. She was addicted to him, his toned and muscular body, his ready smile, his endearing accent. He had promised they would marry and have children and she had clung fast to this belief, even though four years had passed and there had been, until this morning, no sign of a ring or a baby. Now though, she was absolutely ready and it was likely to become a reality.

She reminded herself of the morning as she steeled herself to enter the police station. Andrei had been so gentle as he'd taken her in his arms and held her close, so full of remorse as he'd apologized for his rough words and the way he'd left her to deal with the police the night before, so sincere as he'd dropped to one knee and asked her to marry him. He'd even cried tears of regret for his actions and she'd wiped them away and cradled his head to her breasts. She'd been sorry too for what she'd told the police, but he was willing to forgive her. They made love and it was so full of emotion and passion that she couldn't bear to be parted when finally he held the phone out for her to use. He'd told her what to say to the police officer and she was happy to say it, even though she was now petrified at the possible consequences. He'd convinced her that he had everything under control, that their deception could not be proved, and she believed every word he said. She loved him more than she thought humanly possible and she couldn't wait to become his bride.

She pushed the memory to the back of her mind, controlled her expression and walked towards the police station entrance with the solicitor Andrei had organized for her. Her hands were shaking and she felt sick but she was determined to carry this through. *Say nothing other than what I told you*, Andrei had said and she would do as she was told.

PC Fellowes was awaiting her arrival. His eyes were cold. He knew she was lying, she could see it in his face. He was treating her correctly but with none of the compassion he had shown when she had broken down in front of him the previous night. She knew he was disgusted at her change of heart and she could feel his contempt in every word and action.

She nearly cracked when he told her she was under arrest for conspiracy to pervert the course of justice. Her legs felt weak and her head started to swim but she breathed deeply and held her stance. She wanted to run when she was taken through to the custody office and the facts of the case were spelt out. She felt her privacy violated when a female police officer felt in her pockets and round her body and listed every item, even those of a personal nature, from her handbag. She felt intimidated in the compact interview room with the same two uniformed police officers interrogating her, their eyes scrutinizing her every word and expression, their disbelief and incredulity at her answers palpable.

She stuck to the script though. The car was stolen. Andrei had not been out in it the evening before. She knew nothing about an accident. The rest she declined to answer, making no comment to each and every question.

As she walked from the police station a few hours later the Christmas Eve celebrations were in full swing all around her. Arrangements had been made for her to meet up with Andrei and a group of friends to celebrate the festivities, but she was not in the mood to participate. The interview had been harder than she'd expected and she felt drained. Naively she'd believed PC Fellowes would stop questioning her when she kept answering 'no comment' but he'd persisted, describing in detail the accident and the young victim's injuries. She'd seen him staring straight into her face, his eyes icy but with a hint of desperation, pleading for the truth. She'd averted her gaze, instead concentrating on the memory of Andrei, his words and tearful proposal. Their whole life together was lying within her grasp, and she'd reached out and seized it with little more than a passing thought for the young boy whose potential had effectively been snuffed out, in order that her own future happiness would be ensured.

# Fourteen

It was mid-morning on Christmas Day when Matt finally woke. The house was silent, unlike any Christmas he had ever known. He rolled over and realized he was alone. Jo was not there. Ben was not there. Chloe was not there, instead spending the day with her grandparents in an attempt to make her memories of Christmas Day happy. His family was torn apart and he didn't know whether the wound would ever heal. He closed his eyes and imagined what Christmas morning should have been like, the noise and laughter, the children's faces alight with anticipation and wonderment. He remembered the previous Christmas as he and Jo had lain in bed, watching the reflected sight of Ben hauling his sack of presents along the landing into Chloe's bedroom so they could share the excitement together.

He felt tears of anger pricking the back of his eyes and punched the bed in frustration. All his adult life, he had been the one to make the decisions, to influence his surroundings, to call the shots, but now he was helpless in the face of what had happened. He swung round and got to his feet, stepping wearily down the stairs towards the kitchen. All around was the debris of the season, unlit Christmas lights, stringy tinsel, wonky paper chains, lovingly licked together by Ben a couple of years ago at nursery. A Christmas tree stood tall and erect in the front room, its lower boughs loaded with the decorations that should have been spaced around the uppermost out-of-reach branches too. The children had been so proud of their handiwork; neither he nor Jo had wanted to rearrange it. Unopened presents littered the base. He bent down and picked a few of them up. They were all addressed to him or Jo. His wife had obviously taken time off from her post at Ben's bedside to ensure their children and other friends were not disappointed. He put them back down. He wouldn't be opening any of his until he had something to celebrate.

Walking into the kitchen he poured himself a glass of milk, swallowing it down and feeling the thick liquid coating his throat, taking the taste of the stale alcohol away. It had been almost five o'clock when Jo had persuaded him to return home and get some proper sleep. They had been taking it in turns to spend time at Ben's bedside or on occasional visits to Chloe. She was too young to really know what was going on and thought it all a huge adventure at her grandparents' house. They were trying to keep to her normal routine but she obviously sensed something was different, in the hushed conversations, tears and the way each of the adults clung to each other in grief and shock. She had refused to be prised from his arms when he had got up to leave the previous evening, wanting her daddy to stay with her. Christmas Eve had been spent lying next to her in her small bed, stroking her hair and soothing her tears of confusion, before finally returning to Ben's side when she slept.

When he'd finally returned home in the early hours, a glass of brandy had proved to be his most effective aid to sleep. He climbed the stairs and entered the bathroom, staring at the gaunt face that squinted back from the mirror at him. He hardly recognized himself.

By the time he'd finished showering he felt better. Fresh, clean and shaven, he hoped today would be the day when Ben finally emerged from the coma in which he was trapped. He drove to the hospital feeling a degree of optimism suffuse his body. All around were small groups of people, families walking back from church services, climbing into cars to visit relatives, rushing to parks to try out new bicycles or skateboards. United. As he passed a church, he watched briefly as its congregation spilled out from the doors, embracing and smiling. He was almost tempted to stop and say a prayer, but the urgency of getting to the hospital took away the thought as quickly as it had surfaced.

He parked his car and almost jogged across the car park to the hospital entrance, exchanging greetings with the small groups of relatives arriving to visit their own loved ones. The atmosphere was jolly, decorations and Christmas trees exuding an air of hopefulness and buoyancy. The receptionist wore a colourful paper hat and was surrounded by cards, bringing messages of thanks and good cheer. He waved towards her and continued onwards, feeling his air of optimism pinched by small waves of fear. By the time he arrived at the intensive therapy unit, there were fewer people and the decorations had petered out, replaced by the need for sterility.

He pushed the door open, suddenly petrified that Ben would be gone. But he hadn't moved. He stared across towards the corner where Ben's bed was and felt a rush of gratitude run through him. A nurse was checking his monitors and she looked up as he entered, waving cheerfully towards him.

'Happy Christmas,' she called out, and he greeted her in return as she finished her checks.

Jo sat next to Ben, holding his hand. 'Look, Daddy's here,' she said quietly.

Ben made no response. His eyes were closed and his body was still. It looked far too small for the bed and even smaller, hidden as it was among the mass of tubing and monitors to which he was attached. Matt walked over and bent down, kissing him ever so gently on his cheek. His skin was flushed and warm and alive.

'Happy Christmas, Ben.'

He turned and smiled towards Jo. 'And Happy Christmas to you, too.'

Jo stood up and they embraced, holding each other tightly as if they would fall without each other's support. They said nothing. After a few minutes, they sat down next to the bedside and stared at their young son.

'I've brought some of his presents up,' Jo said eventually. 'I thought it might help if he hears some of the noises they make. The doctors say that hearing is the last sense to go and we should talk to him, to try and bring him out of his coma.'

Matt nodded and watched as Jo pulled a large parcel from a bag and started to unwrap the present. 'Look, Ben,' she said, placing the parcel beside him. 'Look what Father Christmas has brought you.' Ben remained still. She continued un- wrapping until a large box containing a grey, shiny Dr Who dalek appeared. Pulling at the box, she finally extricated it from the metal ties that bound it and placed it on the bed next to him. Ben remained still. She took his hand and placed one of his fingers over a button, pressing it down so that it flashed and sent a robotic command in a loud voice across the ward. Ben remained still. She did it again and again. The dalek lit up and spoke, rotating its turret and exterminator as it did so. Ben remained still.

She took another present from the bag and placed it next to him. 'Look Ben, wake up and see what Granny and Grandad have bought you.' She started to undo the parcel, this time revealing a small electric guitar. 'Ben, look, you can do this. Press this button and see what happens.' He didn't move so she lifted his finger and pushed the button, sending a chorus of rock music blasting across the quiet ward.

Matt couldn't watch any more. Ben remained still and asleep. All his early optimism was dashed. He had so wanted Ben to wake and respond. His chest felt constricted and tight. It almost physically hurt. He couldn't bear seeing his little boy so silent and unmoving.

'Stop it, now,' he snapped at Jo, a little too harshly. 'Leave the other presents until he can open them himself.'

An expression of extreme pain flicked across Jo's face and she turned away quickly. He didn't want to deal with her hurt. He was hurting too much himself. He got up and left the ward for the solitude of the corridor outside.

Christmas lunch came and went without a single slice of turkey or mince pie. The only sustenance needed in the ITU came from a saline drip and feeding tube; consequently there were no cheery auxiliaries, crashing through the doors with trol- leys full of food, no semblance of Christmas Day formalities. None of the patients had TV screens, as none would have been well enough to watch them. Ben was the only child. The ward had filled overnight. Most of the other occupants were elderly, with the exception of a middle-aged man recovering from an emergency operation. A trickle of visitors came and went but only he and Jo remained.

After his insensitive words, Jo stayed quiet when he was around. He could see her speaking to Ben when he left the ward for a break, but she would fall silent when he returned. By mid-afternoon Matt's customary frustration had also returned. He paced the corridor, leaving the building occasionally for a smoke. It seemed only yesterday that he had seen his son imitating his habit on the way to school.

Pulling out his mobile phone, he tapped in Gary Fellowes' number. He hoped Gary would understand his need to be updated, even though it was Christmas Day.

The phone rang and rang and he thought it was going to revert to a recorded message when it was finally answered.

'Hi, is that Matt?' Gary's voice came questioningly across the line.

'Yeah, it is. I'm really sorry to bother you on Christmas Day. I wouldn't usually phone someone up at home, especially not on days like this. But I just had to know how you got on with Sharon and Andrei yesterday.'

'Hang on,' Gary said loudly. Matt could hear the background noise recede as he moved somewhere quieter.

'That's better,' he said. 'Couldn't hear a word you were saying over the noise of the kids. We've got all the in-laws here as well, with their lot.' He stopped abruptly. 'I'm really sorry.' He paused again. 'I didn't think. How's your boy? Is he any better?'

'He's OK. He's still hanging in there. Not the best Christmas I've ever had though.' He let out a small bitter laugh. 'Did you manage to catch up with Andrei?'

'Well, yes we did. In fact he turned up to speak to us, with his solicitor in tow. Not that he said much. I checked with my boss and we conferred with CID, and he was arrested on suspicion of dangerous driving, failing to stop after an accident, theft of a motor vehicle and conspiracy to pervert the course of justice.'

'Theft of a motor vehicle and conspiracy to pervert the course of justice?'

'Yes. Before he arrived I had a phone call from Sharon. She reverted to her previous story, that the car was stolen, and denied any of the conversation she had afterwards about Andrei driving it and saying he'd had an accident.'

'But she can't do that. We all heard it.'

'I know, but did you write it down and get her to sign it?'

'No.'

'Quite, nor did I or Dave. We were all too eager to go after Andrei and try and get any drink or drugs still in his body. She's now saying that she must have misheard Andrei and that he said he was with a friend in their car and when they had an accident, it was in his friend's car, not his own.'

'What a load of bullshit. She can't do this.'

'She can and she has, I'm afraid, mate. I thought we'd still be all right, because there are three of us against one of her, but we might never even be able to use her admission as evidence because we didn't write it down at the time and get her to sign it. We've both done statements now and got them date stamped, but there's a twelve-hour delay.'

'The bitch! How could she do that?' Matt couldn't believe it. 'What did Andrei say?'

'Fuck all. He made no comment throughout the whole interview. Just sat smiling, as if nothing had happened. It's a good job you weren't there. I wanted to punch his lights out, the way he was behaving. God knows what you'd have done.'

'And Sharon? Did you get a statement from her, with her allegation all nicely recorded on it?'

'Yes, we did. She came in afterwards, with her solicitor. Because she'd changed her story twice already, CID said she should be nicked on suspicion of conspiracy to pervert. She looked as if she was going to pass out when I told her she was being arrested but she stuck to the last story in her interview and then made no comment to any other question we asked. She's a hard bitch. Even when I laid it on strong about what happened to your boy, she still didn't flinch. I don't know what the situation is with her and Andrei but I get the impression she won't change her story again.'

Matt took in this information and cursed.

'Shit! We should have cautioned her as soon as she changed her story and started to admit it was Andrei driving. All the things she said afterwards probably won't be admissible, whether or not we wrote them down and she signed them or not. She could even have been arrested at that point. Shit! Why didn't I think of that at the time? I'm a fucking detective sergeant.'

'Come on, Matt. You weren't in a fit state to make decisions

like that. The most important thing was establishing the driver
and tracking him down. She was just ancillary to the offence.
We all missed it. And anyway, it hasn't been ruled out as yet.'

'But you know the way the courts work as well as I do.
We haven't a hope in hell that we'll get that evidence through
to a jury. Sharon knows Andrei was driving the car, he knows
he was driving it and we know it, but the jury will have to
make their decision based on only half the facts, because of
having our hands permanently tied by fucking procedures.'

Gary was quiet and Matt thought for a second he had hung
up. He sighed heavily.

'Sorry, mate. It's not your fault. It's not any of our faults.
It's the way the law works, always protecting the suspect to
the detriment of the truth. It just pisses me off so much when
we're not allowed to even present all the facts. We try our
best with the resources we've got and then the lawyers get
hold of it and cross half of it out. There's more time spent
on trials within trials than there is spent on the actual trial
itself.' He stopped and closed his eyes, forcing himself to
concentrate on the facts of the case. 'What have we got so
far?'

'We've got at least a couple of witnesses at the scene who
saw the driver get out and look back. One of whom took the
registration number. We've still to check for any CCTV in the
vicinity and there's the possibility of witnesses where the car
was found burnt out. I'll be making enquiries at Andrei's work
as to the condition he was in and whether anyone remembers
seeing him with the Peugeot just prior to the accident. Now,
of course there's several other avenues, such as his alibi that
he was involved in an accident in his mate's car. If we can
get a few details about where and when the accident's supposed
to have happened, it would be nice to be able to disprove that
story.'

'What are the chances of that?'

'Not good, admittedly. If it's just a damage-only as I think
it is, it's probably not even been reported to police. We've
only got Kachan's word for it.'

'Are they coming back on bail?'

'Yeah. They've both been bailed pending further enquiries
for two weeks, but Andrei has to come in on December the
twenty-eighth for an emergency ID parade. Let's hope he gets

picked out. Your wife will be one of the witnesses who'll have
to attend.'

'I know, and she's petrified already. I don't know how good
she'll be. She says she was concentrating more on getting to
Ben than what the driver looked like. She was aware he'd
stopped and got out but didn't really get a good look at his
face.'

'She was probably in complete shock as well. Still, we'll
give it a try. You never know. Like I said before, we'll do
everything in our power to get you a conviction.'

'I know, and thanks. Sorry again for disturbing your
Christmas. I'll let you get back to your family.'

'Cheers Matt. We'll speak again soon.'

They hung up and Matt felt the anger and frustration well
up almost immediately. Gary was going back to a loving family
celebration. What was he going back to? He walked slowly
back into the hospital, climbing the stairs and watching with
a sense of gloom as the doors to the ward got closer. Pushing
them open he was aware that nothing had changed. Ben was
still in exactly the same position and Jo was still stationary
at the bedside. She looked up as he returned and tried a small
smile.

'Are you OK?' she said quietly.

'I've just spoken to Gary Fellowes. You know, the guy who's
dealing with the main accident investigation.'

She frowned.

'I thought the Accident Investigation Unit were contacting
us back when they've completed the calculations?'

'Yes they are, but they only deal with the details of actually how the accident happened, as in what speed the driver
was doing, how long before he saw Ben, did he start to brake.
That sort of stuff. Gary is the one who's pulling the whole
lot together, taking statements from witnesses and making
enquiries as to the identity of the driver.'

'Is he working today then?' She seemed surprised.

'No, I just called him at home.'

'You did what? Isn't he in the middle of his Christmas
dinner or something? It's bad enough that we're here, without
Chloe or our family, without you offloading our misery on to
him and his family.'

'He didn't mind. I asked him,' he replied easily.

'He couldn't say anything else, could he?' Jo was angry but he couldn't work out why. He'd apologized for bothering Gary and the man had said he didn't mind. And anyway, it was important.

She turned away and took Ben's hand again, tracing her finger around the shape of each of his small fingers.

'Why can't you just forget about your job for once?' she said quietly. 'It's Christmas Day. Your son's in a critical condition and you're phoning other officers at home. Why can't you concentrate on Ben for once? Talk to him. Talk to him about Christmas.'

'I can't. I don't know what to say.'

'Say anything. Tell him about what's going on all around. Tell him how much Chloe's missing him and wants him back. Tell him how you feel. Tell him that you love him. Tell him that he needs to wake up. Anything.'

She swung round, searching his face with swollen, bloodshot eyes. She'd started to cry again. 'Tell him anything. Just speak to him.'

He looked down into his wife's distraught face and felt a touch of panic.

'But I really don't know what to do. You can do it. You're good at sitting talking to him, reading stories, chatting about what he's been doing at school. I can't. I play football with him. I wrestle with him. I throw him up and down. I *do* things. I can't sit and just chat. I have to do something.'

'Well, do something then. Do anything, but do it with him, instead of running off around the streets trying to catch the culprit.'

A small part of him baulked at the accusation. She wasn't being fair.

'I'm doing what I do best, just as you're doing what you do best. You look after the kids. I go out to work. And on Thursday you're going to have to come to the station and do something that you'll find difficult, just as I find this difficult.'

'What?' she shot back quickly.

'The driver, or at least a man who we believe was the driver, has been arrested and he's going to be put in an ID parade. You're one of the only few witnesses at the scene and you'll have to see if you can identify him.'

'I can't. I didn't see the driver well enough and it was dark.'

'But you've got to try.'

'I can't. There's no point. And anyway, I need to stay with Ben.'

'And I need to get justice for him. Can't you see that? I want him to be better, just as much as you. I wish it had never happened, just as much as you. But I also need to see the man who did this locked away. How could he just walk away and leave our son lying on the road, dead as far as he was concerned?'

She sniffed loudly, wiping at the tears that were falling freely down her cheeks. 'I still can't do it,' she pleaded. 'Don't make me leave Ben.'

'If no one tries to identify him, he'll get away with it. Do you want to see that happen?'

'No I don't, but at the moment the most important thing is Ben. He needs me. I'm the one who looks after him all the time.'

Matt felt his mind snap at her summary dismissal of his role. He turned towards her, his voice angry but controlled.

'It's a shame you didn't look after him properly the other day then, isn't it? It's a shame you didn't stop him running out in front of the car, isn't it? That's why you can't leave him now. That's why you keep going on at me. Because you let it happen! Because you feel guilty! Because it's your fault!'

The words were out before he could stop them. He saw the pain sweep across her brow, the horror dull her eyes and he heard the sob that exploded from her throat into the stillness of the ward. Her hand shot up to her mouth. He watched in horror, recoiling as the enormity of the words he'd spat at her sunk in. He hadn't meant to say it. He didn't really believe it, but in the absence of the driver he needed someone to blame. And he'd not just said the words, he'd hurled them at her in anger. He knew without a shadow of doubt that those words, said as they were, would never be forgotten. They were incapable of being retracted.

'I'm sorry. I didn't mean to say that,' he stuttered, but it was no use. The harm was done.

When Jo turned to face him, her eyes were calm again. Her voice was calm too.

'Don't you think I don't know it's my fault? Don't you

think I don't blame myself for what happened? For the last two nights I've tried to sleep, knowing I should have been holding his hand and that it's my entire fault, but every time I try to sleep, all I can see is his little body as it's tossed up on to the car bonnet, his arms and legs flailing about as he flies through the air. And all I can hear is the thud as he lands in a crumpled heap on the concrete, while I scream.' She lowered her head so she wasn't looking at him.

'So you don't need to tell me. I know and I'm going to have to live with it.'

He reached out and put a hand on her shoulder. She winced and shrugged it away.

'Don't touch me, Matt. Leave me alone. I don't need your blame. I've enough of my own.'

There was nothing more he could do or say, so he turned and started walking. He wanted so much to take her in his arms, to hold her and tell her he didn't blame her, but he knew she wouldn't believe him.

He turned round and saw Jo, her head still bowed in the same position, and he wished with all his heart he could turn the clock back and erase the words he'd said.

But it was done now, and he knew that whatever length of time he had kept the thought suppressed it would finally have come out. However hard he'd rationalized it, however hard he'd told himself that he would have done exactly the same thing, a small part of him did blame Jo, and the niggling criticism would not go away. If only she'd kept hold of him, if only she'd kept control of his impulsiveness, it would never have happened.

He didn't know where to go but he couldn't go home to an empty house full of memories. Although it was still only late afternoon the sky was dark and heavy. His driving was unthinking and his eyes were unseeing as he passed through the empty streets. The knowledge that the houses he passed were full of families, united in their excesses, only served to deepen the suffocating weight that had settled on his shoulders. For a moment he thought of Jake and wondered how his Christmas Day was going. His family too was split, even more terminally than his own, and the boy had been given no idea when or if he would see them again.

His vehicle automatically took him to Brookley Street. Two yellow witness boards were up on either side of where Ben had lain. 'An incident occurred here on Saturday 23rd December. Did you witness it? Did you see what happened?' Can you provide the evidence to nail the bastard, Matt continued to himself. Can you help me put the lying, sneering bastard behind bars where he belongs?

He put the car back in gear and pulled away, his mind going over and over the conversations of the last few hours. A short drive later and his eyes were searching for street names. Martell Street, SE1 came into view and he drove slowly along a shabby, potholed road until he saw Clonsdyke House, looming up to his right. He followed the road further into the estate until he found the entry spur to the car park. The exact spot where the car had been burnt out wasn't difficult to find. Blackened sediment and singed concrete highlighted where it had been abandoned. He switched his lights up to full beam and got out. There was no one around, no sound of conversation from any of the nearby walkways.

The ashes appeared grey in the glare of his headlights and he bent down, sifting through the remnants with his bare hands, searching for anything that might have been missed, anything that might somehow point a finger at Andrei Kachan. There was nothing to be found. He picked up a small piece of contorted plastic and standing up, threw it hard against a wall, watching as it ricocheted innocently down on to the ground. Tears of injustice pricked his eyes again and the tightly controlled emotion of the day finally found a release. He shrunk down on to his knees and sobbed hard, smearing dirty hands over wet cheeks, kneeling among the debris, not caring.

'Are you all right, man?' he heard a voice shout. 'Hey, man. You ill or something?'

The sound came from up above and he looked round, hazily focusing on the person who'd spoken.

'I'm all right,' he returned, wiping his eyes fiercely and feeling both embarrassment and irritation that he had been disturbed.

'You don't look all right to me,' the man called down again. 'Is you something to do with that car that got burnt the other day?'

'That car knocked my boy down. I've been in the hospital

all day with him and needed to get out. Thought I'd come and see if there was anything left here.' He didn't know why he was saying so much to a total stranger but the unexpected voice of concern was drawing it from him. The voice belonged to the epitome of an elderly Caribbean gentleman. He wore a hat, tilted to one side at a jaunty angle, and spoke with a deep Jamaican drawl. His face was pitted, with deep laughter lines showing between the sides of his smiling eyes and his receding grey hair.

'That's right bad, that is! Have they caught the white guy who torched it yet?'

'How do you know it was a white guy?' His attention was immediate.

'Because I saw him. His mate called up to me for a light, but I knew they was up to no good. Didn't want to get involved with nothing of that sort.'

'Did you see the driver?'

'Yes, sir. I saw him pull up. He almost fell out of the seat. He looked mighty drunk to me. He was the one who torched it. He was flicking at a lighter and rolling up some paper. I heard him say something like "this baby's gonna burn".'

'Have you told the police?'

'No, I ain't. Like I said, I don't really want to get involved with those sort. They all looked wrong'uns to me.'

'If I told you that you might be the one person who got a really good look at the driver, would you help? You might be the only witness able to identify him.'

The man frowned, twisting thoughtfully at the edges of his moustache. 'I don't rightly know if I ought. Never got involved like that before.'

Matt was desperate. 'My boy was knocked flying by the driver who was on the wrong side of the road. It's lucky he's still alive but he only just survived. He's still in a coma. The driver just drove off and got his girlfriend to report the car as stolen afterwards. The police don't think it was, but it's proving it, otherwise the driver will get away with it. Please, will you help?'

The old man paused. 'Did the police find the bit he threw away?'

'What bit?'

'I don't know exactly what it was but when I first saw the

car, the driver was pulling at something around the steering wheel. Fell over when it finally came away. He threw it up on top of that building over there.' He pointed to the flat roof of a bin shed underneath a concrete walkway. Matt could see nothing obvious but his curiosity was fired.

'This one?' he enquired, walking swiftly towards it. He hauled himself up on to the top of a wheelie bin and peered into the gloom. A thick layer of dirt lay across the roof felt, with several cans and bottles buried in the grime. It was protected from the weather, nestled in front of a high wall and with a concrete walkway overhead. A piece of plastic was immediately obvious, still relatively clean and bright. Pulling a handkerchief from his pocket he reached over and lifted it carefully from its resting place. He looked down at it, trying to place what it might be, and then it dawned on him in a sudden rush of clarity. It was the ignition cowling, which had obviously been wrenched off in an effort to make it appear that the car had been stolen. Its underside was smooth and shiny and would be a good surface from which to obtain fingerprints. If it could be proved to have come from the suspect vehicle and Andrei's fingerprints were on it, it would be excellent evidence that he had been the driver and was attempting to cover his tracks.

He jumped back down carrying the important piece of interior, and held it up towards the old man.

'Is that what you saw the driver throw?' he called up.

'Yes, sir. It is.' He paused momentarily before continuing. 'And I'd be happy to help you in any way I can.'

Matt couldn't believe his ears. He placed the crucial piece of plastic carefully on a carrier bag in the rear of his car and raced up the stairwell to the old man, shaking his hand gratefully.

'Thank you so much. And Happy Christmas to you.' He smiled, keeping hold of the gnarled old hand.

The old Jamaican smiled broadly and slapped him affably across the shoulder blades. 'Only too glad to be of assistance,' he chuckled back. 'It's Christmas Day! How could I refuse?'

# Fifteen

By the time 28th December arrived Matt's nervousness had grown. He was at the hospital, sitting by his motionless son, running through the activities of the day ahead. Andrei was due back for the ID parade and he was desperate that the Russian should be picked out. The old Jamaican had kept his promise. His name was Beres Morgan and he had lived on the same estate from the time he'd arrived in England in the 1960s. He was to attend, along with several others who had been near the scene of the accident or witnessed the reckless way in which the vehicle had been driven just prior to it.

Jo was also one of those attending, having been persuaded by Gary Fellowes. She didn't want to go and had remonstrated with him, but Gary had succeeded where Matt himself had failed. It was easier to challenge your husband than an independent officer. He and Jo had spoken little since their argument on Christmas Day and the atmosphere between them was tense. They sat opposite each other with Ben between them, both locked in their own thoughts. They were trapped in their opposing positions and even when their eyes met accidentally, each would avert their gaze, unable to even look at the other. He risked a glance at Jo. Her face was a mask, set hard when he spoke, the words she uttered limited to a bare minimum. The only time her expression softened was when she gazed down at Ben.

He knew he was to blame for the damage, that he shouldn't have said what he had, but he didn't know how to talk to her now, whether she would even listen. He ached to hold her and be held, to grieve together, to support each other, to return to how it had always been.

Jo bent down and picked up her bag, glancing over towards him as she stood.

'I suppose I'd better be going then, although I don't see the point. I'll be back as soon as I can.'

She turned without waiting for an answer or offering a kiss, and was gone. Matt watched her slim figure as she walked away and saw the same pain etched deep within her eyes as she turned one last time to check her son.

In the past five days their life had been turned upside down. Ben was still the same. They just had to wait. For however long it would take. Wait to see if he opened his eyes again, if he would ever walk again or chat to them like he always used to, play football, run around, do all the things he always had.

The doctors also had to wait. Ben's brain was still functioning, but to what extent? They would not be able to say whether it had been damaged beyond repair until he roused. His coma was deep, apparently severe. The doctors had explained the Glasgow Coma Scale, a way of measuring the eye, verbal and motor responses and grading the coma accordingly. But everything depended on the severity of the original injury; they were at pains to explain that a severe coma did not necessarily mean Ben's chances of recovery were worse. It wasn't a precise measurement, it was merely an indication, and every case was different.

Ben's condition hadn't really changed but again this was apparently not unusual. Comas, he was told, normally lasted between a few days and a few weeks. After that time the patient would either gradually emerge and start the process of recovery, or would slide into a persistent vegetative state, a state they could stay in for years.

He bent over and put his mouth to his son's sleeping face, kissing each eyelid and taking in his scent.

'Come on, buddy. Wake up. You've been asleep far too long.'

He stared at the motionless face, willing the slightest acknowledgement, but Ben's eyes remained closed. He shut his own, leaning his head in as close as he could, and felt the warm tranquillity of the room take him.

He was still in this position three hours later when Jo returned. She sat down opposite and the scraping of her chair woke him. He sat up smartly, noting immediately the frown on her face.

'That was a waste of time,' she said curtly. 'Have you been talking to Ben?'

He could tell she knew the answer and was just asking to make his guilt more acute. He ignored the question.

'How did it go then?'

'Like I said it would. It was a complete waste of time.'

'Were you able to recognize the driver?'

'No. I said I wouldn't be able to right from the start and I couldn't. I don't know why you all insisted on dragging me though it.'

'Because we have to try! Did any of the others pick him out?'

'I don't know, I didn't ask.'

Matt was incredulous and it showed. He stood up.

'Don't you want the driver caught for this?'

Jo looked away and took Ben's hand, speaking quietly and evenly.

'You know I do, but it's not my priority.'

'And what do you mean by that?'

His voice was raised and he could see heads turned in their direction. Jo didn't look up. He lowered his voice. 'If you think my priority is misplaced, you're wrong. It's not. I would give my own life if it would make Ben better and you know that. I would do anything for him, anything.' He turned away. 'I don't know what's got into you, Jo. I thought we worked together, I thought we were a team and we believed the same things were important, but you've shut me out. I can't do anything right.' He took a step towards the door. 'I can't do anything at the moment to help Ben, so until I can I'm going to make sure the bastard who did this to him doesn't get away with it. If that's all right with you?'

He didn't stop to wait for her answer.

Denise Clarkson breathed in the fresh air. It was good to get away from the claustrophobic, threatening atmosphere of the prison, even if it was to be taken straight to a police station.

Prison life was a nightmare. She shook violently at the thought of her first night, ten days ago, cocooned in a cell with another inmate, intent on finding out the details of the allegation she faced. She had been cagey about the specifics until the other woman – a sunken-cheeked crack addict who went by the name 'Killer' – had pushed her up against a wall and threatened to tell everyone she was a child murderer. Without further hesitation she had confided all about her relationship with Lee, his abuse, his violence, his anger which had culminated in the death of her beautiful three-year-old boy. Her cellmate had rallied to her support then, satisfied in the knowledge that Denise was, like herself, a broken, abused woman. They had plotted Lee's punishment each evening and she had slept each night, apprehensive that the other cons would receive word from a partner, banged up with Lee, that he was saying exactly the same thing about her. It was imperative she be believed, for her own safety. Prisoners weren't immune from getting cut or sliced as a means of retribution by their perversely moralistic fellow inmates.

When she had received word that she was to be returned to the police station to be questioned about the previous neglect and abuse of her children, she had been delighted. Included in the trip was a chance to meet up with Jake, who'd apparently been pleading to be able to see her. DCs Tom Berwick and Alison Richards had promised her a visit during their journey and she was eagerly looking forward to seeing her boy again, even though it would only be a short, supervised meeting.

She watched the heavy prison gates swing shut behind her and grinned with anticipation. The street ahead was bland and grey but despite its appearance, it brought to her a sense of freedom and release.

'How long will I get with Jake?' she asked eagerly.

Tom Berwick was squeezed into the vehicle beside her, his huge frame filling the remaining space on the back seat.

'Not very long, I'm afraid. Fifteen minutes at the most. We've got a lot to get through and Jake will have to go on to school.'

'I can't wait to see him. I've missed him so much. Does he know I'm coming?'

'Yes, and I'm told he's very excited too about seeing you.'

She relaxed back into the seat and smiled again, concentrating on the passing scenery and straining to catch a glimpse of familiar streets or faces. There was so much to say to Jake. She just hoped she would get the chance of a few minutes alone with him. A few precious moments to say the words she didn't want outsiders to hear, words of love and stoicism and advice.

They passed a park with a large boating lake.

'We're nearly there now. The house is just around the corner.'

Her heart was pounding as they pulled into the driveway of a large house. The door opened and she saw Jake standing on the top step, waving in her direction. As her car door was held open, he came running towards her, burying his head in her shoulder as she got out. She lifted her arms and swung them over his head, the handcuffs preventing any easy movement, and held him close. Tears ran down both their faces as they eventually pulled away.

They were escorted into a small room and sat down side by side on a sofa. It was secluded and warm, with only a small window in the corner, the locks of which had been bolted down. Tom was to stay with them as they spoke while Alison spoke with Tyrone, but she didn't care. She was just glad to be with Jake. He'd changed since he'd been there, grown up and filled out, and he seemed happy. A pang of jealousy and regret shot through her.

'I'm sorry I've let you down, Jakey. I didn't think this would happen. I miss you so bad. You know Mummy loves you, don't you? You're my special boy and I'd do anything for you, you know that?'

Jake nodded back, putting a hand on her knee and snuggling in close.

They chatted about how their Christmas had been, what they'd been doing, how they missed each other. She was just glad to be close to him. It was different with him. She felt complete.

She heard a scream from outside the door. It was a high-pitched, angry scream, followed by the sound of smashing glass. More voices could be heard, trying to placate the complainant. Another smash and the voices became louder in response. The cries became more desperate, followed by cursing. She heard a voice say, 'Watch it, she's got a knife!' followed by further crashing and screaming. Tom Berwick glanced out of the door and swore. She saw him glance at the bolted window and back to her.

'Don't move,' he instructed. 'I'll be back in a moment.'

The door shut behind him and she could hear him taking charge.

She turned to face Jake.

'Have you said anything about what happened?' she asked urgently.

'Just that Ryan went quiet when Lee went into the room. I haven't actually said that he did it.'

'And you mustn't. I've had some letters from Lee and I'm frightened of what he'll do to us if we bubble him up proper, like. He's threatened to come after us or send someone else to get us. You know what he's like. We'll never be safe. He won't rest until he's tracked us down and I can't risk it.'

As Matt walked into his office, he saw the looks of surprise.

'What's up, you lot? You look like you've seen a ghost.'

Barry Tate stood up. 'We weren't expecting to see you, Sarge. We heard what happened to your boy. We were told you'd be off for a while. How is he?'

'He's stable at the moment, thanks,' he said defensively. 'There's not much we can do until he comes out of the coma. The driver was up on an ID parade today, so I thought I'd pop in and find out what happened and catch up on anything important with the Clarkson job.'

'There's not much happening really. It's quite quiet. Tom and Alison have been out and brought Denise Clarkson back in for a further interview about Ryan's previous injuries. The CPS wants to see what she has to say before deciding on any further charges of neglect or assault.'

'Has she been interviewed yet?'

'Not that I know of. She was being allowed a visit to see Jake on the way back.'

'Supervised, I hope?'

'Of course.'

'I presume Jake will be re-interviewed as well then, bearing in mind he offered to say what really happened if he got a visit from his mum?'

'Yes, I think that's the plan. But we were having to wait, because he said he'd only speak to you and we weren't sure when you'd be back.'

'I don't know what's happening myself at the moment. Obviously Ben's my priority but while nothing's changing much on that front I'd like to speak to them both. Where's Denise being taken?'

'They're bringing her back to Brixton. She should be there in about half an hour.'

He checked his watch. 'Just time to find out what happened on the ID parade then. Tell Tom or Alison I'll help with the interview.'

He walked briskly through to his own office. Speaking about Ben to people who cared had been more difficult than he thought and he needed some space. He picked up the phone and dialled Gary Fellowes' number.

'Hi, Matt. How're you doing?'

'I'm fine. Just ringing to find out the news on the ID parade. How's it gone?'

'I was expecting a phone call. Andrei was getting a bit cocky until Beres Morgan came up trumps and ID'd him straight away. None of the other witnesses from the actual accident scene were able to, though.'

'That's a shame. We can put him in the car soon afterwards, but not quite at the time. Do you think the CPS will go for it?'

'I don't know. The car is registered to his girlfriend, there's only a short distance between where the accident happened and where the car was found burnt out, and now we can say he was definitely the man who was seen driving into the car park. It'll help if the fingerprints on the ignition cowling come back to him but I couldn't say at the moment. You know how difficult the CPS are. I'm pretty sure they won't allow Sharon's confession to be used, so it's still touch and go. Thank goodness you were there just when Morgan went by, or else we'd stand no chance. That was a real stroke of luck.'

'I know. I couldn't believe it myself. Anyway Gary, thanks for all your work so far. When are we likely to hear back from the lab about the fingerprints? And remind me when Andrei and Sharon are due back?'

'We should get the result of the prints before their return date and they're due to be back on the second of January.'

'Cheers, Gary.'

He hung up with a faint sense of optimism. Things were just beginning to swing in their direction. Maybe they would have enough, but in order to be sure they would still have to wait and see if the forensics came back.

There was a knock on the door and Tom poked his head in.

'Matt, I came straight here after dropping Denise off at

Brixton. How are you and how's Ben? We've all been so worried.'

Matt looked across at his oldest friend and his throat constricted. He swallowed hard, forcing back the lump that was threatening to overwhelm him.

'Not so good.'

Tom was at his side in a moment. 'Try not to worry, mate,' he said, throwing his arm across Matt's shoulder. 'Ben's strong. He's a fighter. I'm sure he'll pull through. How's Jo coping?'

'Not so good either. We had a row about what happened and I said things I shouldn't have. Now we're not talking. We just sit on either side of him in silence. It's awful.' His voice cracked. 'I don't know what to do.'

He pulled away, turning his back on his friend so he couldn't see the pain.

Tom was quiet. 'It'll work out all right in the end, mate. I'm sure it will. Why don't we go out for a drink and you can tell me exactly what's going on.'

Matt nodded. 'I could do with one. It's pretty damn lonely out there at the moment.' He closed his eyes and bit on his lip, pushing the emptiness away. 'Right, let's go and see what Denise has to say.'

'You're in no fit state, mate. Leave it to me. Alison and I will handle it.'

'No. I'll do it. I want to.'

He turned back. He could see that Tom had recognized his determined expression and knew he meant it. He'd sat on his own for too long trying to deal with his emotions. Now, for a short time, he was back where he belonged, in the bosom of his team, doing what he did best. It would allow him a few hours, at least, to feel useful and needed.

Denise Clarkson was pensive when she was brought through. She couldn't have planned the visit with Jake better. The fortuitous background disruption had allowed her several precious minutes to speak properly to him. She knew now exactly what had to be done and she didn't want anyone getting in the way. A volunteer member of the public had been brought in to act as an appropriate adult and that was enough. No one else was required. She wanted to get on with it.

'Are you sure you don't want a solicitor with you?' DS Arnold was saying.

'No. I don't.'

She looked up at him. She liked him and she liked the woman too, Alison. They'd been together when she'd been interviewed in the first place. Tom Berwick was there as well, sat in the corner. She liked him too for allowing her time with Jake.

'Would you like to give me a reason why you don't want a solicitor?' Matt Arnold asked. 'You don't have to give a reason if you don't want to.'

'Because I don't want them getting in the way. I've got things I need to say to you and I don't want them telling me to stop talking.'

Matt Arnold looked up and she caught the glimmer of curiosity that crossed his face.

'I have to remind you that you're still under caution. You know what that means, don't you? Anything you say may be given in evidence.' He said the words slowly and carefully.

She understood completely what he was getting at. He wanted to make sure she was absolutely clear, that he could use whatever it was she might say to her advantage or disadvantage.

'I know what that means,' she replied, equally calmly and slowly.

'I want to ask you about some of the previous injuries that were found on Ryan's body when he was examined. What can you tell me about those?'

'Ryan was always falling over and running into things. He was a three-year-old boy, that's what they do. I never did nothing to hurt him before that night, I swear on my mother's life.'

'What do you mean by "before that night"?'

She had to admit he was good. She'd thrown the comment in on purpose to see if he picked it up and he had, straight away.

'I mean. It was me that killed Ryan. I didn't mean to. It was an accident.'

Matt Arnold stared at her. This time she'd stunned him, she could see it. He wasn't expecting her to say that.

'You're saying that it was you who killed Ryan?'

She wiped at her eyes. 'Yes, it was me. When Lee went upstairs with him, I knew he was going to hurt him. It's him you need to ask about the injuries on his body. He'd started knocking him about, getting much too rough. Sometimes he'd really hurt him, but I didn't know what to do without him taking it out on me or Jake. Anyway, that night, I heard him shouting at Ryan and Ryan was crying and wouldn't stop. I followed him up the stairs and saw him slamming the door shut and locking it. He was in a right temper. He went to the toilet so I thought I would try and stop Ryan crying, 'cause I knew otherwise he would have got hurt real bad.

'He had grazes down his back where Lee had dragged him and I couldn't stop him crying, so I decided to try our special little game that usually makes him laugh. When he has his Spider-Man outfit on, I swing him round and pretend he's flying. He loves it normally.'

She looked up, lifting her arms to show the two policemen how it was done.

'I could hear Lee swearing in the toilet and Ryan wouldn't stop crying and I got a bit desperate. I swung him round even faster and then I heard the toilet flushing. I turned round to see if Lee was coming and lost my balance a bit and stumbled forward. Anyway Ryan's head hit the wall. It was awful. It made a horrible cracking noise and then he went all limp. Lee was still banging around in the toilet and I panicked. I thought he would lay into me for going into the room when he'd locked it. I laid Ryan down on his bed and pulled the duvet up round his neck to make it look as if he was sleeping. Then I left the room. I meant to come back and check on him, I really did.'

She started to cry and sniffed loudly.

'I bumped into Lee on the stairs and he went for me, just like I thought he would. He'd been back into Ryan's bedroom but he'd come out and locked it again. Everything else is like I already told you. He made me go downstairs with him and later on he made me have sex with him, even though I didn't really want to. I was going to go in and check Ryan later but I couldn't. I was too scared. Lee would have gone mad and put me in hospital or something.

'As soon as I could in the morning I did check him. That's when I discovered he was all cold. That's when I phoned the ambulance.'

She looked up through tear-stained eyes. 'I didn't mean to kill him. I really didn't. I just wanted to save him from getting beaten. I loved him to bits, I really did. It was an accident.'

The three police officers were staring at her silently.

'Why didn't you tell us this before?' Matt Arnold said eventually.

'Because I was too scared of what would happen to me. Because I knew Jake would be taken away from me. Because I was frightened of going to prison. I didn't mean to do it. It was an accident.'

She repeated the words.

'And you tried to put the blame for Ryan's death on Lee?'

'Well, it is his fault. If he didn't beat up on us all it would never have happened. He's a vicious bastard and he deserves everything he gets. He's made our lives hell with his drinking and violence. I'm frightened of him and the kids are frightened of him. If he doesn't get exactly what he wants, he'll take it out on everyone, except his own kids of course. He don't hit them, just me and mine. I thought Ryan might escape it as he's Lee's kid, but he's also mine and anything or anyone to do with me suffers.'

'Why have you stayed with him for so long?'

'Because he'd hunt us down and kill us. He's already said that. I'm frightened of what he could do to us.'

She started to cry again, lifting trembling fingers up to her face to wipe at the tears. Her body started to shiver and she shuddered violently.

'I'm going to terminate the interview now to allow you to recover and get legal advice again, if you want it, about what you've just said to us.'

She nodded and allowed the tears to flow once more. She'd said what was required and now she just had to wait. She just hoped it wouldn't take too long.

Matt didn't like what he'd just heard. He closed the door to his office after Tom and Alison had entered and paced across to the window.

'That's the biggest load of bullshit I've heard for a long time. It just doesn't ring true. She's got time to go into Ryan's room, try to stop him crying and swing him round while Lee's in the toilet. Then she just happens to stumble and hits his head against the wall. And then, even though she's in a panic, she's able to calm down sufficiently and have the foresight to lay him down on the bed and cover him up. Most mothers I know would be in one hell of a state if they'd just done that to their kid accidentally.'

'I agree.' Alison nodded. 'Plus both she and Jake said Ryan was still crying when Lee went back into the bedroom and only went quiet while he was in there. She might be changing her story but Jake's account seems to back it up. I wonder why she's changed it though.'

'Did she give any clues that she was going to drop something like this on us when you were with her earlier?'

'No, not at all.' Tom shook his head. 'When we picked her up she was excited at the chance to see Jake. She certainly didn't give anything away about what she was likely to say. She did seem quieter when we were driving away from the home, but I presumed it was just because she was upset at having to leave him. They do seem very close, those two.'

'And they were supervised?'

Tom paused briefly. 'Yes, I was with them.'

'Then I don't know what's happened, but we need to find out. Something's spooked her. It just seems too out of character. She's weak, too much of a victim.'

'Will we be interviewing her again today?'

'Yeah, we sure will. I'll speak to the custody officer and the CPS and let them know what's happened. It may well be that she'll have to be rearrested for murder, based on the new evidence of what she's now said. I'd like to speak to her again though, and try to find out what's caused this change of heart. There's something not right about it and I mean to find out what it is.'

# Sixteen

The custody area at Brixton police station was relatively quiet when Matt, Tom and Alison re-entered. The week between Christmas and New Year saw a lull in the number of prisoners brought in for drink-related offences and by late afternoon most of the shoplifters from the sales had been processed. The custody officer was busy writing up their details.

Denise Clarkson was in her cell. Matt waved towards the sergeant and walked towards it, peering through the spyhole. She was lying prone on the plastic mattress, her eyes closed, seemingly asleep. She certainly didn't appear bothered about the implications of what she had just admitted.

He returned to the reception area.

'Sarge,' he said, waiting for the young sergeant to lift his head from his work. 'Did you book Denise Clarkson in when she first arrived?'

'Yes, I did. Why?'

'Did she say anything strange or make any comments at all about her case?'

'No, not that I recall. She hardly said a word, other than answering what I asked.'

'And how did she seem to you?'

'Fine. Very calm and collected really, considering what she was brought in for.'

'I've got to rearrest her for murder. She admitted in interview to killing her young son. I've spoken to the CPS about it. After she's been questioned further, the chances are she'll be charged with murder and the charge of allowing the death of a child will be dropped when she gets to court.'

The custody sergeant nodded.

'By the way, did she have much with her?'

'I think she had a handbag with a few bits. You can have a look on the property list if you want to.'

He scrolled down to the appropriate page on the custody computer where the entire list of each prisoner's property was noted.

Nothing stood out. A couple of lighters, a purse with a few random cards and a few coppers, a box of cigarettes, cosmetics and correspondence was all there was. He sauntered through to the cabinet where the property was kept and found her bag, checking off the items in the bag against the list. He was interested to see what the items of correspondence were. Peering through the plastic, he could just make out the shape of several envelopes. They were addressed to Denise Clarkson at Holloway Prison and the top one was written in very neat handwriting. He picked up the bag and walked back to the custody area.

'Sarge, I'm going to open this bag and check out the letters. I'll re-bag them when I've finished.'

He tore into the bag and pulled the letters out. There were three of them, bound together with an elastic band. The first was from Jake. He opened it up and read it before passing it to Tom. The words were full of longing but nothing much more of substance. He missed her and looked forward to the time they could be together. A picture of the two of them together was drawn at the bottom of the page and labelled with the words 'Mummy and me', and there were several lines of crosses underneath.

'Poor little blighter!' he commented under his breath.

The other two were from a female whose name he didn't recognize. Reading the first, she appeared to know Denise from the past but predominantly was friendly with Lee. It spoke of how they should get together at Denise's place and that she knew where that was. It spoke of mundane things, of how Christmas had been and how she'd been to visit Lee. It appeared to be a letter from an old friend.

He opened the third letter and started to read it. That too was in the same vein. Normal everyday goings-on were related, names from the past and their current whereabouts mentioned. He was about to give up and repackage the letters when his brain scanned though a paragraph inserted between the chat. He nearly missed it. He reread it, astonished.

*I went to visit Lee the other day and he says to tell you*
*that you'd better take the rap for this, or else he will*
*make sure you regret it. If he isn't able to, he has plenty*
*of friends willing to help. Wherever you and your brat*
*son go, he or his mates will find you.*

The letter then continued in its chatty way and was signed at
the end. *Hoping you make the right decision. Look forward*
*to visiting!!! Brenda.* There was no address shown.

He couldn't believe what he was reading.

'Tom, Alison, look at this,' he said, pointing at the paragraph. 'How the hell was this allowed to get through? I thought
all the letters were supposed to be vetted before they were
allowed in. I think we've just found the reason why Denise
has changed her story.'

Matt sealed both letters in separate property bags and filled
out the forms ready to send them off for urgent DNA examination immediately after the next interview concluded.

'I'll be getting in touch with the prison authorities to find
out how this could have got through,' he muttered to them
both. 'This slip-up could change the whole outcome of the
murder investigation. When I've gone later I want you to
search all our records and see if you can find any link between
Lee and a woman called Brenda. It would be nice to be able
to identify her and get her arrested for witness intimidation
or perverting the course of justice.'

Tom and Alison both nodded in unison.

'What about Lee?' Tom asked. 'Will he need to be arrested
for that too?'

'Is Lee coming back to be questioned about the previous
injuries to Ryan as well?'

'Yes, I've got him pencilled in for the next couple of days.
I don't know exactly when as yet though. It's a difficult time
of year to get anything done. Half the prison staff are off on
leave and there's not too many of us around either. When I
do go and dig him out I'll see if I can find out the names of
any visitors that he's had.'

'Good idea. He can be asked about the threats but he'll no
doubt deny any knowledge of them and put all of the blame on
this Brenda, and at the moment all we've got is what she's said.
If we can't identify her and speak to her it'll be a non-starter,

but we'll see what we can get from the visitor's log and DNA. They might even have CCTV from the prison. Lee seems to be willing to do anything to get himself off this and I'd hate to see the charges against him dropped. He's a violent man and I must admit, for Ryan's sake, I'd love to nail him for this.'

He paused. 'I can't understand how he could inflict the sort of pain and suffering he has on his own son.' He finished the sentence in his head, *while I would do anything to bring my son back.*

'Some men don't deserve to have kids,' Tom agreed, placing a hand sympathetically on Matt's shoulder.

'I know.' Matt stared down guiltily as he thought about the distance between him and Ben's hospital bed. 'I don't know as yet whether I'll be able to help or not but I'm sure you'll do everything that's needed if I'm not there. Now we'd better speak to Denise again.'

They booked her out on her custody record and showed her to the same small interview room. They were to follow the same routine, Matt asking the questions, Alison, his back-up and a friendly female face and Tom staying in the background, in case it got too much for Matt. The same appropriate adult had agreed to sit in, but Denise was still refusing a solicitor, a fact that made him a little uneasy. The last thing he wanted was for her conversation to be deemed inadmissible on some trumped-up idea that she was somehow prevented from obtaining legal advice.

'Are you absolutely sure you don't want a solicitor?' he asked at the first possible moment. 'Not even to speak to on the phone?'

'I don't need one,' she replied.

'We can stop at any time for you to speak with one, you do understand?'

'Yes, I understand completely.'

The interview commenced and immediately it became obvious that she was sticking to her new story. It was her that had killed Ryan, she hadn't meant to do it, she was frightened.

'So frightened of Lee that you felt at ease to say in your first statement that it was him who had killed Ryan?'

'Yes, but I never actually said it was him that had done it. I felt safe when he was arrested.'

'And you don't now?'

She was quiet.

'What's happened that has made you feel unsafe?'

'Nothing.'

'Is it this letter that's made you change your mind?'

He pulled out the bags containing the letters she'd received in prison and put them on the table in front of her. She stared at them, unblinking.

'Who said you could read them?' she asked, looking directly at him.

'We can examine any property that you have with you. Something made you change your story and I wanted to know what. Do you want me to read it out to you?'

'It's not those,' she said, a little too vehemently. 'I'm not frightened of him now. He's locked away.'

'But Brenda's not, is she? And nor is Jake. Were you frightened that someone would get to him?'

She looked down at the table and made no reply. He continued.

'Is that why you've come up with this new story? Because he threatened you and Jake and you thought if you got him off and then said Ryan's death was accidental, you might get found guilty of a lesser charge and be released quickly?'

She stayed silent, so he continued.

'That way he wouldn't come after you and you might be lucky enough, with mitigating circumstances, to be put on probation or given a bit of community service and still be able to be with Jake?'

'I killed him by accident,' she repeated, at last looking up at him. 'I killed Ryan by accident, to stop him getting a beating and because I was afraid.'

Matt's anger was building.

'No one killed him by accident, Denise. Ryan was murdered when his head was smashed against a wall on purpose. And if you want to go on saying that you didn't mean to do it, you can stand up in court, charged with murder, and explain why you did nothing to stop the violence against him, how you finally snapped and hit him against the wall, how you did nothing to get him help until it was too late and how you consistently lied about what happened.'

She made no reply.

'This is your last chance to tell us why you're changing your story. If Lee or anyone connected with him has made threats towards you or Jake, they can be arrested and dealt with. The courts hold a very dim view of anything that prevents the course of justice being served.'

'There's nothing to say. I killed Ryan by accident. It wasn't intentional and I've received nothing that's made me change my story. I changed my story because I want to tell the truth.'

He wanted to stand her up and shake her. Her voice and the words she was saying were rehearsed and automatic. She was patently afraid, unless she was a good actress. Both she and Lee had been in the right place at the right time, both admitted this and it was corroborated by Jake. It could have been either of them. Now, here she was admitting to the worst crime possible, through misplaced loyalty and fear. He was frustrated at the turn of events although he had a pretty good idea what the CPS would say. She's admitted responsibility and should be charged.

Matt grimaced to himself. Lee was due to be interviewed again, but there was no chance of him admitting to anything. He needed to return and visit Jake. He was convinced, more than ever, that this young, vulnerable boy held the answers to the problem.

As they walked back towards his office Matt felt his mobile phone vibrate. A text message appeared on the screen from Jo. He scrolled down with a sense of dread and read the words. *Gave up waiting for you to return after your quick visit to work. Have gone home for a few hours sleep. Try and find the time to go and be with Ben. He's on his own.* The sarcastic tone wasn't lost on him and he sighed heavily.

'Tom, I've got to get back to the hospital. Jo's left and Ben's on his own. Can you and Alison liaise with the guv'nor and CPS and see what they have to say about Denise's confession?'

'Of course we can,' Tom replied. 'You go. And send my love to Jo and the kids, won't you?'

Matt nodded sadly. 'That's if she'll even listen to me long enough for me to tell her, without finding fault.'

Tom placed a hand heavily on his shoulder. 'Mate, you need to try and talk or else you'll go mad. I'll give you a ring and we'll arrange a drink. A few pints will help you to let off steam.'

Alison nodded. 'Or in my case a good stiff gin and tonic. There's nothing like a few glasses to make you forget about troublesome partners.' She smiled miserably, a thin, sad smile that for a brief moment appeared to suck the life from her eyes.

'I didn't realize you'd had problems,' Matt said quietly.

She brightened almost as quickly as she'd grown morose. 'Well, there's not many of us in our job that haven't, at some time or other, is there?' She shrugged. 'Anyway, I try not to discuss my private life at work. You men are worse gossips then all of us women put together!' She pulled her jacket round her and attempted to do up a button. Failing miserably, she smiled again mischievously. 'Shit, knew I should have stuck to my cabbage soup. Oh well, next time.' Turning to leave, she swung back quickly towards Matt. 'But seriously. I'm told I'm very good at sorting out other people's problems, so if you ever needed a chat I'd be only too willing to lend a sympathetic ear.'

She turned again and walked towards the door, stopping one last time as she opened it. 'Just crap at dealing with my own,' she said quietly.

Denise Clarkson stood in the centre of the custody reception. The lights were bright and she fidgeted a little, winding a wayward lock of hair around a finger. The cluster of police staff behind the custody officer had stopped what they were doing and were standing still. Curious eyes craned towards her, as the mixture of prisoners, solicitors and appropriate adults in front of the desk jostled to take a better look. She didn't care.

'Denise Clarkson,' the fresh-faced custody sergeant intoned. 'You are charged that between the third of December 2007 and fourth of December 2007 at 53 Station Road, SW16 you did murder Ryan Clarkson. That is contrary to common law. In answer to the charge, you do not have to say anything, but it may harm your defence if you do not mention, when questioned, something you later rely on in court. Anything you do say will be given in evidence.'

He looked up expectantly but she shook her head. She'd

said everything she needed to say. She had no need to give her watching audience anything further.

'Do you understand the charge?' he queried.

She nodded.

'Sign here that you said nothing,' his voice said.

She signed where she was shown.

'Can I go back down to my cell now?'

'You'll be kept in custody tonight and you'll go to court in the morning.'

She nodded again. 'Can I have some clean clothes to go to court in?'

He shook his head but she wasn't worried. It would have been nice to have some fresh ones but she'd have to make do. The charge didn't bother her either, although the word *murder* sounded harsh. It made her blood run cold. She couldn't believe she'd actually admitted to killing Ryan but the disclosure had been a necessity. Everything would become clear in time. Her confession would be disregarded and she would be free.

She started to hum to herself. It was a tune that she and Jake used to sing together. She felt a hand on her arm, guiding her down the passage, towards her cell. She turned to face the man whose arm was on hers. DC Berwick, DC Tom Berwick. Yes, she definitely liked him. He and the woman officer had collected her from prison that morning and taken her to see Jake. He'd allowed her a few precious moments alone with her boy, just the two of them. She wanted to laugh out loud. They'd be collecting her again soon but next time she'd be reunited with her special son for good.

She wandered into her cell and sat on the bench, humming louder. The song brought back vivid memories of Jake. She shivered and threw her arms around her body, squeezing hard. It wouldn't be long. She just had to wait.

# Seventeen

Lee Clarkson pulled the sheets from around his head and peered out. The view was the same. It was always the same. Grey walls, metal-framed beds, bars. He wanted out. His cellmate was snoring and it was annoying him. He jumped down from his bunk and prodded him hard.

'For fuck's sake. Can't you keep your fucking mouth shut for once?'

The man groaned and turned away, pulling his blanket to one side as he did so and allowing the pasty white flesh of his buttocks and back to be revealed.

'Christ,' Lee muttered.

He pulled on a pair of tracksuit bottoms and a T-shirt, suddenly angry. That fucking bitch had caused this. She'd pay for it and all. He'd enjoy teaching the bitch a lesson in due course and if he couldn't, he'd make sure someone else would. He thought of 'Brenda' and smiled to himself. They'd never find out who she was. He'd instructed his mate well in his letter. Get your missus to come and see me wearing that sexy blonde wig. I need to talk to her. He'd understood straight away what was meant and 'Brenda' had arrived looking completely different to how she usually did.

He'd told her what to write, how to conceal the threat within the niceties of a normal conversation so it would be missed by the screws. The bitch would guess the writer's identity but would be unlikely to tell the cops, for fear of Jake receiving a visit from his mate. He'd instructed 'Brenda' to wear gloves when she wrote, to sign the letter with her pet name and not to lick the envelope. He didn't want her being identified and he sure as hell didn't want his part in the threat being revealed. In any case its discovery was unlikely. The screws had enough of a job reading through all the hundreds of letters to notice one small paragraph. They were more interested in the letters that contained explicit sexual language, much more interested.

The morning alarm sounded across the cell block and lights were switched on. He heard his cellmate groan and pass wind. Instead of bringing a wry smile to his face, it irritated him and made his frustration at his incarceration grow. He'd been content with this life in the past, but this time he didn't want to be there, he shouldn't be there, it was the bitch's turn. Maybe it was the knowledge he was to be collected and taken for further questioning later that had made him wake early. Maybe it was the excitement of getting away from the high walls and barbed wire for a few hours, maybe it was the growing anticipation that, if the threat had got through, he might not be coming back.

He banged on the bars and shouted at the screws to let him out. He wanted to get to the shower block first. He wanted to be ready.

'You'll get out when we say you will, Clarkson, so sit down and wait your bleedin' turn like everyone else,' came the response.

He couldn't sit down though and paced the length of the cell waiting. By the time he heard his door click open he'd completed several hundred lengths and was more impatient than ever. He strode out the door and into the shower block, not noticing the small cluster of men standing to one side, waiting. He stripped off, covering his nakedness with a towel. A shower became free and he dropped the towel and stepped forward into the jet of water. It wasn't hot, but it was warm enough. He closed his eyes and let the water stream over his head.

A sharp pain in his stomach forced his eyes open and he saw a face, directly in front of him. His arms were pulled back behind him and he bucked against the force. The grip remained firm and he was immediately aware of his vulnerability. The face was sneering towards him.

'So you think you're a big man around here, do you? You think you can just jump the fucking queue and get away with it, do you?'

He shook his head. There were at least four men clustered around him and he immediately recognized his odds were not good. A screw stood by the door but his head was turned in the opposite direction.

He felt another punch to his abdomen and his body tensed and recoiled. He was pulled up straight and another blow came in, directly to his ribs. He retched as the pain shot through him.

The man's voice was low and menacing. 'You might be able to push some poor little kid around, but it's not so fucking easy when it's a grown man, is it?'

'I'm sorry. I didn't see you,' he stuttered, desperate to stop the onslaught.

'Well, see this then.'

He glimpsed the fist in front of his eyes in the split second before it landed. As the blow came in to his face, he heard his nose crack open. Blood spurted out and he could taste it in his mouth, feel it running down his neck, see it sprayed into his aggressor's face.

'That'll teach you to fucking pick on someone your own size next time, you spineless bastard,' the man said. 'And just in case you forget . . .'

The sentence was left unfinished and as Lee opened his eyes he saw the knee aimed towards his groin. A white pain shot through the whole of his body as he dropped to the tiles. He pulled his legs up to his chest to protect himself and saw his blood spilling out across the watery floor. The arms that had held him were gone and the group had dispersed, as quickly as it had formed. His stomach went into spasm and he could taste the bile rising up his throat. He expelled it in a loud groan and the sight of the screw running towards him blurred as the whiteness obliterated everything else.

Matt couldn't help a grin as Lee Clarkson was brought through.

'Has someone been giving you a taste of your own medicine then?' he asked, trying to suppress the upturn of his mouth.

'Wasn't expecting to see you here,' came the reply.

He ignored the comment. He hadn't expected to be there himself. Tom had dealt with Lee's production from prison the day before but during the course of a phone call had mentioned the assault on their main suspect. Matt's curiosity had got the better of him and, with Ben's condition remaining unchanged and the situation with Jo still frostier, had decided to take a few hours away from the hospital. He was to conduct the interview and then leave Tom to finish off.

Lee looked a mess. His nose was swollen, with dried blood still on view inside each nostril. Both eyes were blackened, with yellowish bruises emanating outwards. He walked carefully, his hands handcuffed to the front, held close to his body supporting his rib cage. He sat down on the bench, keeping his back straight, panting slightly, obviously in some discomfort. Matt didn't care. It was nice to see his adversary reduced to this level. It was only within the confines of prison that punishment could truly be meted out. Gone were the days when a bit of summary justice could be doled out at police level. He wasn't so sure though whether the vast majority of the public would be averse to a little more rough treatment of prisoners, especially in cases like this.

'What happened then?' he asked, trying to stop the smile creeping back on to his mouth. 'Did the other cons find out what you're in for?'

'I fell down the stairs actually,' Lee replied. He fixed Matt with a stare, raising his eyebrows in an attempt to put an end to any further questions.

'And the stairs happened to lash out and punch you in the face and ribs! Say no more, I think we get the picture.'

Matt donned a fake look of sympathy. Lee's expression was one of pure hatred, but he remained silent.

Matt turned to the custody sergeant. 'Best we get the doctor on his way?'

'There's one here already, just finishing dealing with another prisoner. She should be ready to see Mr Clarkson here in a few minutes.'

The medical examination took longer than normal. Each injury had to be logged and measured and a report completed. The list was impressive. In addition to the obvious facial damage, there was also a broken rib and several large, angry areas of bruising around his abdomen and groin. The accident and emergency department in the local hospital had conducted an initial examination and X-rays had been taken. The conclusion was, however, that the injuries were mainly superficial and a discharge back to the prison had been swift. The police doctor agreed with the initial judgement and Lee Clarkson was declared fit to be interviewed and fit to be detained.

They made their way to an interview room and Tom prepared the tapes. Clarkson had a solicitor present. Matt had with him a file containing every date that Ryan had received treatment and the diagnosis for each injury. In addition to those actually treated, he also had the list of old, previously unreported injuries exposed by the post-mortem, along with photographs of scars and marks that had been found on his body. He was determined to make Clarkson see the full extent of the pain and agony Ryan had suffered at his hands.

First though he needed to put to him his suspicion that Clarkson was the instigator of the threats made to Denise. He showed him the letter and read out the paragraph containing the threat. Lee's response was as expected.

'I never fucking said anything of the sort. If Brenda wants to threaten her, that's up to her, but she can't blame me and nor can you.'

'Who's Brenda?'

'A friend from years ago.'

'What's her surname?'

'I don't know. I only know her as Brenda.'

'Where does she live?'

'No idea. I haven't seen her in years.'

'Unless we can speak to her, how can we dispute what she says about your involvement?'

'That's your problem, ain't it? I'm saying I never said anything like it. You prove that I did.'

He crossed his arms in front of him and his mouth twisted into a self-satisfied smirk. Matt wanted to wipe it off his face so badly. Unless they could track 'Brenda' down, Clarkson was right. They couldn't prove that it had been him who had issued the threat. What was to say Brenda wasn't a disgruntled ex-girlfriend trying to get him into trouble, or even a new woman ready to make a move on the man in front of him? What better way to dispose of the woman in his life than to force her to admit to something she hadn't done?

He opened the file and took the first photograph out, placing it on the table and sliding it towards Clarkson. It showed Ryan's small white hand lying still on a stainless steel slab. A mass of scarring crossed the width of his hand, and a ruler placed next to it showed it to be approximately two inches long and an inch wide.

'On the twenty-fifth of August 2004 Ryan was taken to Hastings District Hospital with a burn to the back of his right hand. He was only eleven months of age at the time. How did he get this injury?'

'No comment.'

'Denise stated at the time that Ryan had fallen against an electric fire. She now says that you caused the injury by holding his hand against the fire.'

'No comment.'

'On April the fourth, the following year, 2005, when Ryan was just over eighteen months old, he was taken to Hastings District Hospital with a fractured lower right rib.' He passed across an X-ray taken at the time. 'How did Ryan come to get this injury?'

'No comment.'

'It was claimed at the time that Ryan fell down the last few stairs and hit his chest on a wooden train that was lying on the floor. Denise now says that he didn't just fall, but that you kicked him down the stairs when he was following you against your wishes.'

'No comment.'

The interview continued in the same vein. There were only a few more hospital attendances before they petered out altogether. The majority of the young boy's injuries had been left to heal by themselves, but the resulting marks had been clearly highlighted in the blaze of the flashlight at his post-mortem.

Clarkson looked down at each picture, no trace of emotion displayed in his expression. Even the photographs showing injuries vivid against the dead face of his son provoked only the slightest of winces.

In answer to every question the man looked directly at him and made no comment. Matt couldn't believe he could be so impassive when presented with this appalling visual evidence.

As he finished the last few photographs in the file, he turned to Tom.

'Is there anything else you want to ask?'

Tom shook his head and grimaced. They both knew what was still left to be said.

'In that case I have to inform you that when Denise was re-interviewed about Ryan's injuries, as well as stating that most had been caused by your assaults, she also stated that it was she that had killed him.'

Clarkson's head shot up and he raised himself half out of his seat, staring straight into Matt's eyes, his mouth turned up in a sneer.

'I told you she was a lying, scheming bitch, didn't I? But you didn't listen. You knew all about this before you showed me all these photographs of my boy, didn't you? You evil bastard! What makes you think she hasn't lied about all these injuries too? If she lied about killing Ryan, why do you think she hasn't lied about these?'

Matt spoke calmly. 'Because I believe you are a bully that uses violence to terrorize your whole family. Because both she and Jake gave the same initial story about Ryan going quiet when you entered the bedroom.'

'Jake!' Lee almost spat out the name. 'He's just a fucking mummy's boy. She probably told him to say that.'

Matt ignored him. 'And because I believe she changed her story having been threatened by you.'

Clarkson was on his feet, pointing a finger directly at his face.

'Well, if that's what you think, you'd better fucking prove it. You won't pin nothing on me, you arsehole, and you never will.'

# Eighteen

He heard her before he saw her. The excited screams reverberated along the corridor, increasing in volume until they exploded into the expectant atmosphere of the ward. His daughter appeared through the swing doors as the peace was shattered, and the faces of other visitors lit up in appreciation of the childish exuberance. Chloe was there to visit her big brother and nothing was going to dampen her enthusiasm. She saw Matt sitting next to Ben's bed and let out a shriek.

'Daddy. Is Ben still sleeping?'

He fought the temptation to put his finger to his lips, enjoying the life that she exuded. Smiling, he held his arms out and she broke into a sprint, leaping heavenwards as she reached him. He lifted her easily, swinging her round until she giggled with delight. As he came to a halt with her small frame clinging around his neck, he saw her expression turn from laughter to sudden earnestness.

'Mummy says I mustn't be too noisy because Ben is sleeping and I mustn't scream and disturb anyone else.'

'I don't think other people will mind too much,' he said equally seriously. 'But you mustn't run around or the nurses won't let us stay.'

Chloe nodded. He looked at her and felt the same rush of love as he experienced whenever he gazed into Ben's face. The only difference was the equally strong emotions of regret and frustration where his son was concerned. He kissed her lightly on the end of the nose and she wrinkled her cheeks in mock horror.

Jo had followed her daughter in and was standing close by, talking to one of the senior nurses.

'Thank you so much for letting Chloe visit.'

'Well, if hearing her voice does the trick and brings Ben out of his coma, it'll be worthwhile. It was a good idea of yours to try it, even though we don't normally allow young children on to the ward.'

'I know, and I do appreciate it. I'll make sure she behaves herself.'

Matt noticed the use of the singular.

'Yes, thank you,' he called across. Jo glanced in his direction but averted her eyes as their gaze met.

Chloe shifted on his lap and leant forward over Ben's bed. He lifted her so she could sit next to him and she bent over and kissed him on the cheek.

'Ben, wake up. Father Christmas came and he's left you lots of presents. And there's a present from me too.' She glanced back towards Matt. 'Why won't he wake up?'

'Because his head was hurt and it's got to mend inside.'

'But when will it be mended?'

The question was so simple but he didn't know how to answer it. It was the question he wanted answered too. He still couldn't consider the alternative, *if it mends at all.*

'I don't know.'

Jo moved across and lifted Chloe from the bed. 'He'll wake up soon,' she said, shooting an angry glare at him. 'We just have to talk to him so he knows we're here. Tell him about what we've been doing so he wants to wake up and join us.'

She sat down on the opposite side of the bed and lowered Chloe carefully down next to Ben. They both leant over him, chatting easily about their news. He sensed his deliberate exclusion immediately. He was cast to one side, with a mass of tubing and equipment between him and his family. He wanted so much to join them and put aside their divide, but he couldn't. He stood up and walked round, standing quietly behind them. He saw Jo tense, maintaining her stance, not reacting to his proximity.

Chloe turned towards him. 'Are you going to join us?' she said innocently.

'I'd love to, but Mummy won't let me.' He regretted the words as soon as they were said.

'Why won't you let Daddy join us?' Chloe turned to Jo, her face full of alarm, and he knew he'd been wrong to drag his daughter into their problems.

'Because Daddy has other things he has to do.' She turned towards him, her expression hard and uncompromising. 'Haven't you?'

His dismissal was abrupt. He couldn't stop the words of bitterness that spilled out from his mouth.

'Yes I have. Sorry darling, I have to go.' He kissed Chloe's curls and smiled towards her. 'I'll see you again very soon.'

'I'll see you again too, Ben.' He leant over and kissed his son's pale cheeks. 'Wake up soon. Let's start the New Year together.'

Jo turned away from him as he said the words. Together seemed like a pipe dream at the moment.

'Happy New Year, Jo,' he said quietly. He meant it. For a fleeting moment he was on the verge of taking her in his arms and attempting to smooth away the bitterness, but then he saw the flash of intense pain that crossed her face. He was confused, but then realized what she'd read into his simple comment. That he was being sarcastic, not sorry. Vindictive, not repentant. That he was clearly labouring the fact that there would be no Happy New Year for them, at least while Ben remained unconscious.

He saw the tears spring to her eyes and put his hand on her back. She swung round, forcing his hand to drop lamely by his side. 'You have a Happy New Year if you want. I'll be here.'

She pulled Chloe on to her lap and twisted away from him so he was left staring at the back of her head. It was no use. He'd mucked up again.

He drove around blindly for several hours, not knowing where to go. He didn't want to face Jo until he was stronger and he couldn't bear to see New Year in at Ben's bedside. He wanted the night over. He would start afresh the next morning, with a New Year's optimism.

He pulled up at an off-licence to buy more cigarettes. The shop was busy with partygoers and revellers, buying copious amounts of alcohol en route to their various destinations. Their voices were loud and full of enthusiasm and drowned out the continual ringing of the entrance bell.

His mobile phone vibrated in his pocket. A familiar but worried voice came on the line. It was Tom.

'Where are you?' he said. 'I've been trying to contact you at home and Jo didn't seem to know where you were either.'

'Tom. Good to hear from you, mate. I'm just driving round. I don't really want to go home and I can't face being at the hospital either.'

'Do you fancy a drink then?'

Within an hour Matt had left his car parked outside his house and been picked up by Tom.

'Is Jo in?' Tom asked as they drove away.

'I think so, at the moment,' he replied. He'd seen the lights on but hadn't wanted to go in. 'Chloe was going to Jo's parents' for the night. I think Jo's going back up to the hospital later. She wants to be there just in case Ben wakes up as the New Year is rung in.' He sighed out loud. 'I don't think she wanted me there to share the celebration.'

'I'm sure she does really, and I'm sure you do too. One of you just has to make the first move.'

'I know, but I just don't know if I can do it.'

'Don't wait too long to try then. Or it might be too late.'

Tom paused. 'I never told you this before, but me and Sue went through a bad patch a few years ago. I thought we were going to split up, it got so bad. It was only because a mutual friend virtually banged our heads together and got us talking that we realized that the problem wasn't so big. We'd just built it up in our heads and neither of us would take the time to sit down and listen to the other one's point of view.'

'I don't think ours is just a difference of a point of view though, Tom. We've both said some awful things that we wish we hadn't.'

'That's the point. You both have. Now you both need to sit down and unsay them. But you won't be able to start until you get talking, and that's the hardest part. The longer you leave it, the harder it'll be. Maybe you should make it a New Year's resolution and tell Jo. Maybe then she'll see you're serious about sorting it out.'

'Maybe,' Matt conceded out loud. *But maybe it's gone too far now*, he thought to himself.

They fell into companionable silence until eventually Tom pulled on the handbrake and they slid to a standstill. 'Here we are. I thought I'd bring you to this pub. It's a bit out of the way and I hope it won't be quite so crowded.'

They got out and Matt recognized where he was. The pub was large, set between two main roads, on a busy roundabout. There were no houses nearby and the pub had fallen into a state of mild disrepair. As expected, the establishment was half empty when they entered. The majority of the patrons were older, the younger drinkers having instead opted for the livelier town pubs. The two bars were quiet. The atmosphere was musty and smelt of stale beer and sweat and the ceilings were discoloured and yellow. A worn path across the patterned carpet led the way to a heavy, darkly stained bar and the furniture was made from the same hard teak. The barman was a thin, middle-aged man with stained teeth and a drooping handlebar moustache. His hair was thinning and greasy and combed across a large expanse of gently flaking scalp.

'What do you want, lads?' he said with barely concealed disinterest.

Tom ordered and they made their way to a table in the far corner, allowing them a full view of the comings and goings while they chatted. It was a habit that was hard to break. The ability to talk and observe the surroundings at the same time came as second nature to them both.

'Any change with Ben?' Tom came straight to the point.

'Not as yet,' Matt sighed. 'It's been almost a fortnight now since the accident. The doctors are hoping that he might rouse this week but they just don't know. Most comas apparently last between a few days and two to three weeks. If nothing happens soon, I don't know what the prognosis will be.'

'What about the driver? Is he likely to be charged?'

'I don't know about that either. It's touch and go whether the CPS will give it a run. The bastard's not saying anything and we fucked up a little with a partial admittance that his girlfriend made. I don't know whether that will be allowed in court. We could just do with a bit more.'

'I'd be tempted to turn up at his place of work and lean on him. He might not be quite so cocky if he had a few facts spelt out. Like how we'll make his life a misery if he doesn't talk and how we'll make sure he loses his job and income if he carries on as he is.'

'I'd like to do that as well, but at the moment I'll wait and see what happens with the CPS. I don't want to go getting heavy handed and risk messing up the whole job.'

Tom nodded. 'Does his girlfriend realize exactly what he's done?'

'I think so. It was spelt out to her quite forcefully at the beginning, but she's just as bad as him. She's changed her story to try and cover for him, the bitch. They're both due back this week for a decision.'

'I'll keep my fingers crossed for you.'

Matt smiled across at his friend. Tom was a good mate to have and there was no doubt in his mind of Tom's desire and ability to visit Andrei Kachan. It would have to wait though. He sure as hell wasn't going to risk his day in court with the bastard for the sake of a few more days' patience. He swilled the last of his pint round in the bottom of the glass and swallowed the frothing liquid down, concentrating on the last few slow-moving trails of bubbles.

'What do you want?' he asked, standing up while he waited for Tom's answer. When it came he walked over to the bar, clutching both glasses in front of him. The barman was busy serving another customer. He was in no hurry as he moved pedantically about behind the bar. Matt stared at the optics, mesmerized by each rush of spirits that filled the vacuum left by the previous measure. He gave his order and concentrated instead on the flow of beer from the tap.

'Well, if it isn't DS fucking Arnold!' He heard his name called out through the fog of his thoughts. 'What brings you here, then?'

He turned round to see Lee Clarkson swaggering towards him, mouth turned up in a sneer, eyes alight with bloodshot energy. His face still bore the remnants of his assault, but the bruises were beginning to fade. He carried with him a half-empty beer glass, from which he gulped periodically. He was clearly drunk and Matt recognized the potential for violence immediately.

He turned the question round. 'What brings you here? I thought you were banged up.'

'I was until this morning. Didn't you know? The kind magistrates let me out.' He smirked. 'Said because the lying bitch had put her hands up to it and the charge of causing Ryan's death had been dropped I should be allowed out.'

'What about the other charges – assault and cruelty?' He thought back to the further recommendations of the CPS as he was about to leave.

Clarkson smirked again. 'What? Do you mean the other charges that I've pleaded not guilty to? You prove it was me and not her, especially now she's admitted lying about Ryan's death.'

Matt felt his temper rising. 'She's only lied because she's frightened of you. I saw the letter and I've got no doubt she's carrying the can for you.'

Clarkson laughed out loud. 'Aw, poor little Denise! Frightened of her big, bad boyfriend, is she?'

Matt tried to ignore the sarcasm in his voice. 'You don't deserve to be a father,' he said contemptuously as he turned away.

'What do you mean? *I* don't deserve to be a father. *You* can talk. What about your son? I hear he's nearly dead because you failed to look after him properly.'

Matt tensed. Clarkson continued.

'How can you stand there, you arsehole, and accuse me, when your own boy's lying in hospital? I found out all about it. I hear your son flies almost as well as mine. Call yourself a good father, do you?'

He heard the loud, taunting laugh and swung round to face his protagonist. Clarkson's face was close to his own, his mouth open, his head tossed back in ridicule. Without thinking Matt swung the now refilled glass of beer towards him, unleashing the full pint over his sneering face. Clarkson was taken by surprise, stumbling backwards a few steps as the beer splashed down over his body and clothes. He looked up momentarily, beer dripping crazily off his nose and chin, and as he launched himself forward Matt could see the hatred in his eyes. A fist landed in his face, smashing into his jaw and throwing his head backwards. Another came in and he landed heavily on the sticky carpet. He saw a boot coming towards him and grabbed hold of it, lifting it upwards as he got back to his feet. Voices were all around him, shouting words he couldn't make out. He heard the smash of glass and saw Clarkson's madness as the broken shards were forced towards him. As they were about to make contact with the skin of his cheek, he felt himself dragged backwards by two strong arms and was vaguely aware of the distance between him and the broken glass growing greater.

'Matt, Matt,' a voice was shouting in his ear. 'For fuck's sake, stop it, he's not worth it.'

Tom was between them, pushing him backwards. His face was throbbing and he reached up and fingered his jaw. It was painful, but didn't feel broken. The point of impact on his cheek was likewise swollen, but malleable. He pressed down on the swelling and winced as a searing pain shot through his head. Tom was edging him towards the exit and he allowed himself to be moved along. He could see Clarkson being restrained by several others as Tom pushed the door open.

'Come on, mate. Let's get you home before we get into any more trouble,' he was saying.

As the door swung shut and the cold air enveloped him he got a last glimpse of Clarkson's rabid face.

'Don't think you're any different to me!' he screamed out. 'You're no better. Remember that, you arsehole, when you're burying your boy.'

The house was in darkness when Tom pulled up outside. Matt was glad. He couldn't face any explanations. Jo was obviously at the hospital. He checked his watch. It was 23.30, half an hour before the New Year was due to be welcomed in.

'Are you sure you'll be OK?' Tom was asking as he turned the key in the lock.

'I'm fine, Tom. You go home and be with Sue. I'll catch up with you in the next few days.'

He pushed the door and stepped up the stairs into the familiarity of his own home. Tom disappeared into the background and Matt heard his car fade into the distance. The house looked and smelt the same but the life had been taken from it. Gone was the noise of the children's screams and the gentle scolding voice of his wife. He switched the TV on and stood watching the pictures from all over the country in the run-up to midnight. Trafalgar Square was heaving with people and the bridges and walkways around the London Eye were packed with expectant crowds awaiting the New Year's fireworks. Edinburgh was alive with Scots preparing to celebrate Hogmanay and streets throughout the British Isles were bustling with revellers.

He left the volume up to try to stifle the silence and walked slowly around the house, switching every light on in a vain attempt to dispel his gloom. He checked his reflection in the bathroom mirror. It wasn't a pretty sight. Dried blood still showed around the outside of his lips and the swellings on his jaw and cheek were turning an ugly mauve. Maybe he was the same as Lee Clarkson. He even looked like the man now. He walked into the bedroom and caught the familiar scent of Jo's perfume. For a second he forgot their troubles and remembered the good times.

He switched the main light on and instantly the emptiness returned. No one was there.

He wandered through the remaining rooms, illuminating his loneliness. The noise of the TV still blared out from downstairs. He opened the door to Ben's room and stepped in. There was no reason to turn the light on in here. He knew every inch of the room, every colour of the decor, every blemish in the paintwork. He half expected to see the duvet, lifted in the centre, covering his son's small body, but it was flat. Uncrumpled. Its smoothness hit him.

He lay down on the bed and pulled the duvet up over him, willing the creases back. It was unwashed since the accident and a faint aroma on the pillow still remained. He thought of Ben and Ryan and Jake. One dead, the other two clinging on to life in different circumstances. He wasn't the same as Lee Clarkson. He loved Ben with a fierceness that until the accident he hadn't realized he possessed. Clarkson was a thug who didn't care about anyone but himself. Never mind his children. They were products of him, but in his mind he owed them nothing. Ryan was dead as a result of his action. Jake and the older children were abandoned in a children's home and their father was getting drunk in a pub.

He pulled the cover further up across his face and closed his eyes. He too had abandoned Ben to go drinking. Maybe Clarkson had been right after all. Maybe he was no better himself. He heard the countdown to the New Year begin from the TV downstairs. Five . . . He would visit Ben first thing in the morning. Four . . . He would find someone to confide in, to get things out of his system. Three . . . He would try and patch things up with Jo. Two . . . He would go and visit Jake again and update him about what had been happening. One . . . Ben would wake up and everything would be all right.

As Big Ben tolled in the New Year, Matt closed his eyes and let his own inner darkness swallow him up.

# Nineteen

Jake received the news of Matt Arnold's impending visit with delight. The last few days had been a nightmare for him. Mikey and Christina were still making his life hell. The jibes were constant and hurtful and he longed to be able to fight back, but they would soon be out of his life and he had to try to ignore them until then.

It was the first day of a New Year, the time to make a fresh start, the time to set in motion the plans.

He heard a knock on the door and Mikey entered without waiting for a response.

'I hear you've got your little mate coming to see you. Now don't you go saying anything you shouldn't, will you?'

'Mikey, go away. I don't want to speak to you now.'

Mikey walked towards him. 'But I want to speak to you! And you haven't got your mummy to help you now. She's locked up for life and you won't ever see her again.'

He laughed, edging closer to Jake. Jake backed away until he was squashed between the wall and the wardrobe. Mikey closed in.

'Your mummy is a lying, murdering bitch who tried to get my dad locked up for ever. But now she's been found out. Now she's admitted it was her. She's never going to get out and you're never going to be allowed to see her again.' He stepped forward, taking hold of Jake's collar and pulling it towards him.

'Who told you that?' Jake shouted. 'That's not true. She's going to get out soon and we'll be together again and then we're going to run away to where you and your bastard dad will never find us. We're better than you. He doesn't care about you or Christina but my mum loves me, only me.' As he said the last words he pushed Mikey hard, sending him reeling backwards, down on to the floor. Mikey looked up in surprise at the blow.

'You wait,' he threatened, climbing to his feet and coming closer. 'You wait till we get let back out with our dad. He won't want you so you'll have to stay. Then you won't be so cocky. Your mummy might love you more than us but you wait till she gets sent down. You won't be able to run away then. You'll be stuck in care for ever.'

'No I won't. I won't. You'll see.' Jake's voice fell almost to a whisper.

'I can't wait,' Mikey sneered, clenching a fist and pushing it into Jake's stomach. 'But until then, you watch what you say. I don't like snitches and if I find out you've been saying anything, anything to drop my dad in it, you'll be sorry.'

He turned abruptly and walked out, slamming the door behind him. Jake threw himself down on his bed. He felt good. He didn't care what Mikey threatened, he had at least fought back. It was the first time he'd ever fought back. He smiled at the thought of his sworn enemy languishing on the floor at his feet. When Matt Arnold heard what he had to say, the tables would be turned and he and his mum would be together again for ever.

He looked forward to seeing Mikey's face then. Maybe then he wouldn't treat him with the same contempt. Maybe then he would leave him alone for good.

The message left on Matt's phone by Gary Fellowes gave no hint of what kind of news was to be expected. It was bland and uninformative and he listened to it several times, trying to gauge whether the voice seemed pleased or regretful. 'Could you come to my office,' it said. 'I have a decision from the CPS on the case of Andrei Kachan and Sharon Cunningham and I'd rather tell you it in person.'

His heart was pounding and a thin film of sweat prickled on his forehead as he walked towards Gary's office. He didn't know what he would do if the CPS had turned them down. Maybe Tom's idea was not so far-fetched as an alternative. But he baulked at the idea. Doling out retribution was a job for the courts, even though these days he believed they increasingly let the victims down. As a police officer he had always felt he should publicly voice his disapproval of vigilantism. Now justice hung in the balance for him, though, he didn't know whether his attitude would change if faced with a negative decision.

He knocked at the door and waited for a response. When it came, he pushed the door open and entered. Gary rose to his feet and held out his hand towards him. They shook and he scanned his colleague's face, trying to decipher the expression. Gary was serious.

'Blimey, Matt. What have you been up to?'

'Let's just say someone took a dislike to me and decided to try and teach me a lesson. I'd rather not talk about it.'

Gary stared for a few seconds at Matt's bruised and swollen mouth and hastily changed the subject.

'Any news on Ben?' he asked.

'Not yet. He's still in a coma, unchanged. I've just been up to visit him. We're still waiting.' As he said the words, he realized how wrong they sounded. The *we* seemed a distant memory, inferring togetherness and solidarity. They *were* still waiting, he and Jo, but separately, in isolation. He thought back to the awkwardness of that morning, the look of distaste apparent on Jo's face when she saw his injuries. She hadn't even asked him how he'd got them, preferring instead to make him feel like a naughty schoolboy caught fighting in the playground. He was glad when he'd been given the excuse to leave and speak to Gary. He paused, hardly daring to ask the question that had been playing on his mind.

'What's the decision from the CPS then?'

Gary turned away and picked up the file, leafing quickly through to the appropriate page. Matt held his breath nervously. When he finally looked up, Gary smiled broadly.

'We've done it. They're willing to give it a run.'

Matt exhaled loudly, closing his eyes. 'Thank God for that. I don't know what I'd have done if they'd turned us down.'

'They nearly did,' Gary interjected. 'If it hadn't been for two last bits of evidence that tipped the balance in the last day or so, I think they would have rejected us.'

'What were they, then?' Matt asked curiously.

'Well firstly, the ignition cowling came back from the lab with Kachan's fingerprints all over the underside. There's no good reason, judging from the position and freshness of the prints, for them to be there. The only explanation for their presence can be when he deliberately removed the cowling to try to give the appearance of the car having been hot-wired. That was a great find of yours.'

'A total stroke of luck. If I hadn't been there at that particular moment I would never have met Beres Morgan and never had the thing pointed out.'

'I feel a bit guilty for missing it.'

'Well, don't. It was tucked well away out of sight. No one would have found it if he hadn't seen it thrown.'

'Thanks, but I still wish I'd found it.'

'It doesn't matter who found it. It was found and that's the most important thing. What's the other piece of evidence?'

Gary grinned triumphantly.

'I got on to various Peugeot garages just to find out how easy it is to steal a Peugeot 106XN. I had a feeling it was difficult, because I'm certainly not aware of many of them being stolen. Anyway, they confirmed that to start that model, the driver would have to key in a security code before the dashboard lights would even come on. There's virtually no way that anyone could steal this model of Peugeot without knowing the code, and certainly not in the amateur way Kachan tried to tamper with the ignition. That, plus the fingerprint evidence, was enough to convince the CPS that the car wasn't stolen. They're going to try and use Sharon's initial statements too, although it might be that they aren't admissible when it comes to court.'

'That's brilliant news. I thought, when he wasn't picked out by any of the witnesses at the crash scene, it would be tough to get a charge. I guess it all hinged on whether we could actually prove the car wasn't stolen.'

'We can put Kachan in the driving seat minutes after the accident, when he was seen getting out of the car at the garages by Beres. The driver at the time of the accident fits his description perfectly, even though he wasn't picked out at the ID parade. He hasn't provided details of anyone else who may have been driving even though he's had every opportunity. He's stuck to the now discredited story that the car was stolen. That must provide the guilty knowledge. We know it was him, he knows it was him, let's just hope the jury believes it was him.'

'At least he'll be put in front of a jury.'

'And so will she.'

'Who? Sharon?'

'Yep. The CPS has recommended they're both charged with conspiracy to pervert the course of justice as well as the driving offences. In addition I've also made enquiries with her insurance company. He's not insured to drive her car at all and she's made a claim against her policy alleging the car was stolen. Now that's effectively been disproved, the CPS has said to have her charged with attempted deception. That'll teach her not to cover up for her partner.'

'So what will he be charged with exactly?'

Gary referred to the file. 'Andrei is to be charged with dangerous driving, failing to stop after an accident, no insurance and conspiracy to pervert the course of justice. It still doesn't really take in the seriousness of Ben's injuries, but it's the best we can do. By all accounts he was clearly drunk. Witnesses at the scene describe his movements as erratic and Beres Morgan says he fell over backwards on to the ground when the cowling came off and his speech was slurred. We lost that charge though, the moment he disappeared.'

Matt nodded his agreement. 'And dangerous driving doesn't really adequately cover what he did either, I agree. If Ben had died, it would be different, but if he's as good as dead, it's the same punishment as if no one was injured. It's so wrong. The courts should be able to change the punishment to fit the results of the crime, not just the actual act.'

'Don't start me on that bandwagon,' Gary agreed. 'The sooner the public and the courts start realizing a car is a lethal weapon, the better. I'm tired of wiping up the results of people going *a little* too fast, or nipping across the lights too late, or forgetting to wear their seat belts or talking on their mobile phones or any of the other pathetic excuses. If people want to take risks, then let them take a proper punishment for the results.'

Matt was quiet. Gary's statement made him uncomfortably aware of all the times he had disregarded the laws of the road. The fact that Andrei Kachan had deliberately been speeding down the wrong side of the road was all that mattered. It didn't matter that Ben had thought it was clear and it certainly didn't matter that Jo wasn't holding on to him. The only person truly responsible was the driver.

'Let's hope when Andrei gets to court he sees the error of his ways and at least spares the witnesses having to relive it all. I hate to think how Jo will cope if she has to go into the box.'

'Well, they're both due back to the police station tomorrow afternoon. She's in first at three and he's due back at four. Let's see if they have second thoughts when they find out they're being charged. I doubt it though. They both seem quite hard and he in particular is quite arrogant. I'm sure he thinks he's got away with it. I'll take great pleasure watching his face when the skipper reads out the charges.'

'I'm going to try and be there when he's charged too,' Matt said seriously.

Gary looked up, alarmed.

'Don't worry.' He put his hands up in mock surrender. 'I promise I won't say anything. I didn't the last time and I certainly won't be doing anything now to jeopardize the case, after all the hard work you've put into it. I just want to look him in the eyes.'

Gary smiled. 'OK, I think I trust you. And you do deserve it.

After all, it was your discovery of the ignition cowling that helped us to achieve the result we've got.'

'Along with all the other stuff you've come up with. Thanks for all your hard work, Gary. I do appreciate it.' They shook hands again. Matt was buoyant. 'And now I have to keep an appointment with another young boy whose life's been torn apart by the actions of others.'

'Sounds interesting,' Gary remarked.

'It is, but it's also a long story. I'll tell you about it over a pint one day, but until then I'll see you tomorrow.'

'I thought you weren't coming,' Jake said sullenly when Matt walked into the office. 'You're late. I thought you'd changed your mind.'

The boy was slouched in an armchair, his buttocks so far forward they only just made contact with the base of the seat. Matt checked his watch. 'I'm sorry for being late, Jake. I had to go to a meeting and it went on a little longer than expected. I promised I'd come though, and you should know by now that I always keep my promises.'

Jake brightened slightly.

'Can we go to the park then?'

'I don't see why not.' He looked towards Tyrone, who gave a nod of approval. 'Come on then. Let's go.'

Jake leapt up from his chair and was the first out through the door. Matt followed, a wry smile plastered across his face.

He didn't know what it was about the boy that was so endearing. He was sparky as well as vulnerable and Matt couldn't help liking him, almost in a paternal way. The day was cold but bright with the midday sun high in the sky. There was no wind, so the branches and boughs of the nearby trees stayed silent. Everything was calm. Jake walked ahead, pacing out in front of Matt who struggled to match his speed.

'Hang on, Jake. Why are you going so fast?'

'Sorry, Matt. I'll slow down. I just want to show you my special places in the park.'

He fell back and they kept pace, their footsteps echoing faintly in the tranquillity all around.

'How are you finding the home?'

'It's not bad I suppose. The food's good and it's great to

have my own room. I miss my mum though and Mikey keeps giving me hassle.'

'In what way?'

'He keeps coming into my room and beating up on me.'

'Have you told anyone about it?'

'No. It would just make things worse. You're the first person I've told.' He surveyed Matt's face. 'Looks like you've been having the same trouble as me.'

Matt rubbed his mouth carefully and smiled apologetically. 'There's me telling you to keep your head down and then I end up having a fight. And guess who it was with? Lee.'

Jake stared at him in awe. 'You fought with Lee! Why?'

'He said some things he really shouldn't have said.'

'I'd love to fight him as well, but he's too strong for me at the moment. One day though, I'll get him back for all the times he beat up on me and my mum.'

They reached the boating lake and stood staring down into the black, murky water.

'I suppose you heard that your mum confessed to killing Ryan?'

Jake kicked at a clod of dirt, sending the fragments spraying across the water. He watched as the ripples spread out across the surface.

'Yeah, I did. That's what Mikey's been ribbing me over. He keeps calling her a lying, murdering bitch.'

'And how does that make you feel?'

'It makes me want to punch his lights out. I pushed him today and took him by surprise. He fell on the floor. It made me feel better. Wait till he finds out what I'm capable of.'

He turned abruptly and ran off before Matt could ask what he meant. He followed Jake along a concrete footpath towards an adventure playground, jogging to keep up. By the time he arrived, Jake was climbing a tower and swinging by his arms along a horizontal metal ladder. He was strong, his wiry frame concealing a hidden power and energy. He got to the middle and dropped down, turning to grin mischievously at Matt. Matt grinned back at the young boy. He was only three years older than Ben and in some ways it was like seeing into the future. Except that he didn't know if Ben would have a future.

'Bet you can't do this!' Jake shouted across to him.

He looked up and saw the boy swaying precariously on a

tyre swing. He was whooping in delight and Matt ran across to join him.

'Go on, it's your turn now,' Jake laughed.

His laughter was infectious and Matt found himself chuckling out loud too, as the tyre slid down the track. It was the first time he'd properly laughed since the accident and it was good. Jake was running from swing to slide to climbing frame with an energy that seemed boundless.

Matt sat down on a bench and watched the young dervish as he circled the playground until, tired and panting, he joined him. Jake leant his head against him and Matt automatically swung his arm over the boy's shoulder. It seemed a natural thing to do, but he was still a little troubled by the gesture.

'Will my mum have to stay in prison for a long time?' Jake suddenly asked. 'Even if she didn't do it?'

'Well, if she didn't kill Ryan why would she admit to it?' The question had been bothering him since Denise's surprise confession.

'Because she was frightened Lee would come after us if she didn't.' He said the words in a matter-of-fact way, as if Matt should have known. 'You don't know Lee or Mikey, do you? He would never let things go. If he went to prison for Ryan's murder he'd make sure either he or a friend would teach Mum a lesson. And he'd make Mikey do the same with me. We'd never be allowed to forget. Mum told me to keep my mouth shut and that it was easier for her to just admit it than always be watching over our shoulder for Lee.'

'Like it threatened in the letter?'

'I think so. Mum told me about the letter but I didn't actually see it.'

He'd suspected that was the reason, but now hearing his suspicions articulated out loud made him angry. How could the letter have been allowed to get through?

As he'd guessed at the time, enquiries with the prison and forensics had drawn a blank. No usable DNA or fingerprints had been found on the paper or envelope and CCTV at the prison had shown a female, obviously in disguise, visiting Lee. The name and address she'd given had proved to be false and the captured image was unidentifiable. Lee had got away with the threat and Jake's bland statement made the truth even more galling.

He turned to face the boy and was surprised to see his eyes wet with suppressed tears.

'I don't want my mum to take the blame though. It's not fair.'

He pulled away and took off, heading towards a wooded area and ducking under low-lying branches. Matt had to run to catch up, tracing his way along a partially trodden footpath and cursing slightly as his shoes sunk into soft, squelchy mud. Brambles tugged at him as he tried to keep up and every now and again a barb penetrated the material of his trousers, causing long scratches across each leg. Jake ran on oblivious, deeper into the foliage, checking every now and then that Matt was still following. Eventually he came to a small clearing with a large tree in the centre. One of its branches had fallen to one side and concealed among its foliage was a hidden recess. Jake was standing in it, beckoning him over. He walked across, climbing over the bulk of the branch and into the cavity. It was larger than he had at first thought and he was able to stand upright in it. Jake pulled some branches over the top and motioned for Matt to sit down on one of several lumps of tree trunk. The den was gloomy and smelt of earth. Dry, brown leaves covered the ground, flattened by the trainer-clad feet of its architect into a brittle woodland carpet.

'Do you like it?' Jake was saying. 'This is my secret hidey hole. No one else has ever been here before. I come here by myself when I want to think, especially about my mum.'

'It's very nice. Did you make it yourself?' he replied, suddenly becoming aware of the photo frame that he himself had given the boy. It was tucked away underneath an overhang, only visible from inside the den.

Jake saw where his eyes were directed and moved across, lifting the photo of Denise up towards a chink of light.

'I brought the picture here because Mikey kept trying to get to it. He was threatening to rip it up.' He stared at it. 'She's very beautiful, isn't she?'

Matt nodded. 'You love her very much, don't you?'

'Yes I do. Lots of other people don't understand. They laugh when I talk about her and call me names, but they don't know what we've been through. It's only ever been her and me. She's got me out of trouble in the past and she doesn't deserve to be locked away for this.'

Matt sensed that this was the time to make his move. It was obvious the boy wanted to talk.

'Tell me what really happened then, Jake. Don't be frightened about Lee or Mikey. I can make sure they never find you or your mum. You'll be safe if you tell me what you obviously need to say.'

Jake was silent. He looked down at his feet and appeared to be weighing up exactly what to do. The whole forest seemed to hold its breath with him; not a twig moved, nothing daring to break the air of expectancy.

'It was me,' he finally said, calm and composed. 'It was me who killed Ryan, not my mum or Lee. She only said that it was her to get Lee off our backs and because she wanted to protect me.'

Matt was in shock. 'What do you mean it was you?' he blurted out. 'It couldn't have been you. You're too young.'

'I had to stop Ryan crying, otherwise Lee would have beaten my mum up again and I couldn't let that happen. He was in a really bad mood. I was only trying to make Ryan laugh. Mum always used to make him laugh when she swung him round. I didn't mean to hit his head on the wall. He slipped when I was holding him.'

'You're not just saying this because you're frightened of Lee, are you?' Matt was desperate. He couldn't believe that anyone other than Lee had killed Ryan.

'No, it's the truth. I'm not frightened of Lee or Mikey any more. I hate them. When they find out what I've done, they might leave me alone.' He smiled briefly before continuing. 'Lee was in the toilet when I did it. I think my mum saw me but she said to make you lot think it was Lee. She told me what to say. She didn't want us to tell you we'd seen Lee actually do it, in case it made him really mad. He's crazy, like. We was frightened he would have come after us. When Mum got the prison letter she knew she had to do something. She really believed he'd get someone to hurt me. She told me she was really scared, like, because she couldn't stop it happening from prison.' He paused and wiped at his eyes. 'She didn't want me to get into trouble for doing it, so she said she'd tell you it was her, to protect me, like. She told me to keep quiet and let her take the blame and that she'd sort it, but I can't let her go to prison for something I did.'

Matt thought for a moment. There was something bothering him. 'When did she get the chance to tell you all this?'

'When she came to visit me at the home.'

'But you were supervised all the time, weren't you?'

'Most of the time we were, but one of the other kids kicked
off just outside the door and the copper that was standing with
us went out to try and stop it. Mum told me what she was
going to do then.'

He couldn't believe what he was hearing. Tom had sworn
that he'd stayed with Denise and Jake all day and they hadn't
been left unsupervised even for a few minutes. Now he realized Denise had not only been given ample opportunity to
concoct a story to fit in with the letter, but had also had time
to school Jake on what to say. Shit. The story was changing
almost daily. Instead of leading the investigation, he and his
squad were the ones being led. They would be made to look
like total idiots when it finally came to court.

'Are you sure you're telling me the truth now?' he asked
impotently.

'Will they let my mum go now?' Jake ignored the question. 'And what will happen to me? Will I be locked up in
prison for what I did?'

Matt's mind was in a whirl, still trying to make sense of
what he'd just been told. 'I don't know yet,' he said honestly.
'If what you're saying is true, we'll need to speak to your
mum again and get your story confirmed. If she backs up
what you've told us she'll probably be released. As for you,
I don't know. You're still only eight years old. That's below
the age of criminal responsibility.'

'I've heard of that. What is it?' A smile flickered across
Jake's face.

'The law says you can't be held responsible for your actions
until you're ten years old because it believes you don't know
the difference between right and wrong until then.'

'So does that mean nothing will happen to me then?'

'I don't know. You won't be charged with anything or have
to go to court or prison but social services will probably want
you to go for counselling.'

'Will I be allowed to live with my mum again?'

'I don't know, but you probably will at some stage. Lee
won't be allowed back though because of how he's treated

you both in the past. He's got to go to court for assault and
cruelty towards Ryan and maybe for some of the violence
he's meted out on you and your mum, so he'll probably get
a prison sentence anyway.'

'So he won't come back, ever?' Jake was grinning. 'And
it'll just be me and my mum again?'

'We'll have to wait for a decision by social services, but I
don't see why not.'

Jake was on his feet, pushing away the fronds and twigs
with which he'd covered the den. The light streamed in and
Matt saw it reflected in Jake's olive-green eyes, which now
glistened with a strange intensity inside the leafy refuge. The
sight made him uneasy, but he couldn't quite put his finger
on why. He hoisted himself up and set off after Jake, who
was pacing out in front of him. However much he didn't like
what he'd just heard, it did make sense. It was reasonable to
assume that Denise would want to take the blame for her
young son, but he found it hard to believe that Jake could be
capable of the killing. It wasn't the actual act, which might
well have been an accident. He could just about justify that.
It was the way he and his mother had acted afterwards. Why
had neither of them done anything to help Ryan? He could
more than likely have been saved. The knowledge made him
uncomfortable. But who was he to even begin to imagine the
fear of violence that had obviously been forever present in
the Clarkson household? Lee may as well have committed
the crime himself. Now an eight-year-old boy was about to
take the rap for his bullying and violence. It didn't seem
right.

He watched Jake almost skipping down the track in front.
He looked pleased to have come clean, even though Matt
couldn't help wishing he hadn't. He would lose all contact
with him now and he didn't want that to happen. Jake was
becoming almost a surrogate son to him. They had laughed
and had fun together and were building a rewarding relationship. He was almost grieving for the forthcoming loss. The
desire to return Jake to the home and never say a word about
what had been said flashed through his mind. Denise deserved
to be inside for allowing her family to be brutalized by Lee
and not moving out. Lee deserved to do time for his past
history of violence and for being the ultimate cause of Ryan's

death. Instead, a young boy who should have been treated as a victim would now be treated as the suspect.

He looked up and saw Jake waiting at the end of the path.

'Can we go straight to the police station now? I want to tell them what I've just told you.'

'Are you quite sure you want to go through with this?' Matt said.

'Oh yes, quite sure,' Jake replied, smiling brightly. 'The sooner they hear my story, the sooner my mum will be let out of prison and we'll be back together.'

# Twenty

January 2nd 2008 was set to be a busy day and Matt was already trying to play down to Jo his involvement in the forthcoming events. He was in the kitchen, making himself and Chloe some toast. Jo was there too. He thought of their fleeting conversations while he watched the butter melt into small patches of yellow before being absorbed. Any mention of Jake seemed to invoke a pained reaction from her. He had been visiting Jake on the day of the accident, on Christmas Day, on New Year's Day. And now that he had mentioned the boy's name again, her mood had changed from frosty to down-right frozen.

'You seem to prefer spending time with a stranger's boy rather than with your own son,' she fired off at him as she walked into the kitchen.

'That's not fair and you know it's not,' he responded with a mix of guilt and rage.

'Then why are you going to be with him this morning, rather than with Ben?'

'Because I have to. Because I promised I would visit him today.'

'And he's more important?'

'Jo, you're twisting things. I'll be popping up to see Ben

before I go in and then I'll try and get back up there later when I've finished.'

'You'll *try* and pop in to see him. Is that the best you can manage?' She spun round to direct the question at him, her face pinched in anger, her voice harsh.

'After today I'll have more time to be around. I promise. I'll have finished dealing with Jake. Andrei Kachan and Sharon Cunningham will have returned on bail and been charged and so there'll be nothing else left to be done. I told Gary I'd be there for that, by the way.' He tried to inject some optimism into the conversation. 'That was good news, wasn't it?'

She ignored the question. 'After today, I'm sure you'll find something else to take up your time, rather than being where you should.'

'And where exactly is that? Because I don't know at the moment.' He tried to hold his temper but he didn't think he could keep calm much longer. 'If I'm not at the hospital you make me feel guilty for not being with Ben, and if I do go, you totally freeze me out. It's as if I'm not there. I don't know what to do. You won't talk to me about what's happening and I can't talk to you at the moment without you jumping down my throat at everything I say.' He paused before plunging on. 'The only people that I can talk to at the moment are Tom and Alison at work. At least they're willing to listen.'

'That's nice for you.' Her tone was mocking. 'All I've asked is that you visit Ben more often and when you do, you talk to him. Is that too much to ask?' She laughed derisively. 'You can go running off and speak to work colleagues but you can't even talk to your own son. You're pathetic!'

The words were like a slap in the face and he was shocked at the vehemence with which they were spat out.

'Well, at least they'll make the effort to sit and talk things through with me. You seem hell bent on destroying every-thing we have. Did you know Tom and Sue went through difficulties a few years back, but they worked things out by talking it through with friends? Maybe you should think about that before it's too late. But then, it depends on *your* priorities.'

He turned and lifted Chloe up in his arms. 'I'm going now. I'll see you opposite Ben's bed, around sixish this evening.'

Jo shrugged. 'Or whenever you get there,' she challenged coolly.

By the time he reached the station it was mid-morning. Nothing had changed at the hospital. Ben was still unconscious and Matt had spent some time trying to talk to him. But it was still difficult to engage in a conversation that went only one way. He was trained in interview techniques, during which observing the responses and body language of the person sitting opposite was as important as the words they formulated. Talking to someone who offered no responses was nigh on impossible. The nurses were sympathetic to his plight, obviously accepting everyone's limitations. They offered support and encouraged him to interact in whatever way he felt most comfortable. He wished Jo could be equally accepting.

Tom was already at work when he arrived. He glanced across sheepishly when Matt walked in.

'Can I speak with you?' they both said in unison.

Tom followed him to his office and shut the door.

'How the hell did you allow Denise and Jake to be unsupervised? And more importantly, why didn't you tell me they were left alone?'

'Matt, I'm really sorry. It was only a few minutes right at the end. Some kid was threatening the staff with a knife right outside the office and I didn't think I had a choice. I had to help. It was such a short amount of time. I didn't think it was important enough to tell you about.'

'It was enough time for them to get their heads together and sort out what to say. We're beginning to look like laughing stocks. First the prison authorities let a threatening letter slip through and suddenly Denise is confessing, with the result that Lee Clarkson is back out on the streets.' He rubbed his cheek. The swelling had gone down but an ugly yellow bruise covered his cheek and jaw, merging at the side of his mouth to form a large kidney-shaped reminder. 'Much to my cost. Then the next thing I know, I take Jake for a trip out in the hope he might spill the beans on Lee and he drops his own bombshell, telling me at the same time that he had a nice, cosy little chat with his mother, just him and her, while you were out acting the hero.'

Tom dropped his head. 'There's nothing more I can say. I

really didn't think they had the time to get their heads together. Which version do you think is the right one?'

Matt sighed. He'd been thinking of nothing much else all night. 'I didn't see this coming at all, but it does make sense, unfortunately. We always thought it was a choice between Lee and Denise because they were the adults and we presumed only an adult would be capable of committing such a crime. Until now Jake was always treated as a witness, but he was there too, on the stairs watching. Or so he said before. Both Denise and he had the opportunity while Lee was in the toilet, but they both intimated it happened when Lee went back into Ryan's room after he'd finished.'

'Why didn't they both just come right out and say he killed Ryan, though? It would have been an easy escape route for both of them and it would have got rid of Lee at the same time.'

'Because they were frightened of the repercussions. I think they hoped that if Lee was pointed out as the main suspect, we would then somehow be able to obtain all the necessary evidence to make sure he went down with it, without them really sticking in the knife. If he thought they'd grassed him up by saying they'd actually seen him kill Ryan, they were worried he'd make sure they were hunted down. Denise probably thought he'd be OK with the lesser offence that they were both charged with, rather than a charge of murder. She didn't realize the new offence came with a fourteen-year maximum term. Nor did she realize just how pissed off Lee was about it until she got the letter.

'As soon as she read that, she realized Lee would make sure she and Jake were hunted down and given a beating. And worse still, she couldn't even protect Jake because she was inside. Only they know what Lee's really capable of, although I have a pretty good idea.' He rubbed his cheek again and raised his eyebrows. Tom laughed.

'The rest then falls into place. Denise admits it, saying that it's an accident to try to protect her only remaining son. She's willing to take the blame in the hope that when Lee's history of violence and physical abuse comes out, a judge and jury would look kindly on her assertion that it was an accident which happened when she was trying to prevent any further assault to herself or Ryan. She would have stood quite a reasonable chance, as well. A good defence counsel would have played on all her previous injuries in order to get her off murder. My guess is it would have been quite easy to cop a plea of manslaughter on grounds of diminished responsibility.'

'So why do you think Jake's come clean with his own confession now? I imagine that's what their conversation was about during the visit. I presume she told him to keep his mouth shut and she would confess.'

'I don't know why exactly. Other than I've always had the feeling he wanted to tell us something. Right from the start, I thought and hoped it would be to bubble Lee up, but this is obviously what it was. Out of all of them he's probably the only one with a guilty conscience. Plus he's always saying how much he loves and misses his mum. Maybe he didn't want to risk being kept in care. It wouldn't take too much working out, even for an eight-year-old boy, that a mother with a conviction for killing a child would be unlikely ever to have any children living with them again, or certainly not for a long, long time. The whole family have had enough dealings with social services to know the score. Unless he was back actually living with Denise, my guess is Jake wouldn't be happy.'

'It was a bit of a risk though, wasn't it? How did he know he wouldn't be sent to prison? Most eight-year-olds wouldn't know about the age of criminal responsibility. Plus, social services could still separate them now if they feel it would be detrimental to allow them back together.'

Matt nodded.

'It was obviously a gamble he was willing to take if it meant he stood an increased chance of being reunited with his mum. He certainly couldn't wait to get on with it once I told him the probable outcome. Of course it will still depend on what Denise says when she's produced from prison for interview.'

'She's arriving this afternoon, by all accounts,' Tom commented.

'You're joking. That's quick. Pity it's not as quick as that when it's the prosecution wanting to ask a few more questions or add a few extra charges. If the defence want something, all they have to do is snap their fingers and it's done ASAP.

Can't keep a poor, innocent woman in prison any longer than necessary, eh?'

'I don't know about innocent,' Tom smiled. 'She's still the last one, on paper at least, to admit to murder.'

'What time is Jake arriving to have his statement taken?'

'Anytime now.'

Matt checked his watch. 'Barry Tate is going to do the honours again and you can assist. I know Jake doesn't really like him and wants me to do the interview, but I've explained that I can't as I'm already too involved. I wrote my initial statement of his admissions last night and date stamped it. I'll let you have that so you can give Barry the heads-up on what he can expect. Let's see when Jake's talking to someone independent whether he comes out with exactly the same story. I will come down and have a few words with him when he arrives, but then it's down to you and Barry. Besides, I promised Gary I'd be at Brixton custody when Sharon Cunningham and Andrei Kachan return on bail and they're due back this afternoon, to be charged.'

Tom got up and started towards the door. 'That's great news, Matt. You must both be delighted.'

'Well, I certainly am.' He didn't mention Jo's unenthusiastic response. From Tom's sympathetic grimace, his mate had picked up on the omission immediately.

'She'll come round. Just give her time. I'll go and get things going with Jake and Denise and keep you informed.' He turned round and the normal cheeky grin was back. 'Maybe those few minutes they had together weren't so bad after all? At least we might finally have got to the truth.'

Jake looked radiant as he was brought through. Not at all like a child about to admit to killing his own brother. His expression flagged somewhat when told that Matt wouldn't be conducting the interview.

'Just tell the truth, Jake,' Matt prompted. 'Tom and Barry will be with you and they'll look after you.'

The boy nodded in response. His freckles stood out in the glare of the office lighting and his fair hair was more unruly than ever. He'd definitely filled out since being in care and his shoulders and back appeared broader than Matt remembered. His olive-green eyes seemed even darker and more intense as he gave his attention to Matt's grave words of instruction.

'I'll tell them exactly what I told you, Matt. I won't let you down.'

'You do realize the seriousness of what you told me yesterday, don't you?'

Jake nodded again and Matt couldn't resist the urge to reach out and tousle the boy's hair.

'I won't be able to see you again until all of this is dealt with, Jake, but good luck. Just tell the truth and after we've spoken to your mum, social services will give you some help to come to terms with what you've done. Hopefully in due course you'll be able to put this behind you and move on with your life.'

'I'll try to. Thanks for all your help,' Jake replied seriously.

Matt held out a hand and Jake took it, shaking it firmly. As they were about to part, the boy pulled away and threw himself at the detective, clinging on round his torso and burying his head in his chest.

Matt wasn't quite sure what to do, particularly with Tom and Barry looking on, and was only rescued from his awkwardness by Tom taking hold of Jake by the shoulder and gently prising him off.

He stood rooted to the spot as Jake was led quietly away. He knew in his heart it would be the last time he ever saw the boy. He watched until the fair hair disappeared from view and turned slowly away, an inexplicable heaviness descending on his shoulders.

# Twenty-One

Andrei Kachan cursed. In just three hours he would find out whether nearly five years spent building a new life for himself, in a new country, were about to be wasted. Five years in which he'd made a name for himself as a hard-working, hard-living man. Five years in which, regrettably, he'd also become renowned as a hard-drinking man. Vodka had always been his consort, wooing him away from reality to a place where he could forget the harshness and poverty of his past. This time though it had led him by the balls towards incarceration.

His fiancée sidled up behind him and threaded her arms through his, undoing the buttons of his shirt with nimble fingers. He held his breath as she moved them slowly round in tiny movements, circling lower and lower, towards the top of his trousers. He tightened his stomach muscles, allowing a gap to form at the waistband, and waited for the fingers to delve deeper. He didn't really have time for this but he'd never been known to turn it down either. He was aware of the fingers tugging gently downwards on his zip and knew that she'd already got the response she was after.

'I love you, Andrei,' she said. 'Don't worry about this afternoon. Everything will be all right.'

He felt himself wilt at the words but her fingers were quickly at work again, gripping him hard, massaging him, undressing him. He hadn't got time, but then he didn't know whether this might be the last time. He turned, forcing a smile to his face, and whispered in her ear what she wanted to hear. Deftly he pulled at her clothing, stripping her naked within seconds, and lowered her carelessly on to the bed. She frowned, but he didn't have time to explain. He pushed his mouth over the frown, kissing, probing, obliterating. He looked at her trusting face and felt only irritation. If she hadn't been so quick to tell the police in the first place that he'd been driving her car, this uncertainty might never have happened. He entered her, pressing in deeply, aware that she was still as yet unprepared. He didn't care though. He didn't have time to wait. He saw another frown cross her brow and looked up, ignoring her silent plea, and concentrated on the increasing momentum. He had to keep going. He felt the pressure growing and drove in deeper and deeper, faster and faster, until the moment of pleasure was reached. His arms and legs buckled beneath him and he slumped down on the bed next to her, panting. She stayed still and again he knew only irritation.

'I'm sorry, darling,' he mumbled. 'I've got things on my mind. I'll make it up to you later, I promise.' She rolled away and got up, pulling a gown over her nakedness. 'I do love you . . . you know that, don't you?' he called out as she walked silently away.

He heard the shower running and waited while she dressed, impatient for her to leave. She took an hour to do her hair and apply her make-up and by the time she eventually emerged he could barely contain his displeasure. He took a deep breath.

'You look lovely. Now remember, when you go back, your solicitor will be waiting. Don't say a word and remember to take the opportunity to phone me as soon as you can and let me know whether we're going to be charged or not.'

She smiled back at him and he leant forward and kissed her on the cheek, winking as he drew away. She could never resist his dark, rugged charm.

'I will. Hopefully it'll be good news and we can go out and celebrate later.'

He kissed her again. 'Hopefully it will. Now, good luck. I'll be waiting for the call so that I can be prepared.'

Five minutes later and she was gone. He heaved a couple of suitcases down from the top of the wardrobe and opened a chest of drawers. The ferry ticket was buried beneath a pile of clothes. He didn't have much time left. He checked his watch again. In half an hour Sharon would be arriving at the police station, within the hour she would be letting him know his fate. In just over two hours he was supposed to be returning on bail. He pulled out a pile of clothes and started folding them carefully into the suitcase. He needed to be prepared.

A shaft of light streamed down through the window into the small, cream box room. She could see nothing out of it except for the sky, which until now had been dirty grey and dismal. It was, however, better than the artificial light she had become used to in prison. While she waited, she sat hypnotized by the steady march of the clouds across the glass, savouring every moment.

Denise Clarkson was ready to be interviewed. Very ready. Since she had been remanded back into custody on 29th December, straight from court, charged with murder, the attitudes of her fellow inmates had changed. Rather than treating her predicament with sympathy they now viewed her with suspicion. Any mother remanded in custody for murdering her own child did not deserve to be given the benefit of the doubt. With one charge she'd jumped up a notch, from victim to aggressor. However much she protested the death was an accident, provoked by the fear of her husband's violence, a growing number of previously friendly inmates were now turning hostile.

It was a situation she hoped would be remedied soon. The last four days had been long and unsettling, with carelessly thrown threats, loud enough to hear, directed towards her. Some of her favourite underwear and cosmetics had been rammed into a soiled toilet bowl. Even her own cellmate had become wary of her, refusing to be seen to be too friendly for fear of reprisals. No one communicated with a child-killer and, until proven otherwise, she was one.

On receiving the information that she was to be re-interviewed, she couldn't help feeling relief that she would at least be given a reprieve from the pressure. She'd taken time with her appearance, clipping her hair back off her face, choosing her most flattering clothes, even applying a little blusher to her pale cheeks.

Now she was ready for whatever was to come. The door clicked open and DS Arnold entered, slipping in next to DC Alison Richards, who was already standing guard. She stood up and held out her hand. He ignored it.

'Sit down, Denise. I'm only going to have a quick chat with you, just to let you know what you're here for. DC Tom Berwick will be conducting the full interview, but he's talking to Jake at the moment.'

'Jake. What's he here for?' She sat up straight and leant forward towards him. 'What's he been saying?'

'I can't go into details. Suffice to say I went to visit him yesterday and he told me a different version of events to the one that you last gave.'

She sunk back against the wall and looked down.

'Denise. I want you to be very careful about what you say when you're interviewed. I think you know what I mean and I think you can guess what Jake has said to me. If what you say corroborates his story, it could change the whole situation. Do you understand?'

She nodded.

DS Arnold stood up to leave. 'Think about it, Denise. I'll try to pop back later to see how it's gone.'

The door shut behind him.

She closed her eyes and an image of Jake floated up into her consciousness. He was a good boy, her very own, special boy.

With little over ten minutes to spare, Sharon Cunningham arrived at Brixton police station. Her solicitor was waiting in reception and they shook hands and moved to the side. A middle-aged, mixed-race man with long dreadlocks and an even longer beard lit up a joint next to them. The smoke spread out across the room, drifting in fragrant wisps among the waiting audience.

'That's taking the piss a bit,' the solicitor whispered across to Sharon. 'I know cannabis has been downgraded but as far as I'm aware it's still illegal to smoke it, especially in a police station.'

Sharon glanced across at the man, who grinned lopsidedly back with brown, discoloured teeth and gave her a thumbs up. She looked away quickly.

'How much longer do we have to wait? It's beginning to go to my head already.' She raised her eyebrows, feigning a swoon, and smiled. 'At least I'll be relaxed when I get in.'

'I'll ring through to custody,' he said, dialling the number as he spoke. 'They normally come and get you if it's a bail return.'

'Do you think I'll be charged?'

'No idea at the moment. Unless they've got some better evidence than last time, I would think it unlikely, but we'll have to see what they come up with.'

The door was soon opened by Gary Fellowes and they were motioned through. Sharon sat where she was told and tried to stay calm. She knew she looked good and it boosted her confidence. *Unless the cops have come up with anything it's unlikely you'll be charged*, that's what her solicitor had just said. She sat upright, her legs crossed and her arms folded on her lap. She had nothing to fear, Andrei had said so and her solicitor had reiterated it too.

Glancing over to where Gary was standing, she noticed the man who had been at her house originally. He was speaking to Gary. She didn't know who he was, but he was staring at her and it made her uncomfortable.

The custody officer called her up to the desk and Gary Fellowes went through the reasons for her original arrest. There was nothing new in what was said. She interrupted them.

'Can you tell me now whether Andrei and I are to be charged with anything?'

The custody sergeant raised his head from the paperwork and smiled.

'We'll get to that once we've gone through your rights and entitlements.'

'But can't you just tell me now?'

She needed to pass the information on to Andrei, like he'd requested. He needed to be ready.

'All in good time,' the sergeant was saying. 'Now, you have the right to have someone informed that you're here, to seek legal advice or to refer to a copy of the codes of practice. You can do any of those things now or at any time while you're here. Do you want to have someone informed that you're here?'

'There's not much point until I know what's happening, but I do need to make a phone call. Andrei wants to know whether he's going to be charged too.'

The procedure dragged on. More prisoners arrived, joining the lengthening queue.

She glanced up at the clock on the wall behind the custody officer. Over half an hour had already elapsed. Andrei would have to be leaving the house by now in order to arrive on time.

'Can you tell me now what's happening? I need to let him know.'

'In a minute, and then we'll go through it all with you.'

She started to worry, but there was nothing she could do. He wouldn't be happy but he'd just have to wait and find out, just as she too had to wait.

Gary was speaking with the custody sergeant, while he typed on to the computer from a prepared form. She tried to listen but she couldn't hear over the commotion all around. Still, she was confident it would all be over soon. Wouldn't they have been gleefully telling her if she was to be charged, watching her squirm, especially in light of the change in her story? She relaxed.

At 3.40 p.m. she was called up to the desk and informed she was to be charged with attempted deception and conspiracy to pervert the course of justice. She felt her legs go weak and shook her head numbly when asked if there was anything she wanted to say. Her solicitor said little more. He jotted down times and nodded back agreeably at Gary Fellowes when told there were no objections to bail.

By 4.05 p.m. she was back out in reception. Cannabis still hung in the air, even though its smoker had departed. She pushed her way out of the claustrophobic atmosphere and scanned the entrance for Andrei. There was no sign of him. She presumed he had already been taken through, but she wanted him there so badly, to reassure her that she had done the right thing and give her strength. She had, after all, done it all for him.

The solicitor took her arm.

'Are you OK?' he said calmly. 'We'll get full disclosure of the case they've got against you before we go to court.'

'Will I really have to go to court?' Sharon was shaking now. 'I've never been in trouble before.'

'I'm afraid so,' the solicitor said, gently prising the folded piece of paper from her hands. He pointed to the type. 'There you go. That's a copy of your charges and the date and time of your court appearance.'

She stared down at the bottom of the form and started to cry as she read the details and inherent warning. *Camberwell Green Magistrates' Court 1000 hours on 10/01/2008. Failure to appear will render you liable to a fine or imprisonment or both.*

Andrei Kachan paced along the street outside their house. He was furious. Furious because his so-called fiancée hadn't phoned, furious because he couldn't find his passport, furious because he had wanted to be gone long before she returned. He still didn't know what decision had been reached, but he couldn't risk returning to the police station unless he knew it was the right one. There was no way he was going to jeopardize his liberty to be banged up on remand in a dirty, stinking prison. He'd done a few small stretches in prison in Russia for fighting and doing it again certainly didn't appeal.

The sky was heavy with rain and black clouds ambled

overhead. A light drizzle was falling and combined with a sudden drop in temperature, the roads and pavements were beginning to become covered in a hard, frozen film. He rubbed his hands together impatiently. Where was the bitch? He'd had his cases packed for what seemed like ages and he was anxious to leave.

He plunged his hands into his pockets, wrapping his fingers around a single car key. His mate's old three-litre Senator stood on the driveway outside his house. Not the best looking car but all he required for a trip to the Continent. Large enough to carry all the belongings and bits acquired from his stay in England, plus a few extras of Sharon's, retrieved from her house as a reward for all the good times he'd given her. He didn't think she'd mind. It was hard luck if she did.

He tucked himself into the shadows as a cab turned into the street and pulled up, stopping only while payment was made. As it disappeared, Sharon crossed the pavement towards the house. He stepped out towards her and she jumped back, a startled expression across her face.

'What are you still doing here?' she stammered, clearly surprised. 'I thought you were at the police station.'

He took no notice of her question. 'Where the hell have you been? Why didn't you phone?'

She still registered shock. 'They wouldn't tell me whether we were going to be charged, so there was no point phoning. When they did eventually tell me, it was too late to let you know. I presumed you'd be on your way. I thought I might see you outside the police station but when you weren't there I guessed you'd already gone in.' She paused and frowned at him. 'They charged me with attempted deception and conspiracy to pervert the course of justice and you were going to be charged too.'

'Just as well I didn't go back then, isn't it?'

'But won't you get in more trouble if you don't?'

She sounded like a pathetic child and for a moment he wanted to laugh. Instead he mimicked her.

'Yes, I probably will get in more trouble, but they'll have to find me first. I'm not letting those bastards lock me away that easily.'

She was wide-eyed with amazement. 'But what are you going to do?'

'I'm leaving. In fact I would already have gone but I can't

find my passport.' He watched as the tears started and felt nothing. It was time to move on. He'd had a good time with her but she'd let him down badly. Nothing she did now could repair the damage. 'Now, be a good girl and show me where my passport is.'

He took her by the arm and guided her towards the front door. The woman was sobbing hard. She was getting herself in a state and it was annoying him.

'But why? Why are you leaving?' she sniffed.

'Because you can't keep your mouth shut, that's why. Because you just had to go and tell the cops that it was me that was driving at the accident, didn't you? Even after I told you not to.'

'But I changed my story for you.'

'It was too late then. The damage was done.'

'Will you be coming back?'

'And end up in jail? I don't think so.'

'But what about me? You can't just leave me here on my own. I've given up everything for you.'

She stumbled through the door and clung on to the frame, fighting to keep herself upright.

'Just find me my passport.'

'What if I don't want to? What if I can't find it?' She was making him angry now. He prised her from the door frame, flinging her into the lounge so that she fell against the sofa. Her eyes shot round the room in alarm and he smiled when he saw a look of resignation gradually replacing the panic. She stared comprehendingly at the empty space in which the plasma television and sound system had been.

'Just find me my passport, before I take everything.'

She nodded mutely and walked stiffly to the bedroom, staring round at the empty drawers and cupboards hanging open. Going straight to the rear of a wardrobe she rummaged about in some clothing and pulled out a plastic file, from which she extricated a passport. She threw it down on the bed and sat on the edge.

Andrei bent down and checked it. His handsome face stared out from the inside and he grinned absently. 'Thanks babe. I thought you might come across to my point of view.'

'Is that all you want now?'

He tucked the passport into his back pocket and leant

towards her, kissing her lightly on the forehead. She tilted her head slightly and he almost laughed out loud. Even now she still wanted him. Even though he was on the verge of leaving her with nothing, she still seemed powerless to resist his charms. She was there for the taking and he was certainly tempted, but on this occasion he really didn't have the time.

She looked defeated, and as he gazed at the dark gashes of mascara streaked down her cheeks and her dishevelment, he was struck by a deep wave of guilt and dishonour. His mother would have been ashamed of his behaviour.

'I'm sorry to leave you like this. I have no choice. I cannot risk the punishment for my crime. Will you forgive me?'

She shook her head slightly. 'If you're truly sorry, you won't go.'

'I have to.'

'Why?'

'I just have to go.'

'Are you leaving straight away?'

'I have arranged to meet Filipp for one last drink and then I will go.' He walked to the door and slipped out into the gloom. The windows of the Senator were beginning to frost over. He scraped a small hole in the centre and squinted through it, rubbing the condensation with an old piece of cloth. He heard the sound of footsteps on the gravel and saw Sharon's face in the misty glass.

'Don't go, Andrei. You don't have to go.'

But it was too late. It was time. With one last glance at her familiar, tear-stained face, he barrelled the car off the driveway and out into the road.

# Twenty-Two

The station officer had been briefed to contact Gary or Matt the moment Andrei Kachan showed at the counter. It was gone ten past four and he was late. It wasn't that unusual though and for the time being they weren't panicking. Traffic was heavy on the main road outside and the January sales were bringing an influx of shoppers to clog up the smaller roads and the car parks. In addition Sharon Cunningham had returned and she had certainly given them no reason to suspect that Andrei would fail to appear. On the contrary, Gary was reassured to hear her pleas to contact him and let him know the decision. He had obviously not forgotten.

While Gary filled out paperwork, Matt slipped into a quieter room to use the phone. He dialled Tom's number and was pleasantly surprised when his friend answered.

'Tom. How's it going your end?'

'Not so bad. I've just this minute finished speaking to them both. Jake pretty much repeated what he said to you. Everything's down on tape now. He admits killing Ryan and says it was an accident. Says he panicked when it happened because he thought he would get in trouble with Lee and laid him in his bed to make him look as if he was asleep.'

'How did he seem to you?'

'He cried when he spoke about it, said he only wanted to help Spider-Man fly, like his mum often did. The rest is history. She told him not to admit it at the beginning in the hope Lee would get done. Then when she received the threatening letter and got scared, she told him to stay quiet and said she would take the rap for it.'

'Did he say why he'd owned up and disobeyed his mum?'

'Not really, other than he didn't think it was fair she should be in prison when it should be him. He seems like a good kid really, especially considering the parents.'

'What about Denise? What did she have to say for herself?'

'She was a bit reticent at first, still claimed it was her, though not particularly vociferously. However when it was reiterated to her that Jake had supplied a different version of events, she took back her confession. Laid it on a bit thick about how Jake should have kept his mouth shut and let her take the blame. We couldn't stop her crying about it. She thought he'd be locked up away from her in a juvenile prison for good. When we explained about the age of criminal responsibility and how he couldn't be sent to prison, it was like she then felt free to talk.'

'Did she corroborate Jake?'

'Yes, almost exactly. Blamed Lee for causing him to do it. I suppose the severity of the impact on Ryan's skull also makes sense now, thinking about it. As an adult you'd have thought Denise would have swung Ryan slower and been more in control. Jake's much smaller and wouldn't have had the strength to keep control. Once the momentum got going, he was probably going a lot faster than an adult would have. Poor Ryan didn't stand a chance when his head hit the wall.'

'Have any decisions been made as to what will happen now?'

'We're just trying to sort it out. Social services are on their way. Judging by the conversation the guv'nor's already had with them, they'll probably be keeping Jake as a ward of court for the foreseeable future. They want to make sure he gets help and counselling to deal with any trauma he might have as a result of the incident. If you ask me, he seems more traumatized at not being allowed straight back to Denise. I think he got the impression he'd be able to run straight into her arms. He's cried more about that than when he was describing what he did.'

'Will he be allowed to speak to her before he leaves?'

'I think they're going to try and arrange a visit.' He paused. 'Fully supervised of course. They'll be allowed to meet up occasionally at first, with a social worker present, and I'm told gradually they'll increase the regularity and length of the visits until they deem them safe to be left together.'

'I suppose, legally, they'd find it hard to stop them being together. They're both really victims of domestic violence, even if Ryan was killed as a direct result of Jake's actions. Denise could launch a legal challenge if they do try to keep them apart. She's not been charged with any other offences and now the murder charge is going to be dropped, she's a free woman in law, though morally I still think she's got a lot to answer for.'

Tom snorted out loud. 'Apparently they're already talking about her receiving a parenting skills course. Yet another new government initiative, I suppose.'

Matt laughed back. 'Anything to try and stop the number of ASBOs getting out of hand. It would be funny if it wasn't so tragic. And Lee, what's happening with him?'

'He's still out on bail until his court date arrives.'

'Hopefully when they hear the list of injuries and assaults he's responsible for he'll be sent down for a few years.'

'And if that happens, I'm told Mikey and Christina will be looked after by a relative of his. Denise certainly wants nothing more to do with any of them and of course, she and Jake are prime witnesses for the prosecution. If he does try to make contact with either of them, he's liable to be remanded in custody.'

'Best place for him. It's a shame he wasn't still on remand on New Year's Eve. I might look more presentable then.'

Tom was silent for a moment.

'Are you all right now, Matt? I've never seen you react like that before.'

He sighed. 'I'm surviving. Just.'

'Well, don't forget us, if you need someone to talk to. I'll be your male back-up and Alison could give you a glimpse into the unfathomable female mind!'

'I'll be with her for a long time then, 'cause I can't understand for the life of me what's going on inside Jo's. Still, maybe that's not such a bad thing.' He paused briefly at the thought of Alison's smiling face. 'Anyway, I won't bore you any longer with my sorry love life. I've got to get back to Gary. He'll be wondering where I am. Kachan is late returning and when he eventually does appear I want to be there.'

'And I'd best be off too. I've got to speak to the CPS about dropping Denise's murder charge. I need to be ready for their decision.'

The phone cut off but Matt stayed rooted to the spot, the receiver still held to his ear. Something in what Tom had just said struck a chord and was troubling him, but he couldn't think what. He ran the sentences back through his mind until he reached the very last one. That was it. *I need to be ready for their decision.* He threw the telephone down and started to run back towards the custody area. That's what Sharon had said. That's what she had said several times. Andrei needed to be ready for their decision. But what did he have to do to be ready? And ready for what?

Gary looked up, startled, as the door burst open.

'Has Kachan arrived yet?'

'Not that I know of. Why?'

He shot a look at the clock. It was nearly 4.58 p.m. Even

allowing time for a few traffic hold-ups, he shouldn't be that late.

'Because I don't think he's got any intention of returning.' He spun round and sprinted towards the front office, scanning the motley assortment of customers waiting in or around reception. Andrei Kachan definitely was not there.

Gary caught up with him.

'What's going on?'

'He's not coming back. It's just hit me. You remember Sharon kept asking whether they were both going to be charged? She kept saying she needed to phone Andrei to let him know the decision so he could be ready. She must have asked three or four times. Well, ready for what? Certainly not to cough to it, he's made no comment all the way through. And now he's not shown. Maybe he wanted to be ready to disappear if the decision went against him.'

'Maybe he just didn't want the shock when he got here?' Gary countered, but Matt knew, knew as certainly as if he was standing next to the man discussing with him his options.

'I'm going to his house to find him. I'm not letting that bastard get away with nearly killing my boy. If he's trying to escape, I'm going to stop him, with or without your help.'

Gary Fellowes needed no convincing. 'I'm right behind you,' he shouted back as the pair of them ran out to the car park. The heavy metal gate swung slowly open and the clock on the dashboard clicked over to 17.02. Matt grimaced.

'I've got just under an hour to find Andrei Kachan, bring him back in and get up to the hospital. I told Jo I'd be there for six.'

The journey to Andrei and Sharon's house wasn't long, but it was fraught. Driving rain impeded the view through the windscreen and queues of stationary traffic baulked their progress. They placed a magnetic blue light on the top of the car and that, combined with flashing grille lights and a shrill, whining siren assisted them a little. In the atrocious weather conditions, however, their dark-coloured, nondescript vehicle did not stand out sufficiently for the still hung-over New Year shoppers to react to their presence.

They crossed the centre of Clapham Common, aware that

the trees lining the avenue were beginning to duck and sway in a strengthening wind.

'Do you think he'll still be there?' Gary shouted above the sound of the siren.

'Let's hope so, the less we have to do out in this weather the better.'

They swung down a side road and Matt turned off the sirens, feeling the back of the car slide out slightly on the freezing, wet road. Beauchamp Road was next on the left. The rain was beginning to peter out, but a light spray was still falling. They stopped outside number thirty-three and saw lights blazing from the windows. The curtains hadn't been drawn and they could see straight inside.

'It looks like someone is home,' Matt muttered.

He pulled his collar up round his neck and ran towards the front door, ringing the bell. There was no answer so he knocked hard on the door. It swung ajar with the pressure and he noticed it had been put on the latch.

'Is anyone there?' he shouted. 'Sharon, Andrei. It's the police.'

'Come in,' replied a woman's voice. 'I've been expecting you.'

He followed the direction of the voice, allowing Gary to enter the lounge first. Sharon was lying on the sofa, staring up at the ceiling. She didn't turn her head as they approached. It was obvious something had happened. He took in the missing plasma screen, the open drawers and the photograph of a swarthy, smiling man, lying on the floor staring up through a shattered glass frame.

'You're too late. He's gone. He's left me. Are you satisfied now?'

She turned bloodshot eyes towards them.

'Do you know where he's gone?' Gary asked evenly.

'No, I don't, and even if I did I wouldn't tell you.'

Gary frowned. 'Why are you being like this?'

'Don't you know? Can't you guess?' She swung her legs off the sofa and sat up abruptly. 'If you hadn't tricked me into telling you he'd been driving my car that first night, he'd still be here. He blames me for getting him into trouble. Now why don't you just go?'

'We're not going until we find out where he is,' Gary said.

'How many more times do I have to tell you? Don't you listen? I wouldn't tell you now even if I did know. You've ruined my life. I had a future with Andrei and now, because of you lot, it's gone.' She stood, almost spitting the words at them. Raising an arm, she pointed towards the front door. 'Now get out.'

The veins in Matt's head were pumping hard. He tried to control the pounding.

She screamed at them again, and in one move he stepped forward and grabbed her outstretched hand, crushing her fingers in his grip.

'Don't tell me we've ruined your life.' His voice was so quiet it was barely audible. 'I don't want to hear about your ruined life. What would you know?'

'Let go of me,' she screamed. Her face was so close that he could feel the warmth of her breath on his cold cheeks. Her expression changed to a sneer. 'So you *can* speak then. I've seen you watching me, like some kind of pervert. You were here the first time. Who the hell are you anyway? And who said you could grab hold of me? I'll sue you for this.'

He let her hand fall and stared straight into her challenging, angry face.

'I'm the father of the little boy your fiancé left for dead in the road. And before you say anything further about your ruined future, maybe you should think about the kind of future my son has, if he has one at all.'

The colour drained from her face as he spoke, but he couldn't stop. 'Maybe you should see the look on his three-year-old sister's face when he won't wake up when she's telling him to, or the Christmas presents still lying under the tree waiting for him, or the pain on his mother's face because she feels guilty for not having prevented him running out in front of your fiancé's speeding car – which incidentally was on the wrong side of the road. Maybe you should come and see him lying attached to a machine in intensive care. Then maybe, just maybe, you might see whose life has really been ruined.'

The pounding had gone and all around was silence. Sharon stood frozen, still staring into his face, but as he watched, her face crumpled and she threw a hand to her mouth.

'Oh my God. Oh my God. I'm so sorry.'

She dropped back down on to the sofa and started to cry.

Gary sat down opposite. 'Now you see why it's so important for us to find Andrei.'

'I really don't know where he is, but he wanted his passport. He'd obviously been planning on going when I was at the station.' She sniffed loudly, dabbing at her nose with a tissue. 'He couldn't find his passport so he had to wait till I returned. When I told him he was going to be charged, that was it, there was no stopping him from leaving. I think he knew he was going to get done anyway. He'd already packed all his stuff. He's taken a lot of my property too, squeezed it into an old car that he'd borrowed.' She looked wildly around, pointing at the spaces. 'Look what he's taken.'

'Can you describe the car at all?' Gary returned her swiftly to the job in hand.

'No, not really. It was big. I think it was a Vauxhall. Dark in colour and it was an S reg.'

'OK, Sharon, that's good. Now I want you to think really carefully. Did he give you any clue about where he was going?'

She concentrated hard, before opening her eyes. They were wide with excitement and flicked from one man to the other. 'He did say he was going for one last drink with Filipp before he leaves. They usually meet at the Horse and Groom in Streatham. You could try there.'

The pub was large, set on a busy main street. The bars at the front catered for occasional drinkers and older patrons. Cushioned seating was laid out around the edges in alcoves and wooden tables catering for larger groups were positioned in the centre. Two doormen stood guard at the front door to discourage troublemakers. They would have been better positioned at the rear entrance; it was there that any disorder was apt to start. The area at the back of the pub was inhabited by the younger generation. Small groups of varying ethnicity gathered to swap stories, exchange news and challenge each other to games of pool and snooker. Until recently the clientele had been mainly of Caribbean origin, but of late groups of Poles, Bulgarians, Russians and other Eastern Europeans had taken root, to the chagrin of the regulars. Games of snooker between the groups had become international matches, with supporters of each player gathered round noisily, cheering their chosen nationality. Occasionally the tension spilt over into fist fights, which inevitably continued in the dimly lit car park that ran the length of the building to the rear.

Matt knew exactly what part of the pub Andrei would be in, if he was there at all, and he wasn't looking forward to the possibility of a welcome party. He briefed Gary about the layout and requested back-up. There was no one spare and he didn't have time to wait. He pulled into the car park and stopped. Although it was still only early evening all light had gone from the sky, erased by the heavy cloud and the rain. It was even darker than usual, a lamp having been rendered useless with a smashed shade. Two men conducting a drugs deal sauntered out from a recess, caught in the headlights of the car. They nodded towards the car and disappeared from view into the glare of the interior.

He scanned the other vehicles. There weren't many as yet and he quickly spotted the old Vauxhall Senator stationary in the far corner. He elbowed Gary and pointed towards it.

'Looks like he's still here then.'

He got out and walked over towards the car, jotting down the registration number on the back of his hand. It was so cold the ink in the pen almost froze on contact with the air. He breathed out and watched his breath swirling around him. He could see the plasma screen TV lying across the rear seat. It was definitely the right car.

'Gary, I haven't actually seen this guy in person yet so I might have to let you point him out. I've only seen his photo.' He remembered the face, grinning out from the frame at Sharon's house. Swarthy and charming but with a hint of arrogance, he'd thought the first time he'd seen it. He preferred to remember how it had just looked, peering out from behind the cracks of the broken glass like an inmate looking through the bars of a prison cell. He wouldn't forget that face. He would never forget that face, but still, it was only a likeness caught on celluloid. He wanted to see the real thing.

He started towards the rear doors, with Gary keeping pace. A waft of rancid humidity belched out from an extractor fan. He tensed, flexing the muscles in both hands, the hunter tracking his prey.

As the door swung open his eyes surveyed the scene, taking in every detail, every movement, every face. The snooker table stood over to the left and he could see only the backs of a small group huddled around it. Various other groups and individuals milled about and a couple leant heavily over the bar. He squinted as his eyes became accustomed to the brightness and stepped forward on to the floorboards. An icy blast followed him in and heads were turned challengingly until he pushed the door shut behind. A jukebox blasted out music from the direction of the snooker table. He headed towards it, immediately drawn towards the anonymity of the players. Three of the onlookers broke away and walked straight towards the toilets. He noticed but he couldn't see their faces.

He leant against a wall and peered at those remaining. They were all white and of Eastern European appearance, stocky and dark with close-cropped hair and muscular physiques. He knew by their regular glances they were aware of his presence, but they didn't seem perturbed at his attention. He ran his hands through his hair trying to smooth down the damp waves and appear nonchalant, but he knew he would soon be identified as a copper, if he hadn't been already. A policeman could always be recognized in this sort of environment. He could see Gary sauntering round the edge, his eyes darting from one customer to the next. He looked like a copper too, paying too much attention to his surroundings, letting his gaze stay a second or two longer on each face than was good for him in a bar.

He risked a good look at the snooker players, trying to fit the photograph to the face, but none had the profile or features of Andrei. Gary was moving round the other bars now and Matt watched him for any indication that he'd recognized his prey, listened for any call for assistance. Gary came back round to join him.

'He's not here,' he said.

'He must be. His car's in the car park.'

'Well, I've checked the whole pub and I can't see him. I would definitely recognize him and, more to the point, he would recognize me.'

Matt nodded. 'The only place we haven't checked is the toilets. Three blokes went into that one as we came in. They haven't come out yet. Come to think of it, it's been too long. They should be out by now.'

'Did any of them look like Andrei?' Gary was interested now.

'I didn't get a chance to see. They had their backs to me and moved off as soon as I came across.'

He knew though that Andrei must be one of them; there was nowhere else he could be. They walked towards the toilets. Matt was aware of heads turning to watch. He could feel his heart beginning to pump more strongly. He flexed his fists and took a deep breath. Pushing the door he stepped in and immediately through another door. Three men were leaning against the far wall in conversation. They stopped talking and stared at the newcomers and the one in the centre smiled languidly. Matt recognized the smile immediately. It was imprinted in his memory. He was glad to be meeting its owner at last.

'Fancy seeing you here.' The comment was directed towards Gary, who was standing directly behind him. The eyes too were fixed on his colleague.

'So you must be Andrei?' The eyes switched to him and the man's face creased in the same indifferent smile.

'I might be. And who are you?'

'My name is DS Arnold. You nearly killed my son.'

Andrei Kachan stood bolt upright, pushing himself off the wall. For a second a flicker of fear crossed his eyes before his face became expressionless again. 'He should not have run out in front of me then. It was his fault.'

Matt tensed. 'It wasn't his fault you were speeding down the wrong side of the road when you hit him and sent him flying through the air. He certainly didn't deserve to be left like an animal on the road while you drove off laughing.'

'So what do you propose to do about it?' Andrei's expression was cold, his eyes icy. Matt responded in equally frosty fashion.

'I propose to take you back to the police station, where you should have returned this afternoon, and I propose to have you charged.'

'And have me put in one of your prisons. I don't think so. You should teach your son how to cross the road safely, or you should tell your wife, if that's who the stupid woman was, how to hold on to him. I'm not going to be punished for your family's foolishness. Now move out of the way and let me out.'

He took a step forward and Matt mirrored it, blocking his way. 'You're not going anywhere, you arrogant bastard.'

Andrei stopped where he was and beckoned to the two other men. 'What you seem to have overlooked is that there are only two of you and at least three of us.' The two other men stepped up behind Andrei. At the same time Matt heard the outside door opening and swung around to see another two men standing to his rear.

'Now, for the last time. Get out of my way.'

Matt couldn't move. He was rooted to the spot, unwilling to allow his suspect to walk away over the horizon without a fight. He also knew, however, that the odds were completely in the other man's favour.

'You don't want to add assaulting a police officer to your list of charges.'

'I won't be,' he smirked back. 'Because you won't have me there to charge with anything.'

He stepped to one side. Matt raised an arm and took hold of him, but he pulled away, twisting so that their faces were close. As Andrei sneered Matt was aware of several other arms reaching out and grabbing him, pulling his arms forcefully behind him. He struggled but couldn't break free. He could smell Andrei's breath on his face, could almost taste the beer fumes. His suspect's expression was full of fury, unlike the smiling likeness in Sharon's house. He looked around at their temporary prison. They were trapped within the confines of the tiled, grubby walls with nowhere to go and five large men as their captors. He pulled again at the arms that held him and felt a blow come into his stomach, making him retch. He tried to pull his legs up to shield himself from further blows but he couldn't. Another blow struck his ribcage and he couldn't breathe. He looked up and all he could see was Andrei's massive frame and fists. The man stepped back and Matt could just make out Gary too, pressed against the wall by the two other males. Andrei turned in his direction and laughed.

'It's your turn now, my friend,' he grinned. 'This will teach you that Andrei Kachan does not receive orders well.' Then he was punching Gary. An explosion of sound filled the small area as the other men jeered and shouted, their faces contorted in delight and encouragement. Gary couldn't move against the onslaught and his shouts became weaker and more pitiful as each blow rained in on him. Blood was spurting from his nose and mouth and splashing down on to the damp tiles. They let him go and he fell to the floor, moaning. Andrei aimed one last kick straight at his head and was gone, striding out into the normality of the bar.

Matt felt the arms that held him drop as the other men slunk away. He ran across to Gary and bent over him. He was moaning and barely conscious. His face was a bloody pulp. The door opened and one of the doormen peered in.

'You're a bit fucking late. It's all over now,' Matt spat furiously. He pulled out his warrant card and held it up. The doorman looked sheepish. 'Call an ambulance and make sure he's well looked after. I've got to go but I'll be back later to make sure it's been done properly. You understand?'

The doorman nodded and shouted across at the other, who was now heading towards them. Matt jumped to his feet and ran. He pulled his radio from his pocket and barked instructions into it. As he flung himself through the back doors, he heard the sound of an engine firing up. He sprinted across the car park towards his own car as the lights of the Senator came on and it lurched forward. His chest and abdomen ached painfully as he drew each breath and he gagged as the icy air hit his lungs. He reached his car and looked up as the Senator passed him. Its driver turned and grinned at him, waving a hand, and he recognized Andrei's sneering face immediately.

The car disappeared around the bend at the end of the car park. It could only turn left when it came to the road, but after that it could disappear easily down any of the side roads off the main street. He couldn't let that happen. He revved his engine and shot forward, wheels screeching. The tyres spun on the freezing concrete and he was aware of how quickly the surface was turning to black ice. He pressed the accelerator and gunned up the driveway. He couldn't see the Senator but knew it must have only just reached the main road. Its rear lights came into his sight just as it swung into a side turning. He accelerated after it and turned just in time to see it disappearing right. He pressed down hard again and felt the back of the car twitch, but as he recovered control he realized he was gaining.

His suspect was turning back on to the main road now and the traffic lights were changing against him. He could see other motorists slow down and stop, blocking his passage.

He reached down and grabbed the blue light, throwing it up on to the roof, and started the sirens. The traffic began to part and he edged through, watching as his target wove his way through the slow-moving vehicles ahead. He was catching him but as he did so, Andrei appeared to become more reckless in his bid to escape. The vehicle was moving from lane to lane as gaps became free. At the next junction, the lights turned to red as Andrei shot through. Traffic on either side of the junction was forced to brake hard as the Senator careered along, using the path cleared by the sirens to forge ahead.

Matt followed. He didn't want to lose sight of his quarry but at the same time Andrei was becoming more dangerous. He wished he would stop. The Senator was on the wrong side of the road now, accelerating down outside the line of traffic. He followed, willing cars in the opposite direction to get out of the way. They parted as he shot towards them, before swinging back on to the correct carriageway. The speed was increasing as they came alongside the Common, forty, fifty, sixty miles an hour. Matt shadowed him, holding back, trying not to push him any harder. He felt his adrenalin surging but at the same time wished it was over. It was too dangerous. Pedestrians watched, their faces alight with fear as the vehicles careered onwards. He saw a mother pull her pushchair back from the kerb as the Senator passed, not too close but close enough for the whine of its engine to signal danger in the woman's mind. He thought of how Jo must have felt as she realized she was too far away from Ben to reach out and pull him to safety.

The Senator veered left, following the road that ran along the other side of the Common. It was darker here, with less traffic. Trees lined the edge and frozen leaves lay glistening on the roadway. Andrei was pushing faster and faster. A mini roundabout appeared at the top of the hill. His brake lights came on and the vehicle slowed, but not enough to stop its rear skidding out across the carriageway, clipping a parked car. Debris spun out into the road in front of Matt. He swerved to avoid it in time to see the Senator accelerate away again, down the hill to the right of the junction. The speed increased to nearly seventy miles per hour as it careered onwards, descending the hill, still following the edge of the Common.

Matt pulled back a little, not wanting to goad him to any greater speed, but Andrei seemed determined to make good his escape. He saw the brake lights come on again at the bottom of the hill. The road made a sharp right-hand bend with a set of pedestrian crossing lights just past it, opposite the entrance to a children's play area. He watched in horror as the lights changed to red. A young child was waiting on the pavement and Matt could just make out the shape of an adult running towards him from inside the park.

Little Jack Bailey was on his way home. It was much later than usual and, at seven years old, it was nearly his bedtime, but he was excited. He and his dad had stopped off at the playground opposite his house as a reward for his being good at the barber's. Several large puddles had turned to ice and he had skidded across them, arms outstretched, pretending to fly. A quick game of hide-and-seek, made more exciting by the darkness, had concluded his adventure and now he was racing to tell his mum and little sister all about it. It was always great fun to be out with his dad.

He pressed the button on the pedestrian crossing and waited, stamping his feet to keep warm. He could hear his dad puffing down the slope towards him. He was waving his arms about and he looked funny. He wanted to get across the road before his dad caught up with him but he knew he had to wait for the green man. It was always being drummed into him by his parents and the teachers at school. Don't cross the road until you see the green man. He saw the lights start to change. Just another few seconds and he'd see the green man and hear the beeping. Then it would be safe. Then he could beat his dad home.

The green man flashed on and he heard the tone start. A car was coming fast down the hill, but it was safe to cross. The green man was flashing. He heard his father shout. He sounded strange. He was catching up. He might beat him if he wasn't quick. The green man was telling him to cross. It was time.

He glanced up as he started to run. The headlights were very close and he could hear tyres squealing but it was safe, the green man said it was.

\*     \*     \*

Colin Bailey saw the situation as it opened up in front of him. Everything was in slow motion and he could do nothing to stop it happening. His son was at the crossing. He'd pushed the button but he didn't seem to be aware of the car. He was looking back towards his father but he wasn't responding to his waving arms. He wasn't responding to the danger.

He could see the lights changing and still the car came. Another car was at the top of the hill. It had a blue light on the top and flashing blue lights on the grille. It must be a police car. He could just hear the sound of sirens above the revving of the first car. The police car must be chasing the first one. The lights were changing to red but the car wasn't slowing down. He was sprinting but he couldn't get there in time. He screamed, 'Jack, stop, stop!' But he wasn't stopping. The green man was flashing in his direction. He could see it clearly. The lights were red for the car but it wasn't stopping either. He saw Jack move forward. He saw his legs move. His head was looking straight ahead. It wasn't looking at the car. He was running. He heard the car tyres screech. It was skidding out of control. It was going straight for his son. He screamed at the top of his voice but nothing came out. Jack was in the road. He'd seen the car at last but now he wasn't moving. He was standing stock still, just looking at it. He waited for the awful thud. He waited to see his little boy on the bonnet, flying through the air like in the adverts, but it didn't come. The car was flying instead. It hit the kerb on the other side of the road and flew through the air. It landed and started to spin, back across the road, back, back across towards a tree.

The noise stopped his nightmare. Jack was still standing in the middle of the road. He ran towards him as bits of metal flew through the air. The sound was awful. It took his breath away. Screaming metal, tearing rubber, leaves and branches snapping all around him. The car ploughed on until with a loud explosion it impacted with a tree. The bonnet was thrown open and smoke and steam rushed out, hissing angrily as its heat mixed with the freezing air. Bits of metal landed among the bushes and a wheel spun off into the darkness. He carried on running until he got to Jack. The police car was coming now and he was afraid it wouldn't stop. He was out of the gate. It was slowing down. He got to Jack and scooped him up in his arms and carried on to the other side of the road. The police car had stopped. It wouldn't have hit him but he had to get Jack out of danger anyway.

Doors were opening and people were coming out of their houses. They were screaming and pointing. He turned towards the first car. It was shunted up against a tree with its bonnet at a crazy angle. Flames licked around the metal and a plume of smoke rose from the mangled engine block.

The policeman was getting out of his car, talking on his radio. He needed to be told. He walked up to the man and grabbed his arm. He was pulling Jack to him and he could feel his son shaking. His face was white with shock. The policeman turned to face him and he had to tell him what he thought.

'What the hell do you think you're playing at, chasing a car down a residential road on a night like this?'

The policeman was silent but he couldn't stop shouting. 'I've read the newspapers. I know what you lot are like. Couldn't you have let him go? Couldn't you have got him another time? You could have killed my son.'

The policeman stared at him. He noticed his face was white too. He saw the shock mirrored in his face. He felt a hand on his shoulder. 'That man almost did kill my son, if you must know. That's why I couldn't let him go.'

Then he was gone, running towards the crash site, and the full impact of his words hit Colin Bailey. He still had his son and he was alive and well. He buried his head in his son's shoulder and sobbed with relief.

The car was beginning to burn as Matt reached it. He was angry. Angry that Andrei hadn't stopped, angry that the bastard had almost killed another child, angry that he himself had been blamed for it. He hadn't wanted to chase Andrei in the first place but in his own mind there had been no option. He couldn't let him escape. It wasn't right. It was his job to bring suspects to justice for the crimes they had committed and he was only trying to do his job. The man had almost killed his son and God only knew what he'd done to Gary.

But the father was right too. Andrei could have killed his son and he would have had to accept part of the blame, however justifiable his actions. He'd thought it was going to end that way as he'd seen the accident play out in front of him. It was like watching his own nightmare occur in front of his very eyes. The boy was Ben, the parent Jo, but the end thankfully was different. He was shocked how close it had been.

For a second, as the father had berated him, he'd been tempted to walk away, leave Andrei Kachan to his fate. But he couldn't. The same sense of duty that had forced him to pursue his quarry was now compelling him to save his enemy.

He was aware of the heat of the car as he neared it. He could hear the blistering and popping of the oil around the engine and the smell of burning filled his nostrils. The car door was hot to the touch and he automatically withdrew his hand from the surface. He could see Andrei's unconscious bulk slumped forward over the steering wheel. He tried the door handle but the door wouldn't open. It was locked. People were shouting at him, telling him to wait until the fire brigade got there. The flames were travelling up the engine towards the driver's compartment. He could feel the heat becoming more intense every second. He didn't have time to wait or it would be too late. Bending down, he grabbed a chunk of paving slab and heaved it at the window. The glass shattered and a wave of heat rushed out. He leant in, pulling the lock up and releasing the catch. The door still wouldn't open. He placed his foot on the hot metal and pulled at the handle, wincing as its heat burnt into his hand. He felt the door give and pulled it wide, listening as the twisted metal creaked and ground.

Andrei was still slumped over the wheel. Matt pulled his body backwards and heard him groan. He was still alive. Leaning in he clamped his arms around the man's torso and lifted. The body hardly moved. Matt could smell his hair singeing and the noise of crackling from underneath the vehicle was getting worse. He tried again, yelling out in his frustration at his inability to shift Andrei's heavy frame. Then he heard shouting next to him. He turned his head and saw Colin Bailey leaning in, offering help. He smiled gratefully at the man. They didn't need to speak. With a loud shout they pulled at Andrei's body again, screaming triumphantly as it was levered out. His foot caught on the door but with one last pull, it came free. They dragged him to the side of the road as the fire took hold, shooting red and white flames high into the night. A fire engine turned the bend at the top of the hill, its siren growing louder as it bore down on them. With a huge blast the petrol tank exploded, sending a wave of sparks airborne.

Matt turned to his helper and the pair shook hands, clasping each other in an emotional embrace.

'Thanks,' he said. There was nothing else he could think of to say.

'No problem,' the father responded. 'Glad I could help you. Now make sure, for both our sons' sakes, that you get him to court.'

'I will,' he nodded in return. 'Don't worry. I will.'

# Twenty-Three

He felt the mobile phone alert vibrate just as the ambulance pulled away. More uniformed police officers had arrived and two were travelling to the hospital with the paramedics, to guard Andrei. Prior to being lifted into the ambulance Matt had gone through his pockets, looking for weapons or means of identification. The ferry ticket had fallen from his wallet and as he'd read the details, the detective realized just how close the man had come to making good his escape. He'd regained consciousness shortly after his rescue and appeared to have no major traumas. The only injuries he had obviously sustained were a broken foot when he'd been pulled from the vehicle, superficial burns and a large bruise to the front of his forehead. Matt's sense of fairness was stretched. It was lucky that anyone could walk from the wreckage of the car still alive. To survive with so few injuries, when his own son had been so badly hurt by the very same man, seemed deeply unjust.

He delved into his trouser pocket and pulled out his phone. A text message from Jo flashed up on the screen. 'Call me when you find time.' Nothing more, nothing less. He checked his watch. Shit. It was gone nine o'clock. He should have been at the hospital three hours before and he hadn't even rung to explain why he was running so late. He was in for another hard time from Jo.

He dialled her number and waited patiently for it to be answered. He didn't have to wait for her to launch into another tirade.

'Jo. I'm so sorry I didn't make it. Andrei Kachan didn't show up at the station so Gary and I have been tracking him down. We got him just as he was trying to drive to Dover and catch a ferry to the Continent. One more hour and he would have been in another country and then we'd never have got him to return. It's good, eh?'

'Yes, it is good,' she replied flatly. 'Unfortunately for you, while you were off chasing after that man, you missed Ben opening his eyes. He's woken up at last.'

He couldn't take it in straight away. His triumph in catching Andrei evaporated in the knowledge he'd missed his son's waking.

'Did he ask for me?' The question was direct and uncompromising, but he needed to know.

'He can't speak very well at the moment, Matt, but he did manage to mouth the word "Daddy". It's a shame you weren't there.'

He thought he could hear a slight edge to the comment, the criticism masked in words of pity. 'I'm coming now. I'll be there very soon.'

He hung up and smiled broadly. 'I've got to go,' he shouted towards the familiar face of the inspector in charge. 'My boy, Ben. He's come out of his coma.'

'That's great news.' The inspector gave a mock salute. 'Hope everything works out for you now.'

He hoped so too. By the time he arrived at the hospital he could barely contain his excitement. He bounded up the stairs and ran along the corridor towards the ward. Jo was sitting next to Ben as he threw himself through the doors. Without thinking he ran up and embraced her, grinning with delight. She tensed a little but smiled back at his enthusiasm. He looked down at Ben. He was sleeping again. He frowned.

'Don't worry,' Jo explained. 'Apparently he'll only wake

for short periods to start with, but gradually the time he'll
stay conscious will get steadily longer and we'll be able to
see what, if any, damage has been done. If you're lucky, he
might open his eyes again while you're still here.'

Her voice had softened and he could detect no hidden
meaning to her words this time. 'I'm sorry for blaming you
for Ben's accident,' he said quietly. 'I nearly witnessed Andrei
Kachan hit another young boy tonight and his father was
powerless to stop it happen. It made me think of you.' She
was silent. 'I'm going to do everything I can to make things
right,' he continued. Her face was blank as she turned away
and he couldn't begin to read what she was thinking.

A small noise stirred him from his thoughts. He glanced
round and saw Ben's small hand begin to move. He took hold
of it and felt a slight twitch. It was so good to feel even this
tiny movement. His son felt properly alive again. He followed
the arm up to his son's face and saw the flush in his cheeks.
His eyes were open and he smiled weakly.

'Ben.' He moved forward to see him better. 'Ben, it's so
good to see you awake again. We've been waiting for you for
so long. When you get better I'll take you to the park and
we'll play football and we'll go fishing for tadpoles.'

He turned and flashed a smile at Jo. She was watching him
intently. He shuddered as an involuntary wave of nervousness
ran down his spine. He didn't know how to read her expression. He glanced back at Ben quickly, anxious not to lose the
moment.

*Speak to him. Encourage him.* That's what she'd said,
wasn't it?

'Don't worry, Ben. You'll be OK. Everything will work out
all right in the end. Mummy and Daddy are here.'

He turned and smiled towards his watching wife, but
somehow he didn't feel quite as confident as the words
declared.

# Twenty-Four

The curtains twitched as Denise Clarkson peered out. March 23rd had not come quickly enough as far as she was concerned. It had been a good ninth birthday party at the children's home but now she was impatient. She couldn't wait to see him again.

A car pulled up outside and she squinted to see its occupants. A middle-aged woman with long, dark hair swept up in a ponytail got out of the driver's side. She went to the boot of the car and pulled out two small suitcases, placing them carefully on the pavement. The passenger door opened and a young boy climbed out, yawning as he did so. He ran his hands through his blond hair and stared up at the house.

She waved from the window and saw the boy's freckled face break into a wide grin. The woman was lifting the suitcases now and walking up her garden path. The boy bounded ahead, rapping on the wood with his fists.

She ran down the stairs and opened the door, laughing with delight as the boy flung himself into her arms.

'Jake, it's so good to have you home again.'

The middle-aged woman smiled at them both and stepped up into the hallway.

'Now, Denise, I just need to come and have a look at the house before I leave the pair of you together.'

She nodded, impatient for the woman to go but knowing the necessity of staying calm and polite.

'I'll show you round,' she replied. She walked slowly from room to room with the woman, pointing out the changes. The house was clean and tidy. She'd spent the last few months preparing it for Jake's return. The social workers said she'd made good progress. She was looking after herself and appeared to be coping well without Lee. He was inside again, having been sent away for six months for child cruelty. With good behaviour he might be out after three and she was already anxious about his release. She didn't want him back. It would jeopardize her relationship with Jake and if he tried to return, she would lose him. She wouldn't allow anything to come between her and Jake again.

'This looks very nice,' the social worker was saying. 'You've made quite an effort.'

She smiled gratefully. 'I'm glad you noticed. I wanted everything to be right for when he returned. I wanted to show you how well I can do without Lee.'

Her voice gave away her anxiety. The woman turned towards her. 'You don't have to worry about him. When he does eventually get out of prison he'll be rehoused in a completely different area, away from you and Jake. He won't be allowed to visit and my guess is he won't want to anyway.' She opened the fridge and peered in, nodding at the food on display. 'This is good, Denise. You've made real progress up until now. Don't let it slip now you've got Jake back. It's only a temporary arrangement until we're absolutely sure you're coping. If you have any problems at all, we're here to help.'

The woman smiled at her and she nodded. She led her up the stairs and opened a bedroom door. 'I've painted Jake's room so it's special and new for him.' She stood proudly to one side while the woman entered. The room still smelt of paint and was tidy and neat. Gone was the padlock on the bottom of the door and gone were the posters on the wall. It housed a solitary bed, instead of the previous two, and a row of toys were laid carefully along one wall. In the corner was a dog basket and a small black and white Staffordshire terrier was looking up expectantly, wagging its tail.

'Scamps,' the boy shouted. He turned to Denise. 'You've got him back.' He let go of his mother and ran to the corner, fussing over the dog and burying his head in its fur. 'This is brilliant, Mum. How did you manage to do all this?'

'I was determined to get you back and I'd do anything to prove I can help you.'

The social worker turned towards her. 'On that subject, you must make sure he continues with his counselling. If he starts missing any sessions we'll have to review the arrangements. Do you understand?'

She nodded again. 'Don't worry. I'll make sure he attends.'

'He's coping excellently with his feelings and the psychologist thinks he's coming to terms very well with the results of his actions. He must continue, though, to be sure he fully understands what he's done.'

They walked downstairs and she stood by the door, willing the social worker to leave.

'I'll come back and visit you tomorrow morning, Denise, and make sure everything has gone well with Jake's first night back home. OK?'

'Yes, thank you. I'm sure we'll be fine though.'

She opened the door and the woman at last took the hint, stepping down towards the road.

'We'll see you tomorrow then.' Denise closed the door abruptly and ran back up the stairs to Jake.

'Happy Birthday, Jake,' she said, smoothing his hair and running a finger over his cheek.

He smiled up at her. 'It's so good to be home properly, Mummy. I've missed you so much.'

'I've missed you too,' she smiled, wiping at the threatening tears.

'What about Mikey and Christina? Will they be joining us?' His voice sounded anxious.

'No, they won't be back. They're not my children. They're Lee's and I don't want nothing to do with him or his family again.'

'Good. I didn't like Mikey. He hit me, like Lee used to, till I said I'd killed Ryan. Then he stopped. He never touched me again. I think he was a bit scared of what I might do, after that.' He laughed out loud suddenly.

'Come downstairs. I've got something to show you,' she said, taking his hand and leading him down to the kitchen below. She opened a cupboard and took out a small birthday cake. There were nine candles spaced out around the edge and the words 'Jake, with love from Mummy' written across the centre. She lit the candles and switched the light off, allowing the flames to shimmer and dance along the walls.

'Go on then, blow them out,' she whispered. He smiled and she saw the flames dancing in the green of his eyes. He leant forward and blew and the room was plunged into darkness. She put an arm around him and pulled him to her, cradling his head to her breast and rocking him gently.

'This is the best birthday present I could have,' Jake murmured, walking slowly into the lounge. They sat down next to each other on the settee and Scamps jumped up on to his lap, licking his hands and face in excitement. Jake threw his head back, laughing at the dog's antics, and Denise laughed too with the pure pleasure of having her son back. When the dog was quiet at last she flung an arm around his shoulders and pulled him towards her, suddenly serious.

'You know how special you are to me. Don't you?' she whispered. 'You've always been Mummy's special boy.'

He nodded and kissed her tenderly on the cheek.

'Thank you for telling the police what you did. You were very brave.'

He smiled at her. 'How did you know I wouldn't get into trouble?'

She turned and looked straight into his eyes. 'Remember when Mummy found you with that pillow over Bryony's face. I thought you might get into trouble then and I was very worried. That nice DS Martin in Hastings asked me whether I thought you could have done it and I said I was sure you could never do such a thing. You were only six years old. Anyway, he must have thought something was wrong. He kept saying if it had been you, you wouldn't get into any trouble as you were below the age of criminal responsibility. I think that's what he called it. You had to be ten years old before you could get into trouble. I didn't say anything though. I just always remembered that age. And they never found out what you'd done, did they? It was our little secret. They just put it down to a cot death. That's when I realized how special you were.'

'I didn't want any babies getting in the way. She was always crying and you always had to be with her. And Lee would get angry when she cried and start hitting you. And I didn't like seeing you getting hurt. I couldn't let it happen any more.'

She kissed him on the forehead and put a finger to his lips. 'I know you couldn't. I know that's why you killed Bryony. Because you love me and you wanted to be with me all the time. And that's why I killed Ryan. Because I love you too and he was getting in the way. And that also has to be our secret, for ever, or else they'll send me to prison.'

He nodded seriously. 'Why did you tell the police you'd

done it then? They could have sent you to prison for ever and that would have been awful.'

'Because I guessed they wouldn't believe me, especially when they found the letter that Lee sent, threatening to come after me and you. I knew they'd think I only said it because I was frightened of what he might do to us.' She paused. 'That letter did us a real favour. I did think they'd only charge me with manslaughter though, which isn't so serious, after I blamed it on Lee's violence. I was a bit worried when they charged me with murder. I knew all along, though, that if you were to say it was you, they couldn't do anything about it, because you were under ten. I was right. That's why I told you what you had to say and do. As soon as you said it was you that had killed Ryan, they just presumed I'd been trying to protect you and let me off.'

She smoothed her fingers through his hair and pulled him towards her, breathing in his scent.

'You were brilliant, Jake. They believed every word you said and now we've got rid of Lee and the other two and it's just us again. You and me, against everyone.'

'Won't Lee come and get us when they let him out, though?'

'We'll be gone again by then. We won't stay here any longer than we have to. We'll keep our heads down for the next couple of months and then we'll move. To another house, in another part of the country. And they'll never find us and we'll change our names. I thought we could change them to Denise and Jake Martin, after that nice policeman in Hastings.'

He smiled and turned his head up towards her.

'Will it just be us together then? I don't want anyone else getting in the way and coming between us.'

She bent her head and kissed his tousled blond hair.

'I promise no one else will ever come between us again, Jake. It's just you and me from now on. I'll make sure of that.'

She looked deep into his olive-green eyes and saw them sparkle in the light from the street outside. Feeling a slight sensation deep within her, she rubbed her growing belly and frowned, as the first flutter of life stirred into her consciousness.